SHADOW OF JUSTICE
A MARA BRENT LEGAL THRILLER

ROBIN JAMES

Copyright © 2025
All Rights Reserved

No part of this book may be reproduced or transmitted in any form or by any means, electronic or mechanical, including photocopying, recording, or by any information storage and retrieval system, without the written permission of the author or publisher, except where permitted by law or for the use of brief quotations in a book review.

This is a work of fiction. Names, characters, businesses, places, events, and incidents are either the products of the author's imagination or used in a fictitious manner. Any resemblance to actual persons, living or dead, or actual events is purely coincidental.

1

I liked his hands. The way he gripped his glass in one, then reached for me across the table with the other. Warm hands. Strong. I traced the lines of the corded veins over his wrist and where they webbed around his knuckles.

"Mara?" he asked. "Did you hear me?"

My focus snapped back to his dark eyes. "What? Oh. Right. Hojo. Yes. I think he'll be okay for the time being."

Sheriff Sam Cruz raised a brow and brought his glass of lemonade to his lips.

"The time being," he repeated. "You think he's gonna run for the open seat outright in January?"

"I doubt it." My colleague, Howard Jordan, had been thrust into the position of acting prosecutor after our last duly elected one ended up recalled for misconduct. "Hojo was starting to set up an exit strategy, not run for higher office. He's doing a serviceable job though. He's better in front of a camera than anyone gave him credit for."

"You know, oddly, Gus and I were saying the same thing just this morning. I don't know why it should surprise anyone. Howard's got that 'aw shucks' charm thing. It serves him well against defense attorneys and in front of juries. You think he's just some local yokel, then he zings you with something."

"That's always been his strong point," I agreed. "Hojo benefits from underestimation. The problem is, I don't think he's handling the stress of it very well. He pops antacids like candy. He's gained weight. I think his girlfriend isn't fully on board with his new role. So, something's going to have to give."

"Are you two ready to order?" Sam and I sat on the outdoor patio of the newest downtown Waynetown eatery, The LadyBird. Right across from the Public Safety Building and the City-County Building, we were each a two-minute walk from our offices. With as busy as things had been for both of us, it was the first time we'd been able to steal an hour for just the two of us in almost two weeks.

"I'll try the chicken salad sandwich," I said.

"Kettle chips or French fries?" the server asked.

"Chips are fine."

"I'll do the Reuben," Sam said. "Chips here too."

The girl took our menus and headed to her next table.

"What about you?" Sam asked. "I know I've asked you before. And I know you know everybody's wondering what you'll do."

"You already know the answer to that," I said. "I like my current job. Running for political office was never an ambition of mine. I like trying cases. I'm *good* at trying cases."

"You're great at trying cases," Sam said. "I'll admit, for my position, I like you right where you are. I like knowing I've got a superstar sitting at the prosecutor's table in that courtroom. But if Hojo doesn't want to run, you leave yourself vulnerable to whoever comes in to take his place."

"I haven't given up hope that Kenya will come back."

A year and a half ago, my former boss, Kenya Spaulding, was ousted in a political upset. She'd spent the intervening time as a woman of leisure but I knew it couldn't last much longer. She did have the political ambitions I lacked. And she was damn good at her job.

"Well, that would be fantastic," Sam said. "If there's anything I can do to help persuade her, you let me know. Still, if you change your mind, you know you'd have my backing. You'd have the entire department's backing."

"You sure that wouldn't cause a conflict for you, Sheriff Cruz?"

"I do not," he said. "And I wouldn't care if it did. And there's nothing that says you couldn't still try as many cases as you want if you took the top job instead of assistant prosecutor. You could run that office any way you wanted."

"I know," I said. "For a while, anyway. But I mean it. I'm not interested in the politics of it."

A shadow crossed his face. "Mara," he said. "I get what you're saying. I do. I just ... I want to make sure you're not saying it because of me. Because of us. Sure. Us being together. Me as sheriff. You if you were elected prosecutor. It could get complicated. But there's no law against it."

"I know that. But I also know people would use it against you in your next election. That's not too far off."

"Mara ..."

"No," I said. "I need you to trust me on this. I'm not turning my back on a potential promotion because of the boy I'm dating."

"Boy?" he said, letting his voice drop low in almost a growl.

"Figure of speech," I said. "Don't change the subject. Sam, have you ever known me to not say what I mean? Or mean what I say?"

He squeezed my hand, sending that little thrill of heat through me. It was like that a lot. Even after months as a bona fide couple, the newness of it still caught my breath.

"I suppose not," he admitted. "I just worry about having an open field. I'd like a known quantity. So if Hojo doesn't want to run and Kenya won't come back, that's a pretty big hole."

"Nah," I said. "Let's be real. The only serious trouble my office would be in is if Caro decided to make good on her threats to retire."

Sam laughed. "Don't say that. She's not seriously considering that, is she? That woman is an institution."

Carolyn Flowers's official title was office manager. But she kept us all running like a well-oiled machine no matter who sat in the big office down the hall from mine.

"I hope not."

"I think Caro's been working for the county longer than anyone else I know."

"She has," I agreed. "Forty-two years. Longer than I've been alive. She turns sixty next month. Though she doesn't want anyone to know. The good news is with Hojo in Kenya's job,

Caro knows he's sunk without her. She loves him. She wants him to succeed. She's the original work mom to all of us. For now, I plan to use her codependency as a weapon."

Our server arrived with our sandwiches. I thanked her and spread my napkin over my lap. Sam managed to take a bite out of his Reuben with such gusto, it made me jealous of the sandwich. God. I was like a teenager around this guy sometimes.

We ate in companionable silence. The chicken salad was delicious. A relief for now. This building had become somewhat of a retail no man's land over the years with every new store coming in cursed to fail within a year. But we could use a good restaurant in this part of town.

"So," Sam said. "Is Will ready for school?"

I crunched a chip and wiped my hands on my napkin. "He may be. I don't know if I am."

"High school." Sam smiled. "How'd we get here?"

We. Just that simple word. I liked it. But it scared me too.

"I'm just worried," I said. "Like always. We got into a pretty good groove at his last school. It's a lot of changes."

"He'll be great, Mara. He's ready. There will be bumps. All kids have bumps. It's part of the experience."

He was right. But my fourteen-year-old son wasn't like all kids. We'd had a long stretch of stable calm, but that hadn't always been true. Even the slightest change in Will's routine could cause a meltdown, or even worse, a shutdown. Sam had been a steadying influence in my son's life. And in mine. But high school was the great unknown.

"He won't let me drive him on his first day," I said. "He wants to ride the bus."

"He told me. I think it's good, don't you?"

"I do," I admitted.

"How about we both take the day off on his first day? Plan something fun and distracting."

"I'd like that," I said. "I'll have to check my schedule ..."

"Sheriff Cruz? That's you, right? You're the sheriff? I've seen you on the news."

I looked up. The girl standing at our table looked to be about eighteen or nineteen. She was tall and thin with wheat-blonde hair and a dusting of freckles across her cheeks. Pretty, but her face was deeply flushed and she trembled so badly I feared she might fall over.

"May I help you?" Sam asked, concern filling his face.

The girl looked at me. "You work ... you're the prosecutor, right? I saw you on the news once, too."

"I am," I said, deciding it wasn't the time to point out the finer points of my job description.

"C-can we ... I'm sorry. I need to talk to someone. I need to get this out." She started to cry.

"Honey," I said, rising, my maternal instincts kicking in. There was something seriously wrong with this girl. She wore a large, crossbody satchel. Whatever was in it looked like it weighed a ton. Sam pulled out another chair and the girl sank into it.

"I'm sorry," she said. "I didn't want to interrupt. But you're both here. I don't know who else to talk to."

"What's your name?" I asked.

She shot a frightened look at Sam, then back at me. "Hayden. Hayden Simmons."

"Okay, Hayden," Sam said. "Are you hurt? Are you ... safe?"

Hayden looked like she was about to be sick. Sweat beaded her brow. The reddish tone to her skin turned positively purple.

"I didn't know what to do," she said. "I didn't want ... I can't ... there isn't ..."

"Honey," I said. "What is it? Did somebody hurt you?"

She shook her head almost violently. "No. No. I'm okay. It's not me. It's ... please. I don't even ... It's ... I have to ... God. I have to report a crime."

Sam and I shared a look. For an instant, I felt certain of what Hayden Simmons would say next. Someone had hurt her. Badly. But the girl finally settled. She went still. She took a breath and turned to Sam. Her voice was low enough that no one but Sam and I could hear it. But she spoke clearly.

"I need to report a crime. I need to tell you. I *have* to tell you. It's my father. He ... my father killed someone. He's a murderer. I brought proof."

2

The girl shivered so badly I worried she might fall out of her chair. Sam set her up in one of the interview rooms on the first floor of the Public Safety Building. She asked for water but had left it untouched in front of her.

"Are you okay?" I asked her. "Would you like me to call someone to be with you? A friend? Do you have family?"

At the mention of the word family, her head snapped up. "No. They won't help me. You don't understand."

"Okay," Sam said. "You can take all the time you need. Whatever you want to talk about, we're here to listen, okay?"

"Okay," she said. She reached for her water bottle but rather than drinking it, she clutched it to her chest.

"Can you tell me your name again?" Sam asked.

"Hayden," she said. "H-A-Y-D-E-N. Simmons."

"Hayden," Sam asked. "Where do you live?"

She cleared her throat. "1492 Gulliver Lane. That's over in Hemingway Estates. The subdivision off Route 7 near Bear Lake."

"I know right where that is," Sam said, his voice calm, soothing. The girl was like a scared kitten. We both felt any sudden movement might startle her and have her diving under the table. She couldn't weigh more than a hundred pounds. The leather satchel she carried had something big and bulky inside of it. She dropped it to the ground at her feet.

"Hayden," I said. "Did someone hurt you? Do you feel safe in your home?"

"No. What? I mean, yes. Nobody hurt me. Nobody's trying to hurt me. This isn't about me."

"Then what's it about, honey?" Sam said. "You said you think your dad killed someone. Did I hear that right?"

Hayden put her water bottle down and laid both hands flat on the table. "Yes," she said.

"Who?" Sam asked.

"How long have you been here?" she asked Sam. "I mean, with the Sheriff's Department?"

"A long time," he said. "I was a detective for a number of years before they elected me sheriff. I've been with the department eighteen years."

"Eighteen," she repeated. "Then you wouldn't have known her. She died before I was born. I just turned nineteen."

"Okay," Sam said. "Maybe you should start from the beginning."

Hayden nodded. "Right. My aunt was Ellie Luke." She said it as if the name should mean something to us. Hayden looked from me to Sam, then realized we were both at a loss.

"Right," she repeated. "So ... nobody in my family ever wants to talk about my Aunt Ellie. My whole life, she was just this ... mythic figure. I didn't even know my mom wasn't an only child until I was maybe ten or eleven. That's how much they don't talk about it. My grandparents are the same. There was this picture in the hallway. Like a senior picture. I just thought it was my mom. I never asked. Then one day, my grandpa was in the hallway staring at it. And he was crying. Like I said, I was maybe ten. I went up to him and asked him why that picture of my mom was making him sad. He looked at me and all the blood drained from his face. He told me that wasn't my mom. That was my Aunt Ellie. And he walked away like that explained everything."

Hayden grabbed the bottle of water and unscrewed the cap. With shaking hands, she took a sip. It seemed to settle her a little.

"I finally asked my mom about it. Maybe a day or two later. We were all staying at Grandma's that weekend because Mom was having the whole house painted. My mom said she had a sister, Ellie. But she died a long time ago and it made everyone too sad so I shouldn't ask any more questions. Well, I was young enough to be satisfied by that. Well, not satisfied. But young enough, I knew not to upset her anymore."

"Who was she?" I asked.

"Ellie Luke," Hayden repeated. "It was the next day. I was out in the yard playing with this girl who used to live next door to my grandparents. She was a year younger than me but we got along. Her mom, April, was baking cookies and we went inside to sample the batter. I don't know what made me do it, but I brought up what my grandpa said. I asked her if she knew I had an Aunt Ellie. Did she used to live next door? Well, April got real quiet. And she started to cry. But she talked about it. She told me somebody hurt Ellie very badly and then she died. I was old enough to know what murder was, for God's sake. So I said that. I asked April if Ellie was murdered. She said yes, but that it was something I needed to talk to my mom about."

"What happened to her?" I asked.

"I looked it up online. Like immediately after I came home that weekend. I found all these articles in the local papers about her. Aunt Ellie just disappeared one day after work. She worked overnight doing home health care for this older lady in Pine Ridge. There were interviews with my grandparents. Their pictures were in the paper. Grandma said Ellie just didn't come home. And she was pleading for somebody to come forward and say what happened to her."

"They didn't find her," Sam said. "I know of the case. It was in the spring. There were search parties. Nobody knew anything. But they found her, what, six months later?"

"Something like that," Hayden said. "Some hunter found her deep in the woods not far from Pine Ridge. Her bones anyway."

"It's a cold case," Sam said. His tone shifted. He'd grown serious. His posture went rigid. "Hayden, I need to make sure I'm understanding what you're saying. Do you believe you have information about what happened to Ellie Luke?"

"Yes," she said. She'd stopped trembling. As the minutes passed, Hayden became more self-assured and purposeful.

"Hayden," he said. "Would you mind waiting here for a couple of minutes? There's someone else I'd like to come and listen to what you have to say. Is that all right with you?"

She took another sip of water. "It's okay. I'm here. I have to get this out."

"Just give us a minute," Sam said. He nudged me under the table. I gave Hayden a reassuring smile, then followed Sam out into the hallway.

"Gus needs to be here," Sam said.

Gus Ritter was the most senior detective with the Maumee County Sheriff's Department. He'd been working homicides for decades.

"Was this his case?" I asked.

"I don't know. Ellie Luke's murder predates me."

I pulled out my phone and opened a browser. Ten seconds later, I found some of the articles a ten-year-old Hayden Simmons must have.

"She was only twenty-one years old," I said.

"Don't let her leave," Sam said. "Keep her talking. I'm going to go find Gus."

"Got it."

I went back into the room with Hayden. She'd picked up her satchel and held it on her lap. The water bottle in front of her was empty now.

"Are you sure you don't want anything else? More water? I'm sure I could scrounge up a sandwich or something."

"No," she said. "I can't even think about food."

"That's understandable. Sheriff Cruz wants one of the detectives to be part of this conversation. If you have information about an unsolved murder, we need to do this the right way."

She let out a huff. "The right way. Ms. Brent, I've been trying to figure out what that is for a long time."

"Do you still live with your parents?" I asked.

"Yes. My mom and my dad."

"And your mom is ..."

"Erin Simmons," she said. "Erin Luke Simmons. Ellie was her older sister. They were three years apart."

The door opened behind me. Sam walked in first followed by Gus. Hayden straightened upon seeing him. Gus could have that effect on people. He had a gruff appearance and a constant scowl. It took a while to get past all of that with him. When you did—if you were one of the lucky few Gus Ritter allowed close to him—he was one of the kindest, most loyal people I knew.

Sam introduced Gus and Hayden. Gus took the seat Sam had occupied. Sam and I moved to the other end of the table.

"I've brought Gus up to speed with what you told us so far," Sam said.

"Okay," she said.

"Ms. Simmons," Gus said. "Do you mind if we record the rest of this conversation?"

"No," she said. "Actually, I would prefer it. I know who you are, Detective Ritter."

"You do?" he said.

"Yes. This was your case. You're the one who worked on my Aunt Ellie's murder all those years ago. Do you remember it?"

Gus did something I wasn't sure I'd ever seen him do. He flinched.

"Yes," he answered. "Ellie Luke was my case."

"Then I think I have as many questions for you as you have for me," Hayden said.

"I'll do my best to answer them," Gus said. "But your aunt's case is still open. Some things I won't be able to discuss. You're okay with that?"

"I'm not okay with any of this. If I had some kind of time machine, I might just want to erase the last two months. That would be easiest. But ... then I think about living in that house with them. And I can't breathe."

"Hayden, I asked you before," I said. "Are you saying you don't feel safe in your home?"

"No," she said. "Nobody wants to hurt me. Not physically. But I don't know what they're going to do when they find out what I told you people."

"One step at a time," Gus said. "What's going on, Hayden?"

"Tell them," she said. "Tell them what happened to Ellie Luke, Detective Ritter."

"We don't have all the answers," he said. "But Ellie was last seen at the home of one of her patients. She worked an eleven to seven a.m. shift. Sometime after she left, something happened to her. She never made it home. Her mother ... I guess your grandmother ... reported her missing just before noon the next day. She just vanished. No trace. Nobody seemed to know anything. Then, a few months later, her remains were found in the woods by a hunter. There wasn't much to go on there. But it was determined she died of blunt force trauma to the back of her head."

Gus's words were cold, clinical. But I knew him well enough to know he was leaving a lot out.

"I was telling Sheriff Cruz and Ms. Brent. For half my life, I didn't even know Ellie Luke existed. I thought my mom was an only child."

"Your mom," Gus said. "Your mom is Erin Luke?"

"Yes."

"Okay. Go on."

"I was always told not to bring it up. My dad would say it made my mom too sad. My mom would say the same thing about her parents. You just don't talk about Ellie. It's too painful. Too hard. I just have so many questions. What happened? Why couldn't you find out who killed her? Who was she? So finally, a few months ago, I started looking for answers online. It didn't take long before I stumbled on this forum. All these people, amateur sleuths. They had sub-forums talking about different unsolved murders in the state. I found one dedicated to my aunt. It was so strange. Strangers knew more about her than I did."

"What was the name of the forum?" Gus asked.

"CCTS. Cold Case Truth Sleuths. I will admit. I got a little obsessed. But it felt like it was the only way I could talk about my aunt. It felt like these people cared more about her and what happened to her than her own family did. I know that's not fair. I know it's just painful for my mom and grandparents. This thing ripped them all apart. And it answered so many questions about how they are. Why my grandma has been so sad. Why she stares off into space sometimes and won't talk. Why my grandpa ended up in AA. Why my mom is such a people pleaser and so nervous all the time."

"That had to be really hard to grow up around," I said. "It's natural you would have questions."

"But they had answers. The people on CCTS. They knew everything about Ellie. That she was a nursing student. She worked nights doing home health care. She had friends. Got straight As. Was a cheerleader. They knew the details of her murder. How she was found months later, nothing but bones. How she was posed under a tree. Morbid stuff. Some of these online sleuths had pictures of my family I'd never seen before."

"What kind of pictures?" Gus asked.

"Yearbook photos. But also all these candid shots of my aunt with her friends. It was this one in particular that just ... got me. I felt hollowed out when I saw it."

Hayden reached into her satchel and pulled out an 8x10 grainy picture reprinted from the internet. I recognized Ellie Luke at the center of it from the photo I'd found online after that ten-second search. Ellie was pretty. Thick, long dark hair and ice-blue eyes. She had a stunner of a smile with dimples in her cheeks. She looked fun. Young. Full of energy. She sat with a group of friends, a mixture of men and women.

"Why this picture?" Sam asked, leaning in close to see it.

"Because of him," Hayden said, tapping the face of a skinny blond guy sitting next to Ellie.

"Who is he?" I asked.

"Jamie Simmons," Hayden answered.

"I'm not sure I follow," Sam said.

"Then you're having the same reaction I am," Hayden said. "Confusion. See, I've talked to my dad and my mom so many times since I found out about Aunt Ellie. Mom would only talk about things that happened when they were growing up. Never about the murder itself. Which was understandable. And my dad would just kind of support her. Tell me how tough it had all been on Mom. He never ever told me that he knew Ellie. That they were friends. That's how he met my mom in the first place."

"Your Aunt Ellie introduced them?" I asked.

"No," she said. "That's what was so wrong about all of it. I found this stuff out from strangers online. My dad was a classmate of Aunt Ellie's. They were in nursing school together. They hung out. They were close. I never knew that."

"You think your dad killed Ellie Luke?" Sam asked.

"No," she said. "That's what I'm trying to tell you. I know it."

Gus looked like he was about to erupt. He grabbed the photo and put on his readers. "I don't see him anywhere in this picture," he muttered. I'm not even sure if he meant for the rest of us to hear it.

"See who?" Sam asked.

"Who the hell is your dad, Hayden?" Gus asked.

"Jamie Simmons," she said, growing exasperated.

Gus took off his glasses and squeezed the bridge of his nose.

"Walk me through it, honey," Gus asked.

"He has a workshop in the basement," Hayden said, her tone filled with distress. "I never go down there. He gets single-minded. He works on these models. Ships in bottles. I always know when he's upset or angry. Because he'll go down there for hours. But it just all kind of built up. Two weeks ago, I went down there. I wanted to talk to him about Ellie. I couldn't find him at first. He wasn't at the bench. Our house is older. There's this room off to the side that used to be a coal bin in the 1930s or something. He was there. The door was cracked and I could see the light on. He was sitting on a stool and he had this box in his hands. I was going to knock. I tripped over a pair of shoes near the boiler. He heard me. He shoved the box under these blankets and he came out. He was enraged. Accusing me of spying on him. Just … completely flipped out. I'd never seen him like that."

Hayden reached down and lifted her satchel onto the table. She rested her hands on top of it.

"My dad didn't finish nursing school. Instead, he works at the hospital as a respiratory therapist. He's been on midnights for the last month. Last week, I went down to the basement. My mom took this trip to Shipshewana with some friends. It was just me alone in the house. I don't know if that's ever happened before. I don't know what made me go back down there. But I knew. I just knew."

She slid a large cardboard box out of her bag. It had a pink lid and flowers painted on the sides.

"I found this," she said. "I didn't want to believe it. But I think on some level, maybe I've always known."

Hayden Simmons rose to her feet. She lifted the lid off the box. At once, Sam, Gus, and I leaned in, our foreheads practically touching each other's.

Gus spoke first. "Son of a bitch!" The shock of it overcame him. He reached out. I grabbed his wrist.

"Stop," I said. "Don't. Just freeze. Don't touch it. Hayden, for the love of God, please close that back up."

3

"Do you see anything I missed?"

I read Gus's search warrant for the third time, looking for anything that might cause problems down the road. But he'd written an airtight legal masterpiece. As usual.

"This is good," I said. "I just got off the phone with Judge Saul's clerk. She's waiting for it. I expect she'll sign it right away."

The three of us stood in Sam's office. Hayden Simmons was with one of the female deputies in a conference room down the hall. Sam scowled as he looked out the window.

Gus poked his head out into the hallway. "Jaffee? It's ready. Take this straight to Saul's courtroom. Don't talk to anybody. Don't make any other stops. Come straight back here when you've got it signed."

"You got it, Ritter." Nick Jaffee Chaney was one of Gus's favorite deputies. He knew the severity of the situation and we all trusted he could keep his mouth shut. Even so, Sam waited until Jaffee left and disappeared down the hall before shutting his office door so we could talk in relative privacy.

Gus took a quick call on his cell while I joined Sam at the window.

"Got it," Gus said. "Thanks. As soon as I get word back from the judge, we'll be down there. Don't let anybody touch anything. Don't look at anything. How's the girl? Good. Keep her there."

He clicked off the call and walked over to Sam's office couch, and sat down hard. He leaned over, assuming a crash position. I knew how he felt.

"What do you remember about this guy, Simmons?" Sam asked.

"Nothing," Gus said, shaking his head. "Or next to nothing. The name doesn't ring any bells but I interviewed a lot of Ellie Luke's friends and classmates during that time frame."

"What do you remember about the case in general?" I asked.

Gus looked up. If it were possible, I watched my friend age about ten years in the span of those few seconds. He rubbed a hand across his face.

"It was one of the bad ones," he said. "Not like there could ever be anything good about something like that. But this kid? Ellie Luke? From everything I learned, she didn't have a single enemy. She was smart. Pretty. Putting herself through nursing school by working as a home health aide for dementia patients. She was as close to an angel as a kid like that could get. Good family. Good grades. Nobody said a bad word about her. She just dropped off the face of the earth one morning."

"Her niece said her grandma reported her missing after she

didn't come home from a shift with one of her home health patients."

"That was it," Gus said. "We found her car abandoned on the side of Chalmers Road facing east like she was heading toward her house. The back right tire was flat. It had been slashed. The theory was somebody grabbed her when she pulled over."

"You think the tire was slashed on purpose? She didn't roll over a piece of glass or something?"

Gus shook his head. "It looked like a clean cut. We didn't find anything embedded in it. I don't know if that'd hold up in court as definitive that it was deliberate. But that sure was my gut at the time."

"You think that somebody stalked her," I said. "Knew she was going to have to pull over."

"Chalmers was a dirt road at the time. There were probably eight houses on it back then. Only local traffic and barely any at that. It's built up now. They put that subdivision back there. Hell, the woods where we found Ellie is a park now."

"You think somebody planned it all out," I said. "Somebody who knew her schedule. When the best time to nab her would be."

"It didn't feel random, no. We had the whole county out looking for her. Volunteers came in from Lucas County. Fulton County. Everywhere. We dragged the river. It went on for weeks. That girl was one of the first homicides I took after I made detective."

"You never had any solid leads?" I asked.

Gus's face darkened. "I didn't say that. That's what makes no sense, Mara. I thought I knew who did it."

"What do you mean?"

"I said Ellie was well liked by almost everybody. But a picture started to emerge. There was a cousin of her mother's. Kid named Dane Fischer. He was maybe three or four years older than Ellie. Troubled kid. Drug problem. His own mother kicked him out and he went to stay with Ellie's family for a summer. This was a couple of years before her murder. Ellie's mom was doing Fischer's mom a favor. The two of them were first cousins. At least I think that's how it went. Anyway, a few weeks after Fischer moved in, Ellie caught him stealing from her parents. Cash out of her dad's wallet. A gold watch. Ellie had a ring that belonged to a great-grandmother or something. A ruby. He stole that too. That's how she caught him. She came home from cheerleading practice or something early and found him in her room rummaging through her things. She told her parents. There was a big fight. Ellie's dad kicked Fischer out. But he didn't call the cops. Ellie did that herself when her parents refused."

"Fischer knew that?" Sam asked.

"Yeah. He came back to the house high and threatened to beat the crap out of Ellie's dad. It was a mess. They didn't want to talk about it. Her parents thought it was in the past. Then Ellie went missing. It took some doing getting this story out of them."

"You interviewed Fischer?" I asked.

"Hell, yes. His story was full of holes. He lied about his alibi. Said he was at some bar. Only it didn't check out. The bar he claimed to be at was closed that day. Then he lied again and said he was home all night. Only his roommate at the time wouldn't back up his story. Said he hadn't seen him for a couple of days. Then, Fischer failed a poly."

"Was there any physical evidence tying him to Ellie's murder?"

Gus shook his head. "That's the thing. Ellie's body didn't turn up for months. There wasn't much there. Bones. Some tissue. Hair. Cause of death wasn't even completely conclusive. Her skull was caved in but there was no way to know if that happened post mortem or not. It's just a working theory. The most plausible thing. Couldn't even tell you whether there'd been a sexual assault. But she was posed."

"What do you mean posed?" I asked.

"It'll take me some time," Gus said. "I'll have to pull all the evidence boxes from the archives. This thing was twenty-two years ago. God. I can't even believe that. Anyway, her body ... what was left of it ... was found leaning up against a tree in a seated position. Her hands folded on her lap. Her legs crossed. The injury was to the back of her skull. Coroner theorized she was hit while she was turned away from her attacker. She was put up against that tree later."

"So there were two crime scenes?" Sam asked.

"Probably. We searched Fischer's apartment and his car. The apartment was clean. But there was blood all over the trunk of his car. But the lab couldn't pull DNA from it. The best we could get was blood type. B positive. Same as Ellie's. But same as Dane Fischer's."

"They're cousins," I said. "None of that's conclusive."

"No."

"I thought I had probable cause to arrest him. But Halsey punted."

Phil Halsey had been the prosecuting attorney in that era. He hired me twelve years ago. Now, he was long gone. His violent death still haunted my dreams from time to time.

"He wouldn't have had a choice," I said. "He never could have gotten a conviction on what you had."

"I just don't get it," Gus said. "Fischer left town after this all went down. He pretty much had to."

"Ellie Luke's family thinks he killed her too?"

"I think so," Gus said. "Her dad told me he knew it in his gut. I was worried he was gonna take matters into his own hands when I told him Fischer wasn't going to be charged. That was one of the worst days of my career, having that conversation with him."

"The case went cold," I said.

"As ice," Gus agreed.

"It wasn't your fault," Sam said.

Gus turned gray. He buried his face in his hands. "Unless I was wrong this whole time."

"One thing at a time," I said. I walked over to Gus and put a hand on his shoulder. He went rigid beneath my touch.

Sam's desk phone buzzed. He went to it and picked it up. "Yeah, Stephanie." He paused. "Good. Thanks. We'll be right down."

"Everything okay?" I asked.

"Jaffee got the warrant signed," he said. "We can legally open the box."

Gus bolted to his feet. I felt my stomach drop. The box. I'd already seen enough to understand the fear Hayden Simmons must have experienced when she opened it.

Gus flung Sam's door open and charged down the hall. Sam and I had to practically sprint to keep up with him.

FIVE MINUTES LATER, WE STOOD IN THE PROPERTY ROOM. Each of us wore latex gloves. Hayden Simmons's box of horrors sat on the table in front of us. Deputy Jaffee had a digital camera, ready to photograph every phase of this.

Gus opened the box and pulled out the first item. He laid it on the table. It was a gold earring. An intricate, dangling circle with tiny heart cutouts and some kind of stone. The second item was a plastic baggie with a lock of dark hair inside of it secured by a purple ribbon. Next, Gus used a small set of tongs to pull out a pair of women's panties. Pink cotton with a daisy pattern. He laid those on the table.

"They look clean," I said. "I don't see any bloodstains."

"We'll have BCI analyze all of this," Sam said.

"Of course," I said. "Was Ellie Luke wearing underwear when she was found?"

Gus shrugged. "I don't think so. I'll pull everything I have. But the mate of that earring was found next to her body. That I remember vividly."

"Christ," Sam muttered.

But there was more in the box. Gus pulled out another baggie, this one larger than the one containing the lock of hair. This one contained a stack of 4x6 pictures. Maybe twenty of them.

I pulled out a chair and sat down. Gus opened the baggie. One by one, he laid the photographs face up on the table in front of us. Every picture was of Ellie Luke.

In the first few, she was sitting at what looked like a cafeteria table. She was laughing, her head thrown back. It was taken in extreme close-up so I couldn't make out who she was talking to or whether there was anyone beside her.

Another few photographs captured her sitting behind the wheel of her car. She had her head turned away from the camera at first, then in quick succession, she looked up. The photographer caught her lifting her hand to tuck a lock of hair behind her ear. Something might have drawn her attention. In another shot, she looked in the direction of the camera, scowling.

In the next series of photos, Ellie was walking out of the main entrance of the county hospital. She carried textbooks in her arms. The wind lifted her hair. She was beautiful. Young. Vibrant. She wore pink scrubs and a student ID badge.

One of the last series of photographs was more disturbing. They appeared to have been taken from a high-powered lens through a window. She was in her bedroom, wearing a robe, her hair wet, probably having just gotten out of the shower.

Gus laid another photograph down. In it, Ellie Luke had slipped out of her robe. She stood in front of her bedroom vanity running a brush through her wet locks. Though taken from behind, the door to her closet had a full-length mirror. She was stark naked in the reflection.

"My God," I whispered. "He stalked her. There are date stamps on these. This was going on for months."

Gus held the final photograph in his hands. His jaw clenched. He shuddered.

"Gus?" I asked.

He squeezed his eyes shut for an instant. Opening them, he slammed the last photograph on the table with the others.

"The date," Gus said. "March 11th. The day before she died. That might be the last photograph ever taken of that poor kid alive."

4

It was almost six before I made it back to the office. I expected it to be empty. But Caro and Hojo sat in the reception area waiting for me. Word had already made its way to them. Sam's concerns about a leak appeared to be well founded.

Hojo pulled a rocks glass and a bottle of scotch I knew he kept in a hidden drawer. He only broke it out after verdicts came in on major trials. He poured two fingers and handed the glass to me.

"How much have you heard?" I asked, taking the glass. I didn't generally like scotch, but appreciated the smooth warmth as I downed it.

"Don't get excited," Caro said. "I talked to Janine over in Judge Saul's courtroom."

"She told you about the warrant?" I asked. "Who else did she tell?"

"Nobody," Caro assured me. "But you can't think that'll last for long. Gus pulled a warrant on a twenty-two-year-old cold case that freaked the whole town out."

"Fill me in," Hojo said. "How soon is this thing going to be something I'll have to deal with?"

I kicked my heels off and perched myself on the empty desk next to Caro's. Hojo sat in one of the reception chairs against the wall.

"Ellie Luke," I said. "Her niece made a fairly convincing case that her own father murdered her and posed her body in a wooded area in Phillips Township. Out by Pine Ridge."

I gave Caro and Hojo the highlights of Hayden Simmons's story, ending with the contents of the box she took from her father's hiding spot.

Hojo whistled. "Man. Caro, you were here then. What do you remember about it?"

"I knew Ellie's mother a little. The Lukes are next-door neighbors to one of my bunco friends. I actually met Ellie once or twice when we played over there. She babysat for my friend's son at the time. This was probably thirty years ago. Sweet girl, from what I recall. Her disappearance really turned things upside down around here for a while."

Caro picked up a red file sitting on her desk. I hadn't noticed it before but my pulse skipped when she handed it to me.

"I haven't seen one of these in a while," I said, thinking about asking Hojo for another shot of scotch. The red files were part of Phil Halsey's idiosyncratic filing system. He used them for open but not active cases. He'd given me an entire box of the things on my first day of work for the prosecutor's office. It felt like a million years ago now.

I opened the front flap and sucked in a breath. Phil loved his sticky notes. He color-coded them. Yellow for action items. Blue for important phone numbers. Pink for appointments or important deadlines. It used to drive Caro crazy collecting all of them and entering them into his digital case files.

"I know," Caro said. "It jarred me a bit seeing those, too. And his writing."

Phil Halsey had died by violent means right in front of me. I didn't often think of it. But now, his last seconds flashed through my mind.

"What do you know about the new suspect?" Hojo asked.

I flipped through Phil's notes as I answered him. There wasn't much there beyond what Gus had already told me. A copy of Ellie Luke's autopsy report, such as it was. Badly decomposed by the time they found her, there'd been no internal organs, DNA, or blood samples to take. No toxicology. No evidence of bullet wounds, stabbing, or strangulation. Only the massive defect to the back of her skull.

"Jamie Simmons," I said. "We don't know much of anything yet. He was a classmate of Ellie's. Based on the photographs in his grisly treasure box, he was obsessed with her."

"And he married her sister?" Caro asked. "That's just ... my God."

"Did you know her?" I asked.

Caro shrugged. "I mean, maybe. I can't say as I remember her. Just Ellie. She was a few years younger, I think. Ellie would have probably been fourteen or fifteen when I knew her. And I don't mean *know* her know her. I just saw her around. But I remember her being very bubbly. Adorable really. Not shy around adults, you know? Funny. My friend Vivian, the one who lived next door to the Lukes. She really liked her."

Phil's file also contained a copy of Dane Fischer's polygraph results. I pulled it out.

"Dane Fischer," I said. "He was the main person of interest at the time."

"I remember that," Caro said. "Some sort of cousin."

I skimmed through the poly. Fischer had been questioned for almost two hours. The examiner detected deception regarding his alibi. His feelings toward Ellie. And finally, his denial of wishing her harm or causing her harm.

"Gus is beside himself," I said. "If he was wrong about Fischer all these years ..."

"Phil wouldn't file charges," Caro said. "I remember that very well. Gus was angry. Lord, he was just a kid then himself. I want to say this was his first solo homicide case. That bothered Phil along with a lot of the rest of it."

"What do you remember about Gus in those days?" I asked. I could barely envision Gus Ritter as a young detective. Twenty-two years ago, he would have been in his early thirties.

"He's always been one of the good ones," Caro said. "Intense, sure. Just like now. But smart. Driven. He's never cared whether he ruffled certain feathers. I mean that as a compliment."

"What did he look like?" Hojo asked. "I just can't picture Gus Ritter looking like anything other than the fire hydrant he is."

Caro laughed. "He hasn't. I've known Gus since he was a street cop just out of the academy. Twenty-five, maybe twenty-six. That man has looked the same for forty years. He could probably grow a full beard in elementary school."

"How long can we keep this under wraps?" Hojo asked. I understood the concern in his tone. If Gus ended up making an arrest, it would be Hojo's first high-profile case since his appointment as acting prosecutor.

"Gus is working on getting search warrants for Simmons's house, phone, computer, car. The whole bit. He wants to serve everything first thing in the morning. We're trying to be as low-key as possible, but if Janine is already talking..."

"She's not talking," Caro said. "She talked to me. It's not the same thing."

"It won't matter," Hojo said. "Judge Saul needs to keep things under seal."

"Jamie Simmons has neighbors," I said. "It'll get out. My best guess, we can keep things quiet until about noon tomorrow. Not much after."

"Okay," Hojo said. "What do you need from me in the meantime?"

"Nothing."

"Where's the girl?" Caro said. "Simmons's daughter?"

"Sam and Gus convinced her not to go home tonight. She's going to stay with a friend. Sam sent a couple of deputies to sit on Simmons's house. Make sure he doesn't try to run."

"Does he know his daughter fingered him for murder?" Hojo asked.

"Not according to her. She hasn't said anything to her mother either. This girl is feeling completely alone right now. She has no idea how her family will react to this news."

"I can't even imagine it," Caro said. "That is one brave kid. Poor thing."

"How does Gus want to handle this?" Hojo said. "Who's going to break it to the wife … er … the sister?"

"Hayden says her mother will probably be at home first thing in the morning. Jamie is a respiratory therapist over at County. He leaves for work at eight thirty. Gus is planning on serving his warrants by seven."

"She can't go back to that house," Hojo said. "This daughter. It's too dangerous for her."

"She knows that. But I've told Gus I want a social worker. Erin Luke is about to find out her husband murdered her sister and her daughter's the one who figured it out."

"You don't think she knows?" Caro said. "You don't think she suspects?"

"Hayden doesn't think so. She says her parents never talk about her aunt. It's a taboo subject."

"I'll just bet it is," Hojo muttered. While we talked, Caro fired her computer back up.

"Simmons, huh?" she said. "How long after Ellie's murder did the sister marry this guy?"

"Well, if Ellie was murdered twenty-two years ago, Hayden's nineteen."

"Yikes," Hojo said. "That is just creepy as hell. So theoretically, Jamie Simmons stalks his classmate. Something happens. He kills her. Maybe raped her before that. We don't know."

"We'll probably never know," I said.

"So then what, Simmons worms his way into Ellie Luke's family? Knocks her little sister up? Mara, this is going to make national news."

"Let's try to prevent that for as long as possible."

"Creepy is right," Caro said. The glow of her computer screen made her face look blue. I could see the reflection of a social media page in her glasses. "My God, Mara, you have to take a look at this."

I slid off the desk and walked up behind Caro. Hojo came up on her other side. Caro had a news article pulled up from when Ellie Luke disappeared. It was the same story I found with Ellie's picture. Those ice-blue eyes just drew you in.

"That's the girl I remember," Caro said. "That smile. Those eyes."

She closed the tab and pulled up another page. It was another picture of what I thought was Ellie Luke but she looked much older.

"Wait," Hojo said. "Did they do an age progression? Why would …"

I felt the blood drain from my head. In our lengthy interview with Hayden Simmons, I'd never thought to ask for a picture of her mother. It never occurred to me to wonder what she looked like. But Caro had pulled up a recent picture of Erin Luke

Simmons, Ellie's younger sister. Hayden's mother. She and Ellie Luke could have been identical twins.

"My God," I said, feeling lightheaded. "He ..."

"Jamie Simmons had a type," Caro whispered. "Good lord, Mara. Did he kill that poor girl and then marry her lookalike sister? Like she's some sort of trophy, too?"

I pulled out my phone. I did a quick browser search until I had the same picture of Erin Luke Simmons pulled up. I shot a text link to Sam then punched in his number. He answered on the second ring.

"Sam," I said. "I need you to look at the photo I just sent you."

"Hang on," he said. I heard him fumble with his phone. "What am I looking at? Wait. That's Ellie Luke. Is that ..."

"It's Erin Luke," I said. "Jamie Simmons's wife. Hayden's mother. Are you seeing what I'm seeing?"

"Christ," he muttered.

"Exactly."

"This thing's going to get messy, quick," he said.

"We can't let it. What's the word on Gus's warrants?"

"All signed," he said. "We're locked and loaded for first thing in the morning. I've got eyes on Jamie Simmons's house. I've got more eyes on Hayden. She just got to her friend's house. I don't want her making any calls or texts to anyone in her family tonight. She understands."

"I hope so," I said. "That poor girl."

"I know," he said. "We're gonna bring Simmons in for questioning, then head over to serve the warrants. I assume you'll want to be in the observation room."

"Definitely," I said. We clicked off. It felt like my legs were encased in cement. Hojo and Caro were statues, too. None of us could take our eyes off Caro's computer screen. There was no need to imagine what Ellie Luke would look like today. In her sister Erin, we could see her face.

5

The next morning, Jamie Simmons walked into the Sheriff's Department with a smile on his face. Sam and I sat in the observation room behind one-way glass.

"What did Gus tell him to get him here?" I asked Sam.

"He told him they found something that might be connected to his sister-in-law's case. Gus asked Simmons if he could run it by him before he brought it to her mother. Simmons was more than happy to oblige."

"I'll bet," I said.

Gus hadn't entered the room. I knew that was part of his tactic. Simmons came dressed for work in dark-blue scrubs. He sat calmly, sipping from a paper coffee cup Gus had offered him when he walked in. Simmons checked his smart watch a couple of times, but didn't seem irritated by the wait.

He was tall, with a trim, lanky build of someone who had exercised regularly his whole life. A basketball player, or someone who biked a lot. He had thinning, dark-blond hair and wore a pair of round, wire-rimmed glasses. I couldn't help staring at the thick wedding band on his left ring finger.

The door opened and Gus walked into the room. He'd left his suit coat in his office and had his shirtsleeves rolled up. That, too, was a tactic.

"Sorry to keep you waiting so long," Gus said. He had a yellow legal pad and put it on the table.

"I don't mind at all," Simmons said. "But I do have to be at work in an hour. Do you think this will take that long?"

"I'll do my best," Gus said. "I was sorry to have to call you out of the blue on something like this."

"Oh, I don't mind one bit. I'm glad you did. The more I know ... the more I can prepare my wife and mother-in-law. They don't like to revisit what happened to Elizabeth. So if you think there's a chance I can help you with what you need without involving them, that would be best."

"We'll see what we can do," Gus said. He flipped through the pages of his legal pad. He had a portion of his original report tucked in between them. He pulled it out.

"We've spoken before," Gus said as he read the excerpt from his report. "I have to admit, I hadn't remembered that. I didn't realize that you were friends with Ellie Luke. I mean, outside of your relationship with her sister."

"We were classmates," Simmons said. "Friendly, yes. Ellie and I were in the same cohort in nursing school."

"Is that how you met her sister?"

"My wife and I became close after. It was one good thing to come out of such tragic circumstances."

"How so?"

"I just got to know her. Her family. There were fundraisers in Ellie's name after her death. I met Erin during that time frame."

"I see."

"Detective, I don't mean to rush you. But as I said, I need to get to work shortly. You said you'd found something you believe is related to my late sister-in-law's case. What was it?"

Gus looked up from his paperwork. He put the pad and report face down in front of him.

"Mr. Simmons, I'm sorry if my memory isn't what it used to be. Twenty-two years is a long time. But I have in my notes that we did speak before. I spoke to many of Ellie's friends after she went missing."

"Yes," Simmons said. "We were all in shock. We all wanted to do whatever we could to try to find her."

"Of course. Do you remember much about that period?"

"What do you mean?"

"Well, how would you describe your relationship with Ellie? How close were you?"

Simmons frowned. "I told you. We were classmates."

"But you hung out socially, too?"

Simmons's posture changed. He leaned back in his chair. "I'm not sure why you're asking that. What is it that you found, Detective?"

"Mr. Simmons, I really need to try to clarify what your

relationship with Ellie was. It'll help me put some things into context."

"What things?"

"Do you remember the last time you saw Ellie?"

Simmons's easy demeanor shifted. He went rigid, his lips pursed tightly together.

Beside me, Sam's text alert went off. He quickly silenced it, but the expression on his face as he read it turned sour.

"Why are you asking me that?" Simmons said. "What does that have to do with anything?"

"Well," Gus said. "I have to admit. I didn't realize you had a relationship with Ellie. I didn't put two and two together until this morning. I wrongly assumed you were just her brother-in-law after the fact, you know? So while I have you here, I just want to maybe have you help me refresh my memory about a few things from back then. You know, just tie up some loose ends so I can put this case to bed once and for all."

"Once and for all?"

"Sorry. Poor choice of words."

"Detective, I really need to wrap this up. So if you could just let me know what it is you need from me, I can be on my way."

Sam slipped his phone back into his pocket.

"What is it?" I whispered to him.

"Trouble. Maybe," he said. "That was Deputy Ryan. I've had her keeping an eye on Hayden Simmons. Her mother showed up at her friend's house twenty minutes ago. Ryan says they got into some kind of argument in the driveway. Hayden was really upset. Crying. She went back inside but Erin Simmons took off. Ryan decided to follow her. Erin Simmons just pulled into the parking lot outside."

"She's here?" I asked.

"I think I don't want to talk to you anymore," Simmons said to Gus. His face was flushed. He pulled at his collar.

"Mr. Simmons, there's nothing to get excited about. I think we're on the same side. I think we both just want to find out once and for all what happened to Ellie Luke. Don't we?"

"Of course," Simmons said. "But you're making me increasingly uncomfortable."

"That's not my intention."

"Then what is your intention?"

"Okay. I'll level with you, Mr. Simmons. You seem like a smart guy. You clearly care a lot about your wife and her family. I can only imagine how tough it's been for them after what happened to Ellie. And to go all this time without really knowing. To have her case go cold."

"I'd say that's your problem," Simmons said. "I do remember talking to you all those years ago. It must eat at you. Knowing you couldn't solve this case. Knowing you're probably the reason her killer might still be out there somewhere."

"Lord," I said. "Sam, Gus can't lose his temper. Simmons is goading him."

"Gus can handle him," Sam said. Sam's phone rang. He answered it.

"Yeah," Sam said. "We'll be right down. Just stick her in the interview room across from Gus's office." He clicked off.

"Jamie?" Gus said. "I think maybe you weren't completely honest with me today. I think maybe you and Ellie Luke were more than just classmates. You did more than just travel in the same social circles, didn't you?"

Jamie Simmons vaulted to his feet. "We're done here. I have nothing else to say to you unless I have a lawyer present."

"Shit," Sam muttered.

"Calm down," Gus said.

"I will not," Simmons said. "I know my rights. And I know the tone of your questions, Detective Ritter. This is an interrogation. You brought me here under false pretenses."

There was a knock on the door behind us. Sam's clerk poked her head in. "I'm sorry. But you really need to get out here."

"Yeah," Sam said. I hated to leave the observation room. Jamie Simmons hadn't yet made good on his threat to walk, but he knew what Gus was after.

"Gus can handle himself," Sam said. I was right on his heels as we went down the hallway and up one floor to Sam's office. We only made it a few steps out of the stairwell before Ellie Luke's lookalike sister nearly ran into me.

It really was uncanny, the resemblance. Erin had those same ice-blue eyes. The same shape to her mouth. Even after all these years, she wore her hair in the same style as her sister had, cut just to the shoulders and parted down the middle.

"Mrs. Simmons," I said. She looked past me, her face red.

"Where is he? Where did you take Jamie?"

"Mrs. Simmons," Sam said. "Why don't we go talk in my office?"

He put a light hand on her shoulder. She jerked away.

"I know what you're doing. I know what my daughter's done. This is insane. I'm calling a lawyer. I'm calling a whole team of them."

We were drawing a crowd. A few deputies turned to see what the commotion was all about.

"Please," I said. "My name is Mara Brent. I work for the prosecutor's office ..."

"I know exactly who you are. Hayden told me. You've poisoned my daughter's brain."

"What? I haven't," I said.

"My daughter is disturbed. That's what you need to know. She's sick. She has no idea what she's stirring up. She didn't even know my sister. She's become obsessed. It's morbid. She needs help."

"Mrs. Simmons, please," Sam said, trying once more to guide her out of the hallway.

She pushed back.

"Don't you dare touch me. I want my husband. He's done talking to you. Any of you. I'll sue the county. I should have done that years ago. You do not have my permission to speak to my daughter outside of my presence. Do you understand that?"

"Mrs. Simmons," I said. "Your daughter is over eighteen."

"She's a kid! A disturbed, confused kid. I'll get a court order if I have to. But this ends today!"

The stairwell doorway opened behind me. By the reaction on Erin Simmons's face, I didn't have to turn to know who just stepped out.

"Jamie!" Erin ran past me and flew into her husband's waiting arms.

"It's okay," he said, comforting his wife.

"Take me home," she said.

Gus stepped off the elevator in front of us. He frowned as he saw Mr. and Mrs. Simmons behind me.

"You!" Erin screamed, pointing to Gus. "I don't want that man anywhere near me. It was you, wasn't it? You planted all that stuff. You told my daughter what to say."

"Erin," Jamie said, his tone filled with alarm. "Honey, let's go. Don't say another word. Not here."

He put his arm around his wife and led her back into the stairwell.

"Mr. Simmons." Gus stepped forward. He stuck his foot in the stairwell door, blocking it from closing. He pulled a folded piece of paper out of his jacket, having grabbed it before coming back upstairs.

"Get away from us!" Erin shouted.

Gus handed the paper to Jamie Simmons. Simmons's eyes darted over it. I already knew what it was. Gus had secured the search warrant for Jamie Simmons's house, car, phone, and computer.

"I'm sending deputies over to your house as we speak," Gus said. "You can be present, but we're searching the house."

"You can't do that!" Erin said. "My God. Jamie, tell them they can't do that! This is insanity. They're treating you like some kind of criminal!"

Jamie Simmons said nothing. He just kept a tight arm around his wife. Before she could say another word, he jerked the door shut, forcing Gus to move out of the way. Then Jamie and Erin Simmons disappeared down the stairwell.

"My God," I said. "She doesn't understand what's coming."

"I think she understands plenty," Sam said. "It sounds like Hayden broke down and told her everything about two hours ago. Jamie Simmons knew exactly why he got called down here. He was trying to play you, Gus."

"Dammit," Gus said. "I need that house secure. I want to make it over there before they do. The deputies are sitting on it, but I want to get there."

"We'll be right behind you," Sam said. I just hoped word of what happened in this building hadn't yet spread beyond it.

6

"Do you really think it's possible he'll find anything else after all this time?" I asked. I sat in the passenger seat of Sam's cruiser. Gus arrived with four other deputies in tow. Two minutes later, Jamie Simmons pulled up, his wife with him.

"No one's touching anything until my lawyer gets here," Jamie said. Sam and I stepped out of the car and walked up to join Gus.

"You've been duly served with a valid warrant," Gus said. "The longer you try to obstruct me from doing my job, the worse this gets."

The front door opened. Hayden Simmons stepped out. She looked like she was about to be sick.

"I've got this," I whispered to Sam. Erin Simmons turned positively purple. She charged across the lawn, trying to get to her daughter before I did.

"Mom, stop," Hayden said.

"You have no idea what you've done," Erin yelled.

I had hoped we could have conducted this without drawing too much attention. Simmons's home was mercifully on a quiet cul-de-sac by itself. No one would have seen all the activity unless they purposely drove by.

Another car pulled in behind the Simmons's. An attorney I recognized from Toledo, an expensive one, stepped out. His name escaped me. But Erin or Jamie must have called him before he even came to the station.

"Mom," Hayden said. "I haven't done anything wrong. I'm not the one you should be mad at."

"Not the one I should be mad at. You're trying to ruin our lives! You have no idea how long it took for all of us to put the pieces back together."

"That's enough." Jamie's lawyer stepped forward, getting in between Erin and Hayden Simmons. For his part, Jamie stayed surprisingly calm. He stood near his vehicle, wearing an almost jovial expression.

"You're Ms. Brent?" the lawyer asked.

"I am," I said. "Mara Brent. I'm the assistant prosecutor."

"Of course. I'm Bennett Cutler." He handed me his business card. "I'd like to see a copy of the warrant."

Gus came up and handed him one. Cutler scowled as he looked it over.

"All right," he said. "But I'll accompany your deputies. They don't go anywhere I can't see them."

"That's not how this works," Gus said.

"It's how it works for my clients, Detective."

I watched every muscle in Gus Ritter's body go rigid. He took a step forward.

"Mr. Cutler, if you so much as breathe in the direction of my deputies, you'll be sitting in the back of one of those cruisers with cuffs on yourself."

"This is ridiculous," Erin said. "This is my home. Our home. Do you see what you've done, Hayden? Whatever you find in there, she put it in there!"

"Erin, that's enough," Cutler advised her. "Why don't you just sit over there with Jamie? Let me do my job."

"I didn't plant anything," Hayden said. "You know exactly what I found, Dad!"

"Stop," Cutler said. "Not another word out of you."

"You're not her lawyer," Gus said. "You don't get to tell her anything."

"Ms. Brent," Hayden said. "I can't be here. I can't stay here. I just came back so I could pack a few things. Can I do that?"

Hayden stepped off the porch and around her mother. She looked ready to collapse. I wanted to throw my arms around her and take her home with me. If what we believed about her father was true, the depths of betrayal Hayden must have felt ... it was unconscionable.

"We need to let the deputies and Detective Ritter do their job," I said to Hayden as I led her out of earshot of Bennett Cutler and her mother. "But yes. You'll be able to pack a bag. I think it's a good idea for you not to be in this house anymore."

"She's going to throw me out anyway. She's completely taken

his side. I don't understand it. Why would she do that? How could she? I know what he did. How could it be anything else?"

"We'll get to the bottom of it," I said. I wanted to tell her everything would be all right. Though I knew it wouldn't. How could it ever be again for this family?

"I don't have a car," she said. "I was borrowing my dad's. I know they're going to search it."

"Where have you arranged to stay?" I asked.

"I have friends with an apartment near the community college. I've been taking a few classes. They said I could crash on the couch for a little while until I figure out what to do."

"Okay. That's a good idea. Let me talk to Detective Ritter and see if we can have one of the deputies go inside with you to pack your things. Wait here in the meantime."

Sam flashed me a quick thumbs up as I led Hayden to the backseat of his cruiser. She could park herself there until I could get her away from here.

Bennett Cutler had pulled Erin away from the front door. She, Jamie, and Cutler huddled together on the other end of the driveway.

I walked in the front door. Gus stood in the living room barking orders to his deputies. Simmons had a desktop computer against the wall. It would be secured, bagged, and taken away today.

"Hayden wants to pack her things," I said. "She can't stay here tonight. Or maybe ever."

"That woman is a menace," Gus said. "The mother. How the hell could she treat her kid that way?"

"She's in shock," I said. "Her sister was murdered. We're basically telling her that her whole life might have been a lie and she's been harboring a killer. Took his name. Bore his child. I don't know how anyone could handle that."

"Yeah," Gus said. "Deputy Linsky's upstairs. She can work with Hayden about packing her things. I'm afraid we're gonna have to take her laptop, too. It's registered under her father's name. It's included in the warrant."

"Hayden's online activity might be relevant to all this, too. She understands that, I think. It sounds like she's got a place to land, at least for now. I'd like to refer her to a social worker. I can call someone from the Silver Angels."

"Good idea," Gus said. "Let the experts help that poor kid out." The Silver Angels were a local victim's advocacy group.

"Experts," I repeated. "I don't know, Gus. Not even they have expertise in this mess."

I heard a new commotion outside. Gus and I looked out the bay window at the same time.

"You gotta be kidding me," he muttered.

A local news live truck pulled in alongside the curb.

"I better get out there," I said. "I don't want anyone sticking a camera in Hayden's face."

Sam beat me to it. He made a beeline for the truck. I wasn't sure whether that would make things better or worse. Having the sheriff himself here at a search warrant wouldn't do much to persuade any reporter that this wasn't a newsworthy event.

"Sam," I called out. He caught my eye. I grabbed one of the deputies as he was making his way back to the house.

"Drake," I said. Deputy Pete Drake leaned in as I whispered to him. "I need you to as discreetly as possible take Hayden Simmons out of Sheriff Cruz's car and put her into yours. Then get her out of here. Drive her around the block. I don't care. I just don't want her face appearing on any news stories tonight."

"You got it, Ms. Brent," Drake assured me. He headed for Hayden. By the time I got to Sam's side, the reporter had stepped out. His cameraman was already recording.

"Sheriff Cruz," the reporter said. He was new to the area. He identified himself as Rob Ellery, Channel Three. "Can you confirm that a new arrest has been made in the murder of Ellie Luke?"

Oh boy. So much for my hopes this was just dumb luck as the news van happened to drive by.

"I'm afraid I can't comment on anything like that yet," Sam said. "For the moment, I'm going to have to ask you to move off. You're in danger of impeding official law enforcement business, son."

Son. It was a nice touch. Rob Ellery looked like his journalism degree might still have wet ink.

"We're parked on a public street," Ellery said. "I'm not breaking any laws."

"Well," Sam said, flashing his killer smile. "I'm asking you nicely."

"I'm afraid I don't care how nice you are, Sheriff. I have every right to be here. I have information that your office has received actionable leads on the murder of Ellie Luke. I'm giving you a chance to comment."

"There will be no comment," Sam said.

"Ms. Brent?" Ellery turned to me. "Would the prosecutor's office care to comment?"

"Not at this time," I said. "You'll have to direct your questions to the acting prosecutor, Howard Jordan."

Even as I said it, I felt myself wince. The last thing Hojo needed ... that any of us needed ... was having the office flooded with press requests on this case. Not yet. It was far too soon. Someone had leaked something. There was no other way this kid could have just fortuitously shown up here. Bennett Cutler had yet to march over here and get his face on camera. It led me to wonder whether he set this whole thing up.

Deputy Drake drove right behind the news truck and around the corner out of sight. I breathed a sigh of relief knowing Hayden, at least, was protected for the moment.

"Just keep rolling," Ellery told his cameraman. Gus's deputies were beginning to make their way out the front door, carrying items from the Simmons's household. Cutler had stashed Jamie and Erin into his car. He had windows tinted dark enough their faces couldn't be seen.

"Will you be making an arrest today?" Ellery asked.

"No comment," Sam said. He put a hand on my shoulder and turned me away from the cameras.

"We need to go," he whispered. "Gus can handle this. The kid can't interview people who aren't here."

"Good point," I said. "Only he's about to watch us get into the same car together. You sure you want that?"

"We're not the ones doing anything wrong," Sam said. "You feel like sticking around for whatever show Simmons's lawyer intends to put on?"

I climbed into the passenger seat. Thankfully, Sam had parked in such a way he wouldn't be blocked getting out.

"I need to get back to the office," I said. "I need to prepare Hojo for what's about to happen. And you need to get with your press liaison and figure out some kind of statement."

"This is getting away from us already," Sam said as he made the turn away from Gulliver Street.

"It's going to be national news," I said. "All anybody's going to have to do is run a picture of Ellie Luke next to one of her sister."

"Yeah," Sam said. "Dammit. Yeah."

"Sam, I can't have this case tried in the press. The minute that starts to happen, we're sunk. No matter what Hayden found in that box. No matter what Gus finds in the house today."

"We'll get a handle on it," he said.

I turned to him. "Great. You mind telling me how?"

7

It was after seven before I finally walked in the door. The heavenly scent of roasted meat went straight to my stomach. I realized I hadn't eaten anything since half a cheese Danish from the pastry box Caro brought in this morning.

"My God," I said. "Do I even have to use a plate or can I just stick a fork in the crock-pot?"

Kat stood at the sink, wiping it down with a red-and-white-checkered hand towel. "I mean I won't stop you. But there's gravy too."

I leaned over the crock-pot. Kat had made a traditional pot roast with carrots, potatoes, and onions. I grabbed the fork next to the pot. The meat came apart.

"That's delicious."

"Glad you like it," she said. "Will's not so sure."

"He's iffy about having his food mixed together," I said. "But this is objectively amazing. He'll deal. Where is he?"

Kat pointed upward. Will's bathroom was directly above the kitchen. "Wanted a shower right when he came back."

My almost fifteen-year-old son had robotics four days a week. They were gearing up for a major competition the third week of school.

"You guys haven't eaten yet?" I asked.

"No. He just got home fifteen minutes ago."

"What about you?" I asked.

"I got here about a half an hour ago. I stopped by on my lunch break and put the roast in. Let's see if we can expand Will's culinary horizons. And this thing was easy. If he likes it, I'll show him how to put it together before he leaves for school."

Since my son was a baby, Will's Aunt Kat, my former sister-in-law, had been an integral part of his life. She started watching him three days a week while my ex, Will's father, and I started our careers here in Waynetown. Will had a hard time getting close to people. But Kat was like a second mother to him. She was my best friend. My sister for life, even though Jason and I were over.

"Hurry up!" Kat went to the stairwell and shouted up. "You don't need that much water for your skinny little body!"

I smiled. Kat had been yelling that exact thing to Will since he was about three years old. A moment later, I heard the faucet upstairs stop.

"How was he when he got home?" I asked.

"Good," she said. "Sounds like he and the new coach worked out their issues. I didn't hear the diatribe."

"That man is just as stubborn as Will is," I said.

"So you've met Mr. Ball?"

"I have."

Kat smiled as she grabbed the plates from the cupboard. "Did he remind you of anyone?"

"He wasn't very friendly. But he seemed more organized than the last coach. Had spreadsheets to hand out and everything."

"Exactly," Kat said, putting the plates on the table. "He reminds me of Will. I think they're both sitting on the same end of the spectrum, Mara. This should be an interesting year."

"You might be right now that I think of it. Well, hopefully they'll gel instead of clash."

"You and me both. Because Mr. Ball has also been named the new special ed algebra teacher. Will's going to have him in class, too. He just got his schedule."

Kat grabbed an envelope off the counter and handed it to me. It had already clearly been opened by Will. My son opened letters, cereal boxes, and chip bags like a raccoon. I read off his schedule. He'd gotten two of the teachers we'd requested but Mr. Ball was new.

Will himself tramped down the stairs, his hair still dripping wet. He reeked of body spray typical of teenage boys. I knew it was better than the alternative.

"How was Mr. Ball today?" I asked.

"Hi, Mom," Will said. Every time I saw him, I swore my boy grew another inch. As it was, he was about half a head taller than me. His father was six foot two. Will would catch up with him by next year at this rate.

"He's getting better," Will said. "Some of the parents complained."

"I'll bet they did," Kat muttered. I shot her a look, hoping Will hadn't overheard. But he was entranced by the contents of the crock-pot.

"Give it a chance," I said.

"Here," Kat said. She spooned Will's portion out, putting the meat, carrots, and potatoes in separate quadrants of his plate. She left the gravy on the table.

"Thanks," I told her. I portioned out my own plate and made one for Kat as well. She had a fourth plate next to the crock-pot.

"We can wait for Bree," I said. Kat's wife worked at the University of Michigan Hospital in Ann Arbor. With nearly an hour commute, she rarely made it for our weekly dinners. I missed her.

"She's working a double today," Kat said. "But then she's got a week off starting tomorrow."

"Good. She deserves it."

I sat next to Will. He pushed his food around on his plate but seemed interested in it. He stabbed his fork into a carrot and ate it. I held my breath for a moment. Before I could ask him what he thought, he went for the meat.

"Good stuff," I said, relieved. Kat's cooking saved the day again. For about a solid year, Will would only eat her homemade spaghetti or macaroni and cheese. But my son was changing. Maturing.

He still had plenty of challenges, but handled his father's absence far better than I could have hoped. Kat thought it had ultimately been a relief for him. So much had been up in the air with Jason for so many years. Now, Will and I had forged a life together. The two of us. With Kat and Bree and now Sam as the significant adults in his life.

My phone buzzed on the counter where I left it. I reached for it. It was a text from Gus.

"Better turn on the local news."

"Crap," I said. "Will, I know we say no screens at the table, but do you mind if I turn on the TV for a second?"

"Is it for work?"

"It's a case that's about to land on my desk," I said.

Will perked up. He'd always taken an interest in my caseload. It worried me sometimes, but I couldn't shield him from it. I grabbed the remote and clicked on the small TV we kept mounted on the wall.

"When there's something I can share, I'll share it!" Hojo stood in front of a bank of microphones in front of the courthouse. Sam stood beside him.

"Sheriff Cruz," a reporter shouted. "When will Jamie Simmons be arrested? We understand Ellie Luke's family is hiring their own attorney. That they are concerned another member of the family has been coerced into providing false evidence against Mr. Simmons."

"What?" I shouted at the television. I picked up my phone and texted Gus back.

"Where is this coming from?"

"Who knows," he said.

I watched Hojo's face cycle through various shades of red, then pale white. He was sweating.

"He doesn't look good up there," Kat said.

"I don't think I can watch," I said, clicking off.

"Ellie Luke," Kat said. "Is that who they said? Are they making an arrest in that case?"

"Maybe," I said.

"Who's Ellie Luke?" Will asked.

"She was a college student," I answered. "She was killed more than twenty years ago. There may be a break in the case. And I say may. None of this is ripe for the media yet."

"Is he in over his head?" Kat asked. "Jordan."

"Not yet," I said. "But this thing is starting to get away from us. That's not to leave this table."

"Of course not," Kat said.

"Ellie Luke," Will said. I knew what he was doing. He would commit her name to memory and start searching the internet.

"Leave it," I warned my son.

"Twenty years is a long time. You probably don't have cell phone forensics to go on. What about DNA? How was she found?"

"Stop," I said. "Don't make me regret telling you as much as I have."

Will shrugged. "It's already in the press. People at school are gonna start asking me about it."

"And you say nothing," I warned him.

"I never do," he assured me. "But that doesn't stop them from asking."

Will had finished his roast. Every single bite. It was as winning an endorsement as we could have hoped for.

"May I be excused?" he asked. "I want to work on my blueprints."

"That depends," I said. "I'm gonna check your laptop, buddy. No doom scrolling on Ellie Luke."

"I won't," he said. Kat shot me a look. Neither of us were convinced. But Will dutifully washed his plate and put it in the dishwasher. He went back upstairs. Kat turned to me.

"You know," she said. "Bree was friends with Ellie Luke."

"She was?"

"They were in nursing school together. They hung out."

"I had no idea," I said, then realized I would have had no reason to. I hadn't dug into Gus's old files. There would be time for that if and when an arrest was made.

"They still do a 5k in her honor at the nursing college," Kat said. "We raced in it two years ago. I think it might have been the twentieth anniversary of her murder, maybe?"

"That would track," I said. "How close were they?"

"They were friends," Kat said. "We only really talked about it the one time. But I know Bree was questioned by the police when that poor girl disappeared."

"Lord," I said. "I had no idea. This may be a dumb question, but did you get the impression it was upsetting to her? I mean, of course it was upsetting. I just mean ... Kat ... this thing is about to blow up. I can't tell you the details, you know that. But there's a slant to it that will probably catch fire in terms of press attention. As in ... national news outlets might run with it."

"Oh wow," Kat said. "Um. Yes. Ellie isn't someone Bree talks about. But it affected her. Shook her up at the time, I think."

"Okay," I said. "Well ... yes. She may have to be reinterviewed, depending on how well she knew Ellie at the time. And if she were interviewed when it happened. I think maybe you should call her. Or I can. I think she should be prepared."

"Okay," Kat said. "I'll talk to her tonight. I'll have her call you tomorrow."

"Thanks," I said. I got another angry text from Gus. It was a stream of obscenities directed at the reporter who showed up at the Simmons's house when he served the warrants.

"We need to meet first thing in the morning," I texted back. "This might get messy."

"It already has," he texted.

8

The next morning, I met Sam and Gus in Gus's new war room dedicated to the Ellie Luke murder. Sam had cleared a space in the office next to his. It had taken two days, but every box of evidence from Ellie's case had been pulled up from the basement. Gus had laid it all out on two tables.

"That was rough yesterday," I said to Sam as he handed me a steaming cup of coffee. It was strong, crappy, and I inhaled it.

"The media already knows too much," Sam said.

"You've got a leak," I said.

"It might not be us," Sam said.

"What difference does it make now?" Gus said. He stood at a third table, laying out photographs. I walked over to him. One by one, he fanned out the crime scene photos. There wasn't much to them. Ellie Luke's remains were nothing but bones. Though it was clear to see how she'd been positioned against that tree. Legs crossed at the ankles, hands linked together in an almost prayer pose.

I picked one up. It had been taken after the ME moved the body. A blue gloved hand pointed to a massive defect at the back of Ellie's skull.

"Did you find anything of value off your search warrants yet?" I asked.

"No," Gus said. "It's gonna take some time for BCI to go through the phones and computer. But I don't expect any real surprises."

"We can't know that," Sam said. "Simmons has probably gotten lazy ... comfortable after all this time."

"We have this," Gus said, handing me a photograph. It was a close-up shot of the ground near the base of the tree where she'd been placed.

"What is this?" I asked, although I knew. I'd seen it before.

Gus picked up an evidence bag from the second table. He handed it to me. Inside was a single earring. A flat hoop with little heart-pattern cutouts.

"That was found at the scene twenty-two years ago," he said. "It looks like a match for the one in Simmons's treasure box."

"And there's this," Sam said, pulling another photograph. It looked like a yearbook photo. Ellie's senior year. She wore her hair up. Those same gold hoop earrings dangled from her ears.

"She wore them a lot," Gus said. "Her favorite pair. Her mother provided other photos of her wearing them. We only ever found the one at the scene."

"You're sending these to BCI as well?" I asked. "Will they be able to determine if they really are a match?"

"I've got an agent en route," Gus said. "Hopefully, they'll come up with something conclusive. They'll test the underwear and the lock of hair. Though it looks cut, not pulled out at the root. Not sure they'll be able to extract any DNA. She colored her hair. I bagged one of her hair brushes back in the day. They'll be able to compare."

"Good," I said. "That's really good."

"Detective Ritter?" Maggie, one of the civilian clerks, poked her head in. "I've got those tapes you wanted."

Maggie walked in holding a flash drive. She handed it to Gus.

"Everything's labeled in separate files," she said.

"Thanks," Gus said. He had a laptop sitting on one of the tables. Maggie excused herself and he slipped the drive into the side port. A moment later, the file menu populated. Each file was labeled with a name. A witness.

"I videotaped every interview," Gus said. "God. I don't even remember interviewing Jamie Simmons. I just went through every name of the people she was in class with. A few people her parents said she hung around with."

Gus pulled up a folding chair. Sam and I did the same. Gus pushed the laptop further back so we could see it. He connected two speakers into another port and pulled up the file on Jamie Simmons.

A moment later, the screen filled with a shot of the interview room just across the hall. After twenty-two years, it scarcely looked different. The image was grainy, an overhead shot. The camera was placed on the ceiling in the corner of the room.

A skinny kid walked in. Simmons. He had a full head of blond hair back then and wore track pants and a Chicago Bears tee shirt.

A moment later, Gus walked in. It was strange to see him like that. Twenty-two years ago he would have been thirty-four years old. Younger than I was now. He was a bit trimmer. Had more color in his face. But it was like Caro said. Gus had probably looked like a middle-aged man since he was eighteen.

"Thanks for coming down," Gus said on the screen.

"Oh, of course," Simmons said. His voice was higher-pitched then. Possibly a function of his youth or the quality of the playback. It might have been nerves but that didn't necessarily mean anything.

"I'm sorry for your loss," Gus said. "I understand you and Ellie Luke were friends."

"Good friends, yes," Simmons answered.

"When was the last time you saw her?"

Simmons sat with his hands folded on the table. Rod straight, it was more the posture of someone sitting in class. Still, I don't know that it would have raised any suspicions in me at the time. Being brought in for questioning by the police would be nerve-wracking for anyone. And his friend had gone missing.

"Um ... I wanna say it was three days ago. What is this? Sunday? We have an anatomy class together on Thursdays."

"Did you talk to her that day?" Gus asked.

"Um ... I mean, sure. We talk when we see each other. It's not a very big class. Ellie sits right in front of me."

"Do you remember what you talked about?"

Simmons shook his head. "Nothing unusual. I can't remember specifically. We had a test coming up that I was stressed out about. We all were. It's a tough class. I think we talked about the material."

"Did she tell you her weekend plans?"

Simmons shrugged. "I just don't remember that. She might have. But Ellie didn't really have much of a social life. None of us do right now. We're so busy with school. Plus, she works weird hours. She's got her CNA license."

Gus hit pause, then rewound. He played back part of Simmons's statement.

"But Ellie didn't really have much of a social life." He hit pause again.

"He's talking about her in the past tense," I said. "You interviewed him before you found Ellie's body?"

"I interviewed everyone before we found Ellie's body," he said. "I should have caught that."

Sam reached for the keyboard and pressed play. A second later, Simmons said, "She works weird hours. She's got her CNA license."

"I wouldn't have caught that," Sam said. "He talks about her in the present tense right after."

"Jamie," Gus said on the tape. "What was Ellie's mood like in class the last time you saw her?"

"Her mood? I don't know. She was ... she's just Ellie. She's a serious girl, you know? Pays attention in class. She's there to learn. She's not ... frivolous. There's no drama with her."

"Gotcha," Gus said. "So nothing seemed unusual? She wasn't acting any different from what you observed?"

"No. I mean, she didn't seem upset. Or distracted. Nothing like that. Nothing that would have made me ask her what's wrong. Not that I'd really be the one she'd tell something like that to. We're friends, but not close, close friends."

"I see. Did you talk to her after class on Thursday?"

"I don't think so, no."

"Jamie, do you know if she was dating anyone?"

Jamie put his hands flat on the table. "I don't know. Not that she told me about."

"Would she have?"

"I don't know. I mean, I would probably have heard about it. Everybody's friends in our cohort. If Ellie hadn't mentioned it herself, I think I would have heard if she was going out with somebody. As far as I know, she wasn't. That doesn't mean she wasn't. You know? Like if she had somebody she wanted to keep secret."

"Would that have been odd? Her keeping a secret like that from your group?"

"Kinda. I guess. Gosh. I'm really sorry if I'm being vague. I'm not trying to be. I just mean if she was starting to date somebody new and didn't want to tell anyone yet. I'm just saying I wouldn't have found that odd. But I'm really just speculating. I have no reason to think Ellie was dating anybody new. I'm sorry. I'm really trying to help in any way I can."

"I appreciate that," Gus said. "And you are. What about enemies? Do you know of anyone who maybe had a beef with Ellie? Anyone she didn't get along with at school?"

"No, sir. Not that I know of. It's like I told you. Ellie's just ... Ellie. She doesn't cause drama. She's serious. She's ... she's like an old soul. She's the one people go to when they need advice. She's like everybody's school mom, you know?"

"I appreciate that. It's helpful. We're almost done. I promise. Jamie, did Ellie ever talk about any drama at home?"

"What, like with her parents? Not that I remember. No."

"Any other family members?"

Jamie pursed his lips and shook his head. "Not that ... hmmm ... I'm not sure. I'm trying to think. She gets along with her folks, I think. She has a brother, maybe?"

"Just a sister," Gus said. "Has she mentioned a cousin to you?"

I felt my pulse quicken. Beside me, Gus leaned far forward in his chair, almost as if he were trying to push himself through the screen.

"A cousin? Hmmm. Maybe."

"Have you ever seen this guy around Ellie?" Gus asked on screen. He laid a photograph on the table. I couldn't make it out, but I could guess who it was.

"Hmm." Jamie Simmons picked up the photograph. "Maybe," he said. "Yeah. Maybe. You think Ellie doesn't like him?"

"Do you think she told you that? She told you she has an issue with her cousin?"

"Christ," Gus said beside me.

"Maybe," Jamie said on screen. "Yeah. I think so. He's some kind of loser, I think. A troublemaker?"

"Dane Fischer," Gus said. "Did she ever mention him to you?"

"I think so. It sounds familiar. But like ... not something she wanted to talk about a lot. Just ... I got the impression he was causing her some stress. I didn't pry. I didn't think it was any of my business. Did he do something? Do you think this guy hurt her? God. I know Ellie. If this guy was causing trouble, then he has to be a real loser. Ellie doesn't have issues with anybody. Like I told you. I wish I could remember more. I just don't."

"It's okay. I appreciate what you've told me so far. I know you probably have to get to class. We're done for now."

"If you think of anything else I can do. Please call me," Jamie said. "I want to help. Do you ... Detective ... is she dead? Do you think Ellie's dead? Do you think this Dane guy hurt her?"

"I can't say, Jamie. But I will reach out if I have any other questions."

There was a knock at the door. Gus stood up, obscuring Jamie from the camera. Gus shook Jamie's hand and excused himself from the room. Jamie Simmons didn't immediately stand up. He put his hands flat on the table again and hung his head. He took a deep breath and exhaled. Almost as if he were relieved about something. Then the screen froze as the recording stopped.

Gus bolted out of his chair beside me and kicked it halfway across the room.

"Gus!" I said.

"I bungled that interview. Christ. I put Dane Fischer in his damn brain. He fed him right back to me and I didn't even see it. That was rookie shit."

"Gus, you can't beat yourself up," Sam said. "You had nothing connecting Jamie Simmons to this. Not then, and not now, if it weren't for what Hayden found."

"I didn't ask him where he was the night Ellie went missing," Gus said. "I didn't even ask him that!"

"He wasn't a person of interest," I said. "You were just trying to get a picture of Ellie's last days. Sam's right. There was nothing about Jamie Simmons that would have tripped your radar. Anyone's radar. Not then."

"I showed him a goddamn picture of Dane Fischer. It was in my mind. Her parents told me Fischer made threats. There was a restraining order. I had tunnel vision."

"You were following the leads you had," Sam said. "If I were in the room with Simmons, I'd have done the same thing. You're being too hard on yourself. Yeah. You were green. Was it the best interview I've ever seen? No. Was it a Gus-Ritter-of-today interview? No. But it wasn't bad. This isn't on you."

"Isn't it?" Gus said.

Maggie poked her head in again. "Gus, I'm really sorry. I've got Agent Willis from BCI on the phone for you. You want to take it in your office?"

"Yeah," he muttered. He looked back at the laptop. For a moment, I thought he might throw it through the window. But he grabbed his jacket off the back of the chair, stabbed his arms through it and headed down to take his phone call.

Sam stood with his hands on his hips, head down. "Mara," he said. "How bad was that?"

"If I play it at trial?" I asked. "It's nothing. It's like Gus said. He doesn't have him commit to an alibi or anything. I think it's neutral at best. Nobody's going to look at that and think oh, there's definitely a killer. But they're not going to think he's innocent from it either. My bigger worry is Gus."

"What do you mean?" Sam looked at me.

"I mean ... he's got to get his head straight. Whatever self-flagellation he wants to do ... he needs to get it out of his system quick. If he takes the stand like that ..."

"He'll be fine," Sam said. "Better than fine. He's solid in that witness box. You've seen him."

"I know," I said.

"Do we have enough?" Sam asked.

"To convict him? Not even close. Hopefully BCI will be able to tie those things in Simmons's treasure box to the crime scene. Even then ... twenty-two years is a long time."

"We'll get there," he said. "But we're arresting him in the next twenty-four hours."

"Good," I said. "Let me know when he's in custody."

9

"I can assure you that my client's main concern is to fully cooperate with law enforcement. He is confident that when the truth comes to light, he will be completely exonerated."

Bennett Cutler stood in front of a bank of microphones outside Jamie Simmons's home.

"Mr. Cutler," one of the reporters shouted. I recognized her as Laura Anderson from Channel Seven. She anchored the six o'clock news and had been a staple in Northwest Ohio for over thirty years. It wasn't usual for her to handle press conferences like this. But twenty-two years ago, she had covered the story of Ellie Luke's murder. Like Gus, she had been a rookie at the time. I'm sure she felt she had come full circle.

"Obviously new evidence has come to light," Anderson said. "You must be privy to the nature of that. Can you confirm my sources that Mr. Simmons's own daughter is the one to have come forward with that evidence?"

Sam walked into my office looking grim. I knew he was preparing his own press conference for later this afternoon. Bennett Cutler had given him no choice. He had the county commissioners breathing down his neck as well.

"Is he done yet?" Sam asked.

"Looks like he's just getting revved up," I said.

"I don't want Hojo anywhere near this today," Sam said.

"He did okay the other day," I said. "He'll be fine."

"I'm not worried about how he'll do," Sam said. "I just think right now it's better if there's one voice talking to the media. Mine. Hojo's ethically bound to keep quiet anyway."

"Fair enough."

Sam stood next to me, scowling as he watched the screen. "Have they said anything yet?" he asked. An elderly couple stood just behind Bennett Cutler. The wife had tears streaming down her face.

"Who put them up to that?" Sam asked. Horror drew deep lines in his face as he realized who the couple was.

Bennett Cutler sidestepped and put an arm around the elderly man.

"Mr. Luke!" Laura Anderson shouted. "Have you been in communication with your son-in-law?"

"He wouldn't," I murmured.

George Luke lifted his chin and leaned forward into the closest microphone. "My family has been through hell," he said. "For twenty-two years, we've been asking for justice for my daughter. I have more questions than answers, just like you. But every member of my family has cooperated with the police. We're going to keep doing that."

Bennett Cutler patted George Luke on the back. To his left, Claudia Luke looked ready to be sick.

"That wasn't what he thinks it was," I said. "Cutler is using that poor couple as a shield. He's trying to make it look like they don't believe Simmons killed their daughter."

"Gus needs to get George Luke in here," Sam said.

"He's got to be feeding them God knows what," I said. "Please tell me nobody has discussed the new evidence with them."

"I have no idea what Simmons is telling his wife or his in-laws," Sam said.

"I need to know. The sooner the better. I can't compel Simmons to testify at trial, but I can certainly use any statement he made to family members. That's not privileged. Lord, Bennett Cutler knows that. Has Gus questioned Erin Luke again yet?"

"Cutler got in the way of that."

"He can't represent both of them. That's a clear conflict of interest."

"I suppose that's Erin Luke's problem, not ours."

"It's like he's gaslighted that whole family for two decades," I said. "I need to understand the power he has over them. Simmons did more than collect a box of souvenirs from that murder, Sam. He's collected Erin Luke's whole family."

Sam's phone buzzed. He looked at the screen.

"It's Gus," he said. "Bennett Cutler called him an hour ago and said he's bringing Simmons in right after that circus in front of their house. The arrest warrant has been signed."

"And Cutler is setting up the photo op as we speak," I said. I couldn't watch anymore. I clicked off the television and tossed the remote on my desk. "Well, at least his strategy won't come as a surprise. Cutler wants to taint the jury pool as much as he can."

"I'd like to shake him," Sam said. "He's using that poor family as pawns. It doesn't matter what George Luke actually said. Just the optic of him standing beside Simmons's defense attorney is going to make it look like they're supporting that bastard."

"Give it time," I said. "We really don't know what Simmons has been telling him or telling Bennett Cutler. My bigger concern is Hayden. If Cutler gets to her, he could poison this whole thing. The Lukes need to understand what happened. Where are we on BCI and the analysis of that earring and the other bits from Simmons's box?"

"They've moved it all to the front of the queue," Sam said. "I expect some preliminary findings in the next couple of days. I don't expect any DNA. But if they can definitely match those earrings, at least."

"And the underwear," I said. "If the Lukes can't yet bring themselves to believe they've been harboring their daughter's murderer all these years, they can at least start believing what an absolute creep he is. I'm really worried about Hayden. If they all turn against her ..."

"I know," Sam said. "She's the key to this in a lot of ways. We need her solid."

"Mara." Caro poked her head in. "I'm sorry to interrupt you. But there's someone out here asking for you."

"I'll leave you to it," Sam said.

"You'll be there when they bring Simmons in?" I asked.

"Absolutely."

"Actually, no," Caro said. "I really am sorry. We tried to get him to leave. He won't. He's here looking for you, Sam."

"Where is he?" We heard a shout from out in the hallway. "I know he's back there. I have a right to speak to the sheriff. I have a right to punch his damn lights out for what's been done to me."

Sam went rigid, drawing his shoulders back.

"Sam," I said. "Whoever ..."

Sam ignored me, walking out of my office in two short strides. Caro shot me a look that seemed to say, "You better follow him and make sure he doesn't make things worse."

I stepped around my desk and followed Sam out into the hallway.

"You have to wait in the lobby!" Justine, one of our new interns, raced after a tall, muscular, middle-aged man wearing a blue flannel shirt, jeans, and work boots. He had thinning brown hair and a permanent scowl on his face.

"Hold on there," Sam said, his voice booming with authority. "I'm going to need you to take a step back, turn around, and walk out that door. If you're looking for me, this isn't where we're going to have our conversation."

The man stopped short. Sam had a couple of inches on him, but it looked like it might be a fair fight if it came to it.

"We'll have our conversation right here," the man said. "I'm tired of waiting. I'm tired of being jerked around and having my name dragged through the mud. I want some answers. Now."

"I'm sorry," I said. "Would you like to tell us who you are?"

"You're the prosecutor?" he asked.

"I'm Mara Brent, yes," I said. I put a light hand on Sam's arm. His bicep was hard as granite. His right hand played at the handle of his holstered sidearm.

"You don't know who I am?" he asked.

"Right now, I don't care who you are. I care about you taking a few steps back," Sam said. This time, the authority in his voice seemed to have an impact. The man blinked and dropped his shoulders.

"I just want to talk," he said. "I deserve to know what's happening."

"What can we help you with?" I asked.

He put his head in his hands. The man went from nearly open aggression to weeping in two seconds flat.

"The conference room is open," Caro said, using her most motherly tone. "It's just through here."

The man nodded. He let Caro put a hand on his arm and guide him to the room across the hall. Sam shot me a look. He was by no means ready to stand down himself, but he let me lead the way as we walked into the conference room. Caro plopped our new guest down in a chair at the end of the table.

Sam stood sentry by the door, ready to spring into action if he sensed any further aggression. I took the seat on the other side of the table.

"Can I get you anything?" Caro asked. "Water, coffee?"

The man shook his head. He looked up at me, eyes pleading.

"You really don't know who I am?"

"I really don't," I said.

"My name is Dane Fischer. And I need you to tell me. Did Jamie Simmons kill my cousin?"

Sam and I exchanged a look. Dane Fischer. It took half a second for the synapses in my brain to fully fire. Dane Fischer. Ellie Luke's cousin. This was the man Gus thought had killed Ellie all these years, but could never prove.

"I'm sorry, Mr. Fischer," I said. "We can't comment on an ongoing investigation."

"But I saw the news," he said. "You're arresting Simmons for Ellie's murder. Right?"

"Yes," Sam said. There was no point in trying to put him off. He was right. It was in the news. The arrest would be public record in a matter of minutes.

"He killed her." Fischer repeated it like a mantra. "He killed her. I told them. I told them. Do you have any idea what the last twenty years of my life have been like? Are you going to do something about that?"

"Mr. Fischer," I said. "I can't imagine how difficult this has been for your family. I really wish we could talk more. But it's as we said …"

"I need you to tell me something. That detective. Gus Ritter. He was mentioned on the news too. Is he going to be the one to handle this case?"

"Yes," Sam said. "Gus Ritter is the lead detective on Ellie Luke's case. Yes."

Fischer's face went white. "Do I need a lawyer?"

"For what?" I asked.

"I don't think you get it," Fischer said. "They all think I did this. My whole family. That detective made them think I did this. I never hurt Ellie. I would never have hurt Ellie. I would never hurt anyone. Nobody would believe me. Ritter let them think the worst of me. All this time. Are you going to tell them the truth?"

"Mr. Fischer," Sam said. "You were never charged with Ellie's killing. I don't know what you think it is we can do for you. My only interest is in getting justice for that girl."

"I should sue you," he said, rising from his chair. "I should sue you both. Sue the county. Maybe even Ellie's family. You all have destroyed my life. Made me live under this cloud. You have no idea what it took for me to get sober. To stay sober. They've painted me as this devil. I lost everything. Do you understand that? Everything. I didn't do anything wrong. Nobody believed me because you people didn't care. That detective told them he thought I killed her. My aunt and uncle believed that. Ellie's sister believed that. Even now, they're out there protecting Jamie Simmons. They'd rather believe the worst of me than face the fact they got it wrong. They don't care about Ellie. They don't care about justice. None of you do."

"I assure you," I said. "That's not true. I'm truly sorry we can't discuss this at greater length with you."

"I don't know why I came here," he said. "I don't know why I thought either of you would be more decent than the last sheriff. The last prosecutor. Gus Ritter is still wearing a badge. We're not finished. Know that. I'm getting a lawyer."

"You don't need one," I said. "You're not under suspicion anymore, Mr. Fischer."

The bravado was back. Fischer puffed his chest out, daring Sam to make a move on him.

"You've said your piece," Sam said. "Now I'd like you to walk out of this office, Mr. Fischer."

Fischer jerked his chin at Sam. A challenge. To his credit, Sam stayed rigid, letting him pass. Fischer stormed down the hall. He knocked a plant off Caro's desk as he passed it.

"That mother—" Sam started. I put a hand on his arm.

"Let it go," I said. "He's in the wrong, but he's not wrong that he's probably been treated terribly by Ellie's family all these years. Let's not do anything to make this thing even worse than it is."

Sam shook his head. "I have a feeling this thing is going to get a lot worse before it gets better. I'm just worried the circus is going to make it that much harder for all of us to get justice for that girl, Mara."

"I know," I said. "Just ... stay on BCI. Get me that evidence."

I went up on my tiptoes and kissed his cheek. "We're going to figure this all out. We're going to make sure Hayden Simmons has all the support we can give her. And I'm going to do my job."

Sam smiled. "You're pretty good at it."

"Yes," I said. "I am. And so are you. So is Gus. Do me a favor and remind him of that."

Sam's face darkened. "I better get across the street and be there when Simmons surrenders."

"Yes. You better. But then after that, you're going to come over to my house, remember? Will's at a friend's house tonight. We'll make dinner."

Sam kissed me and patted his stomach. "I can't wait. Just make me a promise."

"Of course."

"I won't let you talk about the Luke case. And you won't let me."

"Deal," I said. But as Sam left the conference room, I wondered how good either of us would be about keeping that promise.

10

Every fear I had about the Luke case taking on a circus quality seemed to come true that afternoon. Bennett Cutler made sure Jamie Simmons surrendered in full view of the cameras in front of the Maumee County Sheriff's Department. Hojo was accosted by reporters on his way to his car. He managed to keep his cool and say no comment as he drove away. As I took the lasagna I'd made out of the fridge and waited for the oven to heat up, I flipped to one of the cable news channels just in time to see a teaser for Ellie Luke's case.

"A cold case killer may have just been exposed ... by his own daughter ..."

I slammed the oven door shut just as Sam walked in the back door.

"Did you see it?" I asked, pointing to the television.

"I heard about it," he said. Sam pulled at his tie. He looked as angry as I felt.

"Well, there's no hope for it now. Hayden Simmons is going to be a household name along with her father and aunt by week's end," I said.

"Have you talked to her?" he asked.

"No. But I've sent Nicole Silver to her. They're working on getting Hayden someplace to stay. It won't take long before the media figures out who her friends are and starts knocking on doors."

"Good," Sam said. "No. That's real good. We need her solid, Mara."

"You don't have to tell me that. What about Simmons? Is he talking?"

"No. And he won't. Bennett Cutler has made sure of that."

Sam was still wrestling with his tie. I went over to him and gently pulled his hands away. He was coiled tight. The pulse in his temple beat at a furious pace.

"You've done all you can do today," I said. "This thing is just going to have to play out."

"BCI has pulled out the big guns. Lois Palmieri is going to handle it herself. She's a national legend in crime scene investigation. She can't make me a concrete promise, but she thinks she'll have something for me the early part of next week on the evidence we sent her. She's moving a few things to the front of the line."

"Good," I said. "But are you really expecting any surprises?"

"No," Sam said. He kissed me on the forehead. "Sorry. I came in here loaded for bear. We promised each other we weren't gonna discuss the case tonight."

"It's okay. It's going to be hard not to."

"You mind if I grab a shower before dinner?"

I wrinkled my nose, teasing him. "I'd prefer it if you did."

Sam gave me a playful swat on my backside that sent a thrill through me. "You sure we're uh ... in the clear?"

"Will's at a sleepover," I said. "He and one of his teammates from robotics have been joined at the hip all summer. They went to the science museum today. He'll be back tomorrow around lunchtime."

"Okay." Sam ran a hand through my hair. "But pretty soon, don't you think we need to have a conversation with him?"

"He knows you're part of my life," I said. "And you're part of his life, too. What else do you think he needs to know? Go on. Wash up. That lasagna only needs to be heated up. It'll be ready in about twenty minutes. You feeling like beer or wine tonight?"

"Beer if you've got it," he said. Sam unbuttoned his shirt. He wore a plain white tee underneath and filled it out nicely.

"You can throw everything in the washing machine if you want," I said. "I was going to run a load tonight anyway."

"I can do my own laundry, Mara."

"Maybe I don't mind." I smiled.

Sam pulled off his tee shirt. He was broad-shouldered, muscular, and trim. I wondered if I'd ever get tired of looking at him. We'd taken things slow for so many reasons. I was recently divorced. There was Will. There was the potential political fallout of him being the sheriff and me working for the prosecutor's office. But tonight, it felt good to just have him here all to myself. To not have to edit myself or worry about who might have an opinion of our relationship.

He tossed his clothes in my washing machine off the kitchen, then kissed me in passing as he made his way up the stairs.

I started a load. Will had brought his things down from his hamper this morning. He'd grown like a weed this summer. Though he didn't have the build of an athlete, like Sam, they wore the same size tee shirts. My little boy was fast growing into a man.

I heard the shower running in the bathroom directly above me. A wicked thought crossed my mind. I decided to act on it. I turned the heat down on the oven but decided I didn't care one bit if the lasagna burned.

"I LIKE IT HERE," SAM SAID THE NEXT MORNING AS HE LAY beside me. "Maybe too much."

I threaded my fingers through his, leaning back against his solid chest. I traced the lines of his palms. He had big hands. The kind that could span my waist. I tried not to compare him with the man I used to share this very bed with. Jason. My ex. Will's father. There was a time I never thought I'd be with anyone else. Now, I was beginning to feel the same about Sam. He was right. Sometime soon, we'd have to have a conversation with Will. But first we might have to have one between us.

"I like you here too," I said. It was only the third time he'd spent the night. "I just wonder if maybe we shouldn't ... you know ... take the risk. With all this attention on the Luke case."

"I really don't care what people think on that score."

"It could become a distraction. We both know I'm going to be the one trying this case if it gets that far. I've had reporters camped outside my house for lower profile cases. This one's already made national news. Cutler made sure of that. I just don't want to run the risk of either of us becoming the story."

"You sure that's all it is?" Sam asked.

I leaned up on my elbow. "Yes. Don't forget. In another year you have to run for election. You're still filling out Bill Clancy's term. The wagons are starting to circle and we'd be naïve to think you'll run unopposed. I just don't want to give anyone fodder."

"I can handle it," he said. "Can you?"

"It wouldn't be the first time I've had my love life used against me. There are plenty of people who still think I should be punished for the crimes Jason committed."

"Is that the real reason you won't run for prosecutor?"

"What? No. I've told you a thousand times. I like the job I have. I've never had the slightest interest in elected office."

"Fine," he said, pulling me closer to him. "But I'm not going to sneak around because of closed-minded people's opinions. I love you. Period. I don't care who knows it."

I felt a rush of heat. We'd said it before to each other. It wasn't that. It was just here ... in the early morning, in my bed. It felt even more intimate than before.

I rested my head back against him, liking the way we fit together. Part of me wished I could stop time. We stayed that way for a while. Sam made me feel safe, warm, at peace. I don't think I'd ever felt that way with Jason. Not in all the years we were married. It wasn't in me to say it. But it would have felt like sacrilege, invoking Jason's name in this space and time.

Finally, I don't know who moved first. But we did. Sam had space in a drawer. He put on a pair of jeans and a fresh tee shirt. I found a pair of yoga pants and a hoodie. Downstairs, I could smell the coffee brewing.

Sam made us both an English muffin. The coffee was good. Strong. But he frowned as he read something on his tablet.

"Bennett Cutler plans on holding another press conference after Simmons's arraignment," he said.

"Are you surprised? He's going to take every opportunity he can to parade Ellie Luke's family out there. It's only a matter of time before they realize what he's doing."

"Gus is going to flip out," Sam said.

"I'm worried about that too," I said. "Do you think he's taking this one too personally?"

Sam met my eyes. "Don't worry ..."

"Stop," I said. "This is me. I'm not wearing my prosecutor hat. And you can stop wearing your sheriff's hat. I'm talking about Gus. I know your noises, Sam. Your facial expressions. And I'm asking you. As Gus's friend too ... what do you *think*?"

Sam put his tablet down. His face softened. "I think Gus probably hasn't slept since Hayden Simmons brought that damn box into our office."

"This was his one, wasn't it?" I asked.

"His one?"

"The case he couldn't solve. The one that got away."

"Gus has been a detective for a long time. He doesn't have just one. He's not a superhero. There are plenty of cold cases in our archives."

"Sam ... please. Don't do that. You don't have to protect Gus. Not from me. I told you. I'm asking as a friend. Is he okay?"

Sam frowned. "I think he will be. He'll do his job. He'll do it better than anybody. I'm sure I've said this before. If someone I loved was murdered, Gus Ritter is who I'd want on the case. Nothing about that has changed."

"He feels responsible for Dane Fischer," I said. "I know Gus. He'll blame himself for ruining that man's life."

"Nobody ruined Dane Fischer. He didn't go to jail. He was never even charged. Whatever issues Fischer has with his family, those are his alone."

"Sam, come on. It's not that simple. You heard him. It feels like Ellie's family still thinks Fischer's guilty. Despite what Hayden found."

"They'll have to get over it."

"Just promise me you'll keep an eye on Gus."

"Are you asking me to look over his shoulder on this case?"

"No," I said. "I'm asking ... I don't know what I'm asking. I'm just worried about him. And I know you are too."

"He'll be okay. He'll be more than okay."

"But if ..." I didn't get to finish the sentence. The garage door swung open and Will bounded in.

Sam started to rise. Will froze, surprised to see him.

"You're home early," I said. "Nick's mom said she was taking you guys to the museum. I was ..."

"It was closed," Will said, his eyes darting between me and Sam. "Some kind of water main leak in the ladies' room. Nick's mom offered to take us to the zoo instead but I just wanted to come home. Did you have your own sleepover?"

"Did we ..." My jaw dropped. He said it so innocently. Then I saw a twinkle in my teenage son's eye. He enjoyed making me uncomfortable.

"Will," Sam said. "If ..."

"Relax," Will said. "I'm not a baby. You don't have to treat me like one. And you don't have to wait until I'm out of here to come over. I'm good with it. Are there any English muffins left?"

"Er ... yeah," Sam said. He went over to the toaster. "You want me to make you some?"

"Yeah," Will said. "Can you do it as a sandwich? I think we've got eggs and bacon in the fridge."

"Sure can," Sam said. He went to the fridge while Will got a frying pan from the cupboard.

"You want one, Mom?" Will asked.

As I sat there with my mouth agape, as Sam and Will cooked me breakfast.

11

My sister-in-law, Kat, lived on the outskirts of town in a brand-new home she'd built for her and her wife, Bree. On Sunday afternoon, Gus met me in the driveway. I could smell Kat's cooking from there. Gus's stomach growled as he got out of his car. But then, there was always something growling about Gus.

Kat stood in the doorway, giving us a friendly wave. They'd just put sod around the front of the house. She had fifteen acres of natural woods and a pond in the back.

"Come on in!" she called out. "Sorry about the mud."

I stepped gingerly around a few puddles in the gravel driveway. Gus put a hand out when I nearly caught my heel.

"You hungry?" Kat asked. "I've got pork chops and mashed potatoes."

Gus patted his stomach. "I could stand to skip a meal."

"Nonsense," she said. "It's the least I can do now that your poor car's caked with mud."

Gus and I kicked our shoes off at the door. Deeper in the house, I could hear Bree singing along to a Patsy Cline song. She had a strong, clear soprano and sang in her church choir.

We followed Kat through the hallway into her newly built gourmet kitchen. We would celebrate Christmas here. Bree had a big family with six brothers and sisters, and countless nieces and nephews. It was good for Will. It had been just us and Kat for so long. He now had instant cousins near his own age.

Bree stood at the sink still wearing her blue scrubs. She'd just completed a sixteen-hour shift but didn't have to go back for three days. She switched off her Bluetooth speaker.

"Wine?" she asked.

"I'm fine," I said.

"I'm technically on duty," Gus said. "Thanks for letting us come out. I didn't mean to disrupt your meal."

"You're not," Kat said.

"Kat would take it as an insult if you didn't enjoy some of her cooking," I said.

"Well, I'm not going to argue," Gus said. He let Kat usher him into a seat on their giant farm table in the center of the room. It could seat twelve.

Bree brought over a bottle of wine and poured herself a glass. A few minutes later, Kat put dinner in front of Gus and me. He unfolded the cloth napkin and spread it on his lap. I wasn't the least bit hungry, but knew not to protest.

"I'll make up a plate for Will," Kat said. "He doesn't love pork chops but I made them with that apple glaze he likes."

Bree sat down at one end of the table. Kat disappeared back into the bowels of the kitchen.

"You're not eating?" I asked.

"Kat and I will eat together later," she said. "She made all this just for you guys."

A wave of guilt washed through me. "I didn't want to put her to any trouble."

Bree rolled her eyes. "You've met your sister-in-law, right? She lives for this."

"She doesn't have to make herself scarce," Gus said. He took one bite of his pork chops and I swear his eyes rolled back into his head.

"She'll flit in and out," Bree said. "She's worried about me."

"We don't want to dredge up bad memories," I said. "I had no idea you were close to Ellie Luke."

Bree shrugged. "I only knew her for those couple of years we were in college together. But we were close enough. There was a group of us that kind of found each other in nursing school."

Gus pulled out his phone and scrolled to a picture I'd seen at least a hundred times now. It was the one Hayden showed us from the amateur sleuth forum she'd frequented. One of the online users had connected with another student in Bree and Ellie's cohort. A group of twenty-somethings smiling for the camera as they sat on a cement wall outside the main entrance to the university. Ellie Luke sat at the center. Jamie Simmons was on the edge, his arm around another of her classmates.

"That's me," Bree said, pointing to the pretty brunette in the back. The first time I saw the photo, I hadn't even recognized her. She wore her hair long then. Her face was turned away from the camera.

"I know I talked to you before," Gus said.

"A million years ago, yeah," Bree said. "You talked to all of us. I remember wishing I could do something to help you. I felt useless back then. I just didn't know anything. Now ..."

"It's okay," Gus said. "You did help, as I recall. You did the best you could."

"So did you," Bree said, sensing something in Gus's tone, maybe. I was still worried about him. Though Gus was always gruff, something haunted his eyes more than usual today.

"I have a copy of the statement you gave me," Gus said. He pulled a folded piece of paper out of his jacket pocket. It was several pages long. I'd read it over myself before coming. His interview with Bree had been thorough.

"I can have you read it," he said. "But first I'd like to see what you remember on your own."

"I remember everything," she said. "That week has always stayed kind of frozen in my mind. Losing Ellie was such a shock. I mean, I was in nursing school. I'd already done a couple of clinical rotations. I was used to being around sick and dying people by then. But Ellie was the first person I knew who died. I know that's crazy. I was twenty-one years old. But she was."

"Okay," Gus said. "So walk me through what you remember again. How did Ellie seem to you that week?"

"She seemed normal," Bree said. "We had an anatomy class that was torturing all of us. We were meeting once a week to study for it. Ellie was the brain of the group. No question. She aced everything. She was one of those people who just remembered everything she read. And she was calm. Never freaked out. That's kind of why a bunch of us gravitated toward her in the beginning. She was like the class hype girl. Everyone's cheerleader."

"You told me back then she wasn't dating anyone that you knew of," Gus said.

"Nope. Ellie was very serious. We would joke that she was twenty-one going on fifty. At the time, I would question whether this was really what I wanted to do with the rest of my life. Everyone did. Not Ellie. She was driven. Focused. Had a plan for her life and she just methodically followed the steps to get there."

"Okay," Gus said. "What about Jamie Simmons? What do you remember about him?"

Bree's face fell. Kat came back into the room and put her hands on Bree's shoulders.

"I just didn't think anything of it," she said. "I never would have thought Jamie had anything to do with this."

"Forget that," Gus said. "Try to forget what you've seen on the news. I know it's a shock. But try not to reframe your memories with what you think you know about Simmons now."

"Okay," she said. "But that's hard. It's almost impossible not to think I should have seen it."

"Why?" I asked.

Bree took a deep breath. "Jamie was a creep. That's as plain as I can say it. In the beginning, our first year, he was just this goofy guy in our group. A cut-up. Harmless. Just affable. He made us laugh. But after a while, he got annoying."

"In what way?" Gus asked.

"Just kind of in your face a lot. So there were eight of us in our group. Jamie and Paul Mansfield were the only men. But Paul was married to Sarah Mansfield. They were going to school together. So Paul was just paired off. Jamie was the single guy and he started going through the group."

"What do you mean?" Gus asked.

"Just ... that he'd start paying particular attention to the other five girls in the group. Like he'd pick a favorite and just pester her to death. I mean, he started with me but found out pretty quick he wasn't my type. But everyone else, he burned through. Just calling all the time. Texting. Giving gifts that weren't appropriate."

"What kind of gifts?" I asked.

"Well, with me, when it started, it was just dumb stuff. Candles. A day planner I didn't want. When he realized it was a waste of time, he'd move on to the next girl in our group. We started trying to freeze him out. Only Ellie was just nice. She felt sorry for him. Jamie just didn't seem to know how to talk to girls. He was awkward. The class clown routine got old. And he was just one of those guys who didn't know how to read the room or take no for an answer. At one point, our friend Shante confronted him. He'd been pretty merciless asking her out."

"Shante Jones," Gus said, checking his notes.

"Yeah. She's Shante Rawlins now, I think. She's not local anymore. I don't know what happened to her. We lost touch. She dropped out of school the next year. She married this guy who went into the Army and last I heard she was living overseas somewhere. But that had to be almost twenty years ago now. I couldn't even tell you if she was still married to him."

Gus wrote down what he could.

"Tell me what you know about that?" Gus said. "This confrontation?"

"Just that Shante finally told Jamie what we'd all been thinking. That he was coming on too strong and it wasn't cool of him to try to go through our friend group trying to hook up. None of us liked him like that. We just wanted him to chill out."

"Did he?" I asked.

"Kind of. He certainly stopped bothering me. And he stopped coming to our study sessions. I assumed he'd finally taken the hint. But that was all at least a year before Ellie went missing. That's why I never thought much about Jamie during all of that. His behavior wasn't a problem. He was just this dorky guy in our classes. We were friendly. But he was on the periphery."

"So Ellie never told you she was having issues with him?" Gus asked.

"Not specifically, no. She stayed friendly the longest with him out of anyone. I remember asking her about it. It was right before Christmas break, a couple of months before Ellie disappeared. She mentioned she was going to meet him for coffee. I think I asked her why she was still giving that creep the time of day. I don't remember what she said. But I got the sense she felt sorry for him. Like he had no other friends. Then when we got back ... now this I *do* remember pretty well. I was sitting next to her and she got a call from him on her cell. She didn't say anything but she clicked it off. Didn't answer. The vibe I got was that she was annoyed with him. I wished I'd have asked her about that. I just didn't. I didn't like talking about him. Giving oxygen to it. We talked about classes. We talked about our plans. Ellie was working for a home health care agency. She liked it. She was just on her path, you know? Ellie was not someone I ever worried about. She didn't do drugs. Didn't drink. Didn't date losers. Didn't date at all as far as I knew. Not seriously. There was just not an ounce of drama where she was concerned and that's why I liked her so much."

"Okay," Gus said. "What about when she disappeared? I asked you then if you knew anyone who might want to hurt her."

Bree shook her head. "And my answer today is still no."

"What about Jamie Simmons after the fact?" Gus said. "Did you have any communication with him after Ellie went missing?"

"Yes," Bree said quickly. "And this is the part that's haunting me the most now."

Gus and I exchanged a look.

"What do you mean?" I asked. All Bree knew was that Jamie had been arrested. The media knew that his daughter had turned in evidence implicating him. But so far, we'd been lucky that the substance of that evidence had not been leaked.

"Jamie was just really upset. And it's not that that in itself raised any suspicions on my part. We were all completely freaked out. Ellie was the last person I would ever have predicted that happening to. She was careful. Responsible. I told you all that. Anyway, Jamie was just at the forefront of everything. Calling us all. Telling us when and where different search parties were being organized."

Gus wrote something in his notepad.

"He brought those missing person flyers to school," Bree said. "Handed them out and got everyone to tack them up everywhere. Went to every vigil. I mean, we all did. Definitely in the beginning. As the weeks went on, we all knew there was no hope. Ellie was never coming back. Jamie took the whole thing really hard."

"And that seemed out of character?" I asked.

"No. That's just it. It seemed very *in* character. That's why I didn't think a whole lot about it. I just rolled my eyes. I knew Ellie didn't like Jamie. I knew he annoyed her as much as the rest of us. She was nicer than the rest of us about telling him to buzz off. If you ask me, she was too nice. I've never been the kind of person who's had issues setting boundaries. Ellie was always more worried about hurting people's feelings. She put up with Jamie more than the rest of us did. So when she went missing, it made a certain amount of sense to me that Jamie would take it so hard. But he was just ... I don't know. Really intense about it. Once when Paul and Sarah said they couldn't be at the search party one weekend ... Sarah's grandma died or something. They had to go to Fort Wayne for a funeral. Jamie was livid. Snapped at them in the courtyard. Said they didn't care about Ellie as much as the rest of us. Paul put him in his place. We chalked it up to stress. Moved on."

Gus wrote a few notes, then closed his book.

"I'm sorry," Bree said. "I just didn't think to mention any of this back then. Jamie was intense. It wasn't out of character in my mind. Now ... if he really did have something to do with hurting Ellie, it makes a different kind of sense. I could see it as the behavior of someone guilty. Now ... I think maybe Jamie hadn't moved on from Ellie. I think maybe he was still in her shit, you know? Still trying to get with her like he did everyone else in the group before that. And if she did something to finally set that boundary ... maybe he ..."

"You can't do that," I said. "You can't second guess yourself."

"You answered the questions I asked of you," Gus said, his tone bitter.

"Did he ever seem violent?" I asked. "Do you know if any of the other girls in your friend group were afraid of him?"

Bree shook her head. "I just know that we were getting creeped out enough to freeze him out. And we did. Jamie did have a temper. That day in the courtyard with Paul and Sarah, he made a scene. Yelling at the top of his lungs. Calling them names. It was scary. But like I said, I just wrote it off as stress. Ellie was Jamie's friend, too. At least as far as he was concerned."

"I really appreciate this," Gus said.

"I haven't done anything. Maybe if I'd have told you all this twenty years ago, it could have made a difference."

"None of this would have raised reasonable suspicion against Jamie Simmons," I said, as much for Gus as Bree. "It's like you said. You were all grieving. You were all traumatized by losing your friend."

"Then when she was found all those months later," Bree said. "I don't know. It never occurred to me it could have been someone in our group. I'm sorry."

"Did you know Jamie ended up marrying Ellie's sister?" I asked.

"No," Bree said quickly. "I mean, I know it's a small town. But I didn't stay in touch with the people from college. I moved to Ann Arbor. Started my own life. Our paths didn't cross. Jamie didn't pursue nursing as far as I know. But when I found out last week, I was horrified. Just horrified. I remember Ellie's sister Erin from the funeral later that year. She looks just like her. My God. If I'd known Jamie married her ... I don't know. It might have got my wheels turning."

"It's okay," Gus said. "You can't beat yourself up. This has been helpful. I may have more questions later. For now, just try to put it behind you."

"I loved her," Bree said. "Ellie was special. And this is all such a waste."

"I know," I said, reaching for Bree's hand.

"You have to make him pay," she said. "If Jamie really killed Ellie, then wormed his way into her family like that ... well, there's no punishment too harsh for him. I mean that. I just wish I could have seen it twenty years ago."

I saw Gus's face harden to stone across the table. I knew the same thought would torture him until the grave.

12

"This is accurate," I said, my eyes scanning the forensic report in front of me. "They're sure?"

"They're sure," Gus said. "The lab geeks were excited by this one. There's all kinds of stuff in there about wear patterns. The type of metal. But yeah. They're sure. The earring Jamie Simmons had in that box is the mate to the one found with Ellie's remains. There's even some stuff in there about the photographs of her wearing them. Again, the wear patterns are a match. It'll hold up."

"It'll hold up past a suppression hearing," I said. "At least I hope. I'm still gonna have a fight convincing a jury of all this. I just need somebody on the stand that can get through the science of it without boring them to death. But this is good, Gus. This is ... I don't even know what this is. We can't tell the family. We can't let this get out. We've had enough leaks."

"It won't come from my office," he said. "Still waiting on some labs. The lock of hair Simmons had in his possession didn't have roots attached. So DNA's a no go. But Ellie Luke dyed her hair.

They're working on matching the coloring to what Ellie used. There were also two pubic hairs embedded into the threads of the underwear Simmons had in that drawer. Those *did* have roots attached. We might get a hit off them."

"But we don't know when he got those," I said. "We don't know if Ellie was wearing them the night she died or if he collected them later when he was at her house. At best, we can prove he was obsessed with her."

"You can prove he knew where her body was and went treasure hunting off it, Mara." Gus's whole posture reminded me of a cobra about to strike. He puffed his chest out, shoulders back. I knew he didn't want to hear what I had to say. But I had to think like a prosecutor. It only mattered what I could prove in court.

"This is good," I said. "Let me know when you have the rest of the labs back. But I'm confident in the charging document. Hojo's going to sign off on aggravated murder. We'll go from there."

Gus's shoulders relaxed. I knew that was what he wanted to hear. I didn't say the rest of it. Though I was confident in what to charge Jamie Simmons with, I was far less confident about what I could convict him of.

"You'll know what I know as soon as I know it," Gus said. "Tell Hojo he's doing a good job."

"So are you," I said. Gus didn't answer. I knew he carried too much guilt about not zeroing in on Simmons sooner. For now, there was no point trying to convince him otherwise. That would take time.

"I'll be in touch," he said, then turned on his heel. He nearly ran into Caro as she stood in the doorway. They exchanged brief pleasantries, but whatever Caro wanted, she clearly didn't want Gus to hear it. She waited until he'd disappeared down the hall, then turned to me.

"Mara," she said. "Bennett Cutler is in the conference room. He wants a few minutes with you."

Cutler? What the hell was Simmons's defense lawyer doing here already? Thank God Caro had the presence of mind to get him out of sight before Gus saw him.

"Simmons hasn't even been arraigned yet," I muttered. "He can't possibly be here begging for some plea deal."

"He was pretty adamant about seeing you," she said. "As if you've got nothing better to do."

"It's okay," I said, hoping it was.

"You want him where he is or should I walk him back here?"

"I'll go to the conference room. I don't want him getting too comfortable."

I grabbed a pad of paper and pen, then walked down the hall. Cutler stood in front of the book shelves, perusing our collection. He smiled when I walked in and declined Caro's offer of refreshments.

"I won't take up too much of your time," Cutler said. "I have another appointment."

"I'm surprised you didn't make one with me," I said.

"Didn't think I needed one. I can't imagine you've got anything more pressing than Ellie Luke's case."

"That's pretty presumptuous of you, Mr. Cutler," Caro snapped.

"It's okay," I whispered to her.

"You've got fifteen minutes," Caro said. "Ms. Brent is due in court." She closed the door behind her and gave me a sharp look. God bless her for having my back.

"What's this about, then?" I asked.

"I wanted to hear it directly from you. Because I just couldn't believe the rumors. You're not seriously considering charging my client with aggravated murder, are you?"

How the hell did he know that already? I kept my face neutral.

"I am," I said. "Ellie Luke was abducted. Brutally beaten. Left to rot in the woods alone. She was stalked. Hunted. By your client, Mr. Cutler."

"And you won't be able to prove any of that. Not a single bit of it. At best, you might be able to prove there were some items in the Simmons's home that raised suspicions. But you can't even prove how they got there. Or who put them there. Frankly, I'm surprised your boss is even willing to charge at all on this one."

"I'll worry about my case. You can worry about yours. That *is* how this works, after all. Is your client willing to admit what he did?"

Cutler laughed. "He hasn't done anything. Nothing illegal."

"Okay. Well, you can save all this for the jury. I really do have to get to court."

"Evidence tampering," he said. "That's about as egregious an act as you'll be able to prove. And I'm not saying you *will* prove it. But this has ripped Jamie Simmons's family apart. He's eager to try to put things back together."

"I'm not offering a deal," I said. "Not now. Probably not ever."

"That isn't entirely your call to make," he said. "And maybe you shouldn't be so dismissive so soon. You have plenty at stake on a personal level, Ms. Brent."

"What?"

"Your office can't afford what this case could do to it. Hell, I don't think the entire county is ready for what's coming."

"Okay. I think we're done here. I'm not offering your client any deals at this point. He murdered Ellie Luke. And what he's done to her family ..."

"Her family supports him. They know he didn't kill that girl. And he's been a strong, supportive husband to their surviving daughter. They're united in that."

"Except for Hayden," I snapped.

"I'm glad you brought her up. I know you understand what this trial will do to that girl. I can assure you that's the last thing Jamie Simmons wants for his daughter."

"Then he should do the right thing and confess," I said.

"Hayden Simmons is a troubled girl who has become obsessed with her aunt's murder to the point of ghoulishness. It's sad, Ms. Brent."

And he would try to paint that picture at trial. It was his only play really. The only way to try to explain what Jamie Simmons kept in that box. Cutler would try to imply Hayden planted it. Made it up. The forensics would say otherwise. Soon enough, when I had the full report, I would have to disclose all of it to Cutler. Maybe then he could talk some sense into his client.

"I don't think we can help each other today, Mr. Cutler. Now if you'll excuse me ..."

"The other reason I wanted to talk to you in person," he said. "You need to prepare yourself. Mr. Simmons is not willing to waive his right to a speedy trial. He wants this whole ordeal over as quickly as possible. He deserves that."

Of all the things Cutler said, that one shocked me. It meant we'd likely be in front of a jury in a matter of weeks, not months.

"Well, as you said, that is his right. I appreciate the heads-up. I'll see you at his formal arraignment next week."

"We'll be seeking bail," he said.

"That is also your right. We'll push back on that. Hard."

"I didn't expect anything less. I'm just curious. How do you think it's going to look when the public realizes you're sleeping with the sheriff?"

His words stung me like a slap across the face. I knew that was his intention.

"You need to leave now, Mr. Cutler," I said.

"And you need to think very carefully about what you're trying to accomplish with this case."

"What I'm trying ... Jamie Simmons murdered Ellie Luke. I'm going to prove it and seek the maximum penalty afforded by law. That's what I'm trying to accomplish."

"Sam Cruz is running for reelection in a year. I'm supposed to believe this whole thing is a coincidence? Ellie Luke is one of the most infamous cold cases in the county. Two weeks ago, you,

Sam Cruz, and Hayden Simmons had lunch together. All the while, you and the sheriff were playing footsie under the table by all accounts. Then all of a sudden Hayden Simmons dreams up this headline-grabbing story about her father and Aunt Ellie ..."

He took a step toward me. Then another. I'd known many men like Bennett Cutler before. He wasn't physically threatening me, per se. But he was using our size and strength difference to claim more and more space around him. Expecting me to take a step back. I wouldn't.

"I'd say we're done talking," I said.

"Even if you win, you'll lose," he said. "We haven't even stepped inside the courtroom and I can see appealable error taking shape. This case could ruin your career if you ever want to run for office."

"Lucky for me, I don't."

"Your boyfriend does. Look, I won't want to do it. But a man's life is at stake. I'm not going to have a choice."

Cutler put a hand flat on the wall next to my ear. He was no more than three inches from my face. I had the urge to punch him in the groin.

"It's not like this office has a stellar reputation," he said. "You've been under investigation before."

I felt the air shift beside me. A hand came around my face and grabbed Bennett Cutler by the lapel. Sam forced him backward until he was up against the table.

"Is there a problem?" Sam asked, his voice a low, threatening growl.

Bennett Cutler's face split into a satisfied grin. "No problem at all. I'd say I've seen all I need to see. You've pretty much confirmed everything I suspected about you two."

Sam curled his fist. He was all corded muscle and coiled rage. I'd never even heard him walk up, but there could be no doubt he'd heard every vile thing Cutler had said to me.

"Sam!" I shouted. Lunging forward, I pulled Sam's arm back. I don't know if he actually would have struck Cutler, but didn't want to find out.

"Time to go," Sam said. "You need to talk to her, you do it by phone or email."

Cutler straightened his suit jacket. Still grinning, he picked up his briefcase off the floor and showed himself out.

"You okay?" Sam said, turning to me.

"Of course. He's a blowhard."

"What was that?"

"That? Cutler's trying to get a rise out of me. He certainly got one out of you. He also tipped his hand a little. He's going to try to make Hayden Simmons out as an attention-seeking nutcase. I need to talk to her. I need to make sure she's in a mentally strong place. This is going to get very ugly, Sam."

"I don't care."

"Maybe you should. Maybe we both should. I'm assuming you stood there long enough to hear Cutler's theory about our lunch date with Hayden Simmons. He's right that it could cause you issues."

"What?"

"Us," I said.

Sam waved me off. "Enough. I'm not afraid of that weasel. I know you're not. You'll eat him for breakfast if this goes to trial."

"Oh, it's going. That's the other thing he wanted me to know. Simmons isn't waiving a speedy trial. They want this thing in front of a jury as fast as possible."

"What? Why? He's could face the death penalty."

"Probably because Cutler thinks I won't be ready in time."

Sam leaned against the table. His face was still flushed with anger.

"Will you?" he asked.

I smiled. "Of course. I just need to make sure your office is. That Gus is."

Sam came to me. He looked over my shoulder. Through the wall of windows, he could see straight to the lobby. Caro wasn't at her desk. No one could see in. Sam kissed me.

"Gus is ready."

"Good. But maybe we should heed one piece of advice from Cutler. Maybe we should make sure we don't become part of the story."

"Cutler can go screw himself. I don't make decisions based on empty threats from scumbag defense lawyers like him. Neither should you."

He put an arm around me and drew me close. I loved his warm, solid strength. It was comforting to think he was willing to fight my battles for me. Only I knew ultimately this was one I would have to fight alone.

13

Three weeks before Jamie Simmons was set to go on trial for his life, I received a call I never thought I'd get. George and Claudia Luke wanted to talk.

We met on a Saturday evening in my office. They wanted to come when no one else would be in the building. When no one might see them walk through the parking lot. And they came alone.

I waited for them in the lobby, keying them in. At my insistence, Sam had called back the deputies who normally patrolled the grounds on the weekend. Sam himself waited across the street in his own office, ready to dispatch anyone I needed at a moment's notice.

If it was possible, George and Claudia looked as if they'd aged ten years in the last two months. Late October now, I couldn't imagine how difficult the upcoming holiday season would be for them.

George rested a protective hand on his wife's back as I showed them into the conference room, turning on the hall lights as we went.

"Can I get either of you anything?" I asked, then kicked myself for not thinking about starting a pot of coffee. It was late though. Almost seven thirty.

"We're okay," George said. "We just want to get this over with."

They chose two chairs at the long table, putting their backs to the bookshelves. I left my notepad in my office. Silenced my phone. I wanted this meeting to feel as informal as possible given the circumstances. I took my seat opposite them.

"I appreciate you coming in," I started. "I'm here to answer any questions you may have. I can give you some idea of what to expect once the trial starts."

Claudia cast a nervous glance at her husband. "I don't think we can help you."

"I'm saying I'm here to help you, Mrs. Luke."

"Call me Claudia. Mrs. Luke was my mother-in-law. She was …"

George put a hand over his wife's. "My mother was a hard woman to like."

"Okay. Claudia. I really cannot imagine how stressful this has all been for you. I can understand why you've been reluctant to talk to me or Detective Ritter."

"Can you?" Claudia snapped. "We didn't just lose our daughter, Ms. Brent. This thing … this hideous thing … I feel like I'm losing my mind. That I'm in some nightmare but I can't wake up."

"Shh," George consoled his wife. "It's going to be okay. This will be over soon."

Claudia's hands trembled. She reached for a tissue box at the center of the table, took one, and blew her nose.

"What we want to know is," George said. "Do you really think our son-in-law hurt Ellie?"

His question tore through me. I could only imagine what Bennett Cutler must have told them. It was in his interest to keep them believing Jamie Simmons had been framed. Railroaded. They'd accepted him into their family. Treated him like a son.

"Yes," I said bluntly. "Jamie Simmons stalked and murdered your daughter. He's kept it a secret all these years. I would not take this case to trial if I didn't think he was guilty."

"But Detective Ritter told us," Claudia said. "He said my nephew was the one who did this. Dane threatened her. You don't understand what was going on. I brought him into our home. George and I tried to help him turn his life around. Then he stole from us. He got violent with George. Did you know that?"

"No, I didn't."

"He did. George, tell her. Dane pushed him up against a wall. I thought he was going to strangle him. We threw him out. Ellie tried to warn us. She was never comfortable around Dane. Then he took my engagement ring. Stole money out of George's wallet. Ellie found him searching her room looking for more money. She was the one who insisted we call the police. Dane hurt Ellie. I know it. And I let him into our home!"

"I'm sorry," I said. "Claudia, you did what you thought was right. You tried to help your cousin. There's nothing wrong with any of that. I believe you that Dane Fischer was a bad element. But he isn't the one who killed Ellie. Detective Ritter knew twenty years ago he didn't have enough for probable cause to arrest Dane. He was a lead. A person of interest. Nothing more. But Jamie ... you have to understand I'm not at liberty to discuss some of the elements of my case. The evidence. But I assure you, I will be able to tie Jamie to Ellie's murder."

I stopped short of making any promises. The Lukes were grappling with so much more than the loss of their daughter. They'd been cloaked in Jamie Simmons's lies for twenty-two years.

"You want me to lose everything," Claudia said. "Do you understand that?"

"I don't. I'm not doing any of this to hurt you."

"Hayden," George said. "There are some things you need to understand about our granddaughter."

"All right," I said. Though I suspected I already knew where this was going, I decided patient, active listening would be the best way to defuse a potentially volatile situation.

"It's our fault," George continued. "Losing Ellie ... the *way* we lost Ellie. It was so painful. It's not just us missing her. Torturing ourselves over what her last minutes on earth must have been like. Did she call for help? Did she call for us? She had to have. That would be normal, wouldn't it? You're a mother. It would be natural for a child to cry out for her parents when they're in pain. When they're frightened. That alone is enough to destroy me. Us. But then to find out that someone we let into Ellie's life was the one who did this to her."

"Only you didn't," I said, contradicting my intentions. "Dane Fischer didn't do this."

George put up a hand. "We can put that aside for now. Let's assume that's true. What I'm trying to tell you about is my granddaughter. We didn't talk about Ellie. After Detective Ritter told us he couldn't arrest Dane ... after we realized there would be no justice for Ellie ... we shut down. We couldn't cope. The only way we survived was by locking that part of our life away. Not forgetting her. Never that. But it was just too painful to talk about. And we were losing Erin, too. That's what you have to understand. Erin was trying so hard to make everything okay for us. She was just a kid. Eighteen. That's a tremendous burden. Erin felt like she had to be all things for us. And God help us, we let her."

"I'm so sorry," I said.

"Jamie was a friend to her," Claudia said. "He watched out for her. For all of us. Erin grew to rely on him. He was like a big brother to her and that was such a comfort. She needed that. I think she felt comfortable talking to him about things she couldn't say to us. Then ... I don't know. Things grew between them. Almost two years after Ellie died, Erin found out she was pregnant. I was terrified for her. She was so young. But Jamie took care of her. Jamie is the reason my family survived. Do you understand?"

"I do," I said. "If you think I'm judging you for anything, I promise you, I'm not."

"He couldn't have done this," George said. "Jamie loves us. He's part of our family. We made a mistake not being open with Hayden about her Aunt Ellie. Her curiosity was natural. What she did about it wasn't."

"What is it you think she did?" I asked.

"She was sick," Claudia spat. "Looking online at those awful pictures of poor Ellie's body. Ellie was nothing to her. Bones. A curiosity. My granddaughter is a disturbed young girl. She needs help."

It broke my heart to think how Hayden's family had turned on her. Jamie Simmons's talons were sunk so deeply into Ellie Luke's parents. And Erin Luke had lived as his wife for twenty years. I wouldn't say the words. It served no purpose to antagonize them. But Jamie Simmons had managed to groom and brainwash Ellie's parents. There was no telling what he'd done to a young, grieving, vulnerable Erin Luke. She was just as much a victim as Ellie had been. That is what I would need the jury to see.

"Have you spoken to her?" I asked. "To Hayden?"

"You can't talk to her," Claudia said. "She won't listen. She's got some therapist that tells her she has to set boundaries. What do they call it, George? What she's done?"

"No contact," he said bitterly. "Hayden won't engage with us."

Good for her, I thought. I would never say it. The Lukes were victims too.

"You need to be prepared," I said. "It's as I've told you. I wouldn't pursue a conviction against your son-in-law if I didn't think he was guilty. I can connect him to the crime scene. I have witnesses who will testify about the inappropriate attention he paid your daughter. The lies he told."

"You're harassing him," Claudia jumped in. "We know what this is. How important it is for the new sheriff to notch a conviction before the election next year." She was parroting Bennett Cutler.

"This isn't about that. And we didn't seek this out. When new, credible evidence emerged, we pursued it. It has nothing to do with the timing of an election. You have my word on that."

"Your word," George said. "Can you understand why that doesn't mean much to us? From where we sit, the Sheriff's Department has done nothing to instill confidence in us."

"Sam Cruz wasn't the sheriff when your daughter was murdered," I said. "And I wasn't the prosecutor. Neither of us has any personal connection to this case. We're only interested in getting justice for your daughter. I am telling you today, Jamie's trial is the way to get it."

"We're going to lose her!" Claudia shouted. "Don't you see that?"

"Hayden," I asked. "She loves you. She's hurt. But she loves you. She understands how traumatic this is for you."

"Not Hayden," George said quietly. "She's talking about Erin. She's afraid of losing Erin. This whole thing ... Erin's fragile. She always has been. Ellie used to look out for her. She mothered her as much as my wife did."

"Then Jamie took on that role," I said.

Squeezing his eyes shut, George Luke nodded.

"Maybe Erin's stronger than you think," I offered. "I know you want the truth. I know you must want to know what happened to Ellie once and for all."

"Truth," George spat. "Seems to me the truth is whatever someone twists it to be."

That sounded like Jamie Simmons talking. Lord, he really had done a number on this family. No wonder Hayden had been so terrified. No wonder she decided to confront Sam and me out in the open in a public place.

"No," I said. "The truth is what the physical evidence in this case revealed. Jamie Simmons murdered Ellie. I'm so sorry for that. And even more sorry for what he's done to your family since then. It's hard to accept. Of course it is. But I am telling you. We have the right man. We know what happened to Ellie."

"How could you?" Claudia said. "All you have is assumptions. You know what Mr. Cutler says? He says Hayden knew exactly what they found at Ellie's crime scene. It's all online. She knew what she'd need to make it look like her father was some kind of monster. The internet is the devil. It's taken my granddaughter away from me."

This was going nowhere. Claudia and George Luke wrapped themselves in Jamie Simmons's lies for protection. The truth was far too awful for them to accept. I could only hope the jury could see through it. And that Hayden Simmons could hold up to Bennett Cutler's withering cross-examination. I could hear it in my mind.

Cutler would try to demonize Hayden on the stand. He would sever whatever thin ties she had to her family. She would be the villain. The whack job. If she wasn't strong enough to withstand the onslaught ... Jamie Simmons might just get away with murder.

Claudia and George Luke stood abruptly, ending our meeting. I didn't try to stop them. There was no point. There was only one thing left to do. I had to prepare Hayden Simmons for the brutal attack headed her way. And all she'd done was tell the truth.

14

Seventy-two hours before opening statements, Hayden Simmons sat in my office worrying a long beaded necklace between her fingers. She had an opened envelope on her lap when I walked in.

"Sorry to keep you waiting," I said. "Do you need something? Coffee? Juice? Have you eaten?"

"I'm okay," she said, but didn't look it. I hadn't seen Hayden in a few weeks but she was much thinner. Her hair hung lifeless around her face. Her forehead had broken out. She tried to cover it with thick makeup that was too dark for her pale complexion. This nineteen-year-old girl looked forty today. I feared it would only get worse.

I sat down behind my desk. "Thanks for coming in. I just wanted to touch base with you and answer any questions you might still have heading into Monday."

She shook her head. "I just want to get this over with."

"I spoke to your grandparents a couple of weeks ago. Did they tell you that?"

Hayden looked down. "It's awkward with them. My grandma tries to stay in contact. But we don't talk about anything real. It's just surface stuff. She asked me how I'm doing in school, if I need anything." Hayden let out a bitter laugh.

"I can't imagine how tough this has been on you, Hayden. But you know you're doing the right thing."

She picked the envelope up off her lap and reached across my desk to hand it to me. Frowning, I took it from her.

"That was delivered the day before yesterday," she said. "A man came to my work. I thought he was putting in his coffee order but he came behind the counter and put that in my hand. My boss saw. My coworker."

I recognized the court caption across the top. Erin Luke had filed for a restraining order against her own daughter. I skimmed it.

"This is only a petition," I said. "It's not a court order. This means the judge wouldn't grant it without a hearing."

I read the bottom of the form. A hearing had been set for two weeks from now, smack in the middle of the trial.

"Have you had contact with your mom?" I asked.

She shook her head. "No. I've tried to call her. Text her. She blocked my number. I asked my grandma to give her a letter from me but she said she didn't feel comfortable getting in the middle."

Anger bubbled through me. This smacked of a Bennett Cutler

tactic, though he wasn't the one who'd signed the petition. Erin Luke had done that presumably on her own.

"She wants to make it illegal for me to talk to her?" Hayden asked.

"This is a stunt," I said. "This is so Bennett Cutler can ask you about it on the witness stand. An attempt to poison the jury's impression of you. As much as you can, I need you to not let this rattle you, Hayden."

"It's not her," she said. "My mom wouldn't think to do this on her own."

"Probably not."

"I feel like such an idiot. There are so many things that I should have picked up on over the years. It's only in the three months since I've been out of that house that it's starting to be clear."

"What things, Hayden?" I asked.

"The way my dad manipulates my mom. My grandparents. He decides everything. Always has. My mom has always just deferred to him. Never argues with him."

"Have you ever seen him get physically violent with your mom?" I asked.

"No. Not like that. It's been more subtle. She goes to him for everything. She doesn't keep her own bank account. She's never worked outside the home. She did some online medical data entry for a while but when that started taking up her time, my dad made her quit. I don't know why I never really questioned any of it. God. He does that. He just takes over. I've lived my whole life with him in charge. Until now."

I wanted to be careful not to put words in Hayden's mouth. I couldn't afford anyone thinking I'd coached her. This case would greatly hinge on how well she could stand up to Bennett Cutler's cross-examination.

"If I asked you about that on the stand, do you think you could give specific examples?"

"Of how he manipulates her? Yes. I just never thought anything of it. I didn't know any better. But my mom doesn't have friends of her own. Everyone they socialize with are people my dad is friends with. People he works with. That shopping trip she took when I found the box in the basement? She was with two wives of my dad's friends. And she called my father practically every hour while she was gone. That was the first time I can remember her going somewhere without him. My mom has lived in and around Waynetown her whole life. She went to high school here. But she doesn't keep in touch with any of *her* old friends. For as long as I can remember, she never has."

The more I knew about the Simmons family dynamic, the more I realized Ellie Luke had only been Jamie's first victim, not his last.

"What about your grandparents?" I asked. I would not tell Hayden what they'd said about her. If they took the stand, she'd hear it soon enough. Let her reaction be genuine. Let the jury see it for themselves.

"They worship the ground my dad walks on. Even my grandpa. He runs every financial decision by my dad. When I was little, I remember going over there watching him balance their checkbook. If there was something in the house that needed fixing, my grandpa would call my dad and he'd call the plumber or the furnace guy. Whatever. It's like they've all been children and he's the parent. I don't know why I never questioned it."

"Hayden, you've been a kid yourself this whole time. Why would you question it?"

"That's what my therapist says," she said.

"How's that going?"

"I don't know. It's hard. I cry a lot. But my shrink has been helping me realize how oppressive my household was growing up."

"It's going to take time," I said. "You need to be gentle with yourself. None of this is your fault, Hayden."

"I know. At least I think I know. I just don't see how my mom and grandparents are ever going to understand who my dad really is."

"As hard as it is," I said, "you're going to have to accept that it's not your job to make them."

She smiled. "My therapist said that too. She reminds me of you."

"Thanks. I think."

"I just … I'm sorry. I can't help wondering if I've done the right thing. If I'd have just left that box where it was. If I'd just packed my things, moved away, never said what I believed. Just gone no contact sooner. Maybe that would have been better."

"Do you really believe that?"

She squeezed her eyes shut. "No. I guess I don't. He hurt Aunt Ellie."

Hurt. That's not how she described it before. I knew Cutler would capitalize on her phrasing if that's what she said on the stand. Hurt doesn't mean killed.

Hayden looked at me. "I know what he's capable of now. Even if my family doesn't. They can't admit what he is because then they have to admit how wrong they've been. That they've let him control them. Then their whole lives since Ellie died is a lie."

"It's so much, Hayden. And you're carrying the weight of it on your own."

"What about that?" she asked, pointing to the petition.

I looked over Hayden's shoulder. I could see out into the hallway. A familiar face had just walked in. Caro had thrown her arms around her. I quickly suppressed my own smile.

"I can't get directly involved with this," I said. "I'm still the prosecutor. But if you don't want to go to the hearing on your own, I can recommend someone to go with you."

"Okay. Thank you."

I wanted to tell her it would be okay. Not to worry. But those would be empty words. There was no precedent for what Hayden Simmons would face. Though she looked frail, I knew this girl had a spine of steel. She would need it.

I walked Hayden down the hall to the employee exit. I didn't want her leaving the building through the lobby. Though I hadn't seen any when I came in this morning, I couldn't promise there wouldn't be a reporter or two lurking out there.

"I'll see you Monday," I said. "If anything comes up over the weekend, you call me."

I gave her a hug. It seemed appropriate. Hayden choked back a sob. I watched through the window until Hayden got into her car. Then I started back toward the empty office beside mine. I'd turned it into my trial prep room. Caro had taken our visitor there.

She stood in front of my whiteboard, hands on her hips.

"Kenya," I beamed. She turned around. Kenya Spaulding, my former boss, looked radiant in wide-legged red pants and a black blouse. Her gold bangles rattled as she threw her arms wide and pulled me into a hug.

"You're a sight for sore eyes," I said.

"I had a feeling you could use a cheerleader," she said. She wore her hair piled high on top of her head, her intricate braids looped tightly into a spiral.

"I could use a lot more than that," I said. We were alone, but Kenya stepped around me and closed the door.

"How's it really going?" she asked.

"How much do you know?"

"Only what I've read on the news. I talked to Caro a bit. She says you're holding up just fine."

"I don't know. This case isn't as strong as I want it to be."

"They never are."

"Do you remember much about this one?" I asked.

"Ellie Luke," she sighed. "No. This one predates me by a few years. I mean, I'd heard of it. Gus Ritter's great white whale. How's he holding up?"

Kenya must have read something in my face. "Geesh. That bad?"

"No. I don't know. I'm worried about him. I won't lie. He's wound pretty tight with this one. And Jamie Simmons's defense lawyer isn't messing around."

"He's gonna try to filet Gus on the stand," she said.

"Exactly."

"Well, don't count Gus out just yet. He can be abrasive one on one, but you know how good he is in the witness box."

"This one's different, Kenya. Gus blames himself for it."

"There was no physical evidence tying this Simmons guy to the murders twenty-two years ago. He wasn't on anyone's radar. The family led Gus to somebody else. He can't think any of this is his fault."

"You know Gus," I said.

"Yep. Poor guy. I'll check in on him. See if I can give him a pep talk."

I smiled. "Like the one you're giving me? Come clean. Was it Caro's idea?"

Kenya grinned.

"I knew it," I said. "Is she that worried about me?"

"Not worried. Just making sure you remember that you're Mara Effing Brent. You've got this."

"I don't know. That's the truth. Most of this is going to fall on Hayden Simmons's nineteen-year-old shoulders. If she shuts down, this whole case does."

"Was that her walking out when I came in?"

"Yes."

Kenya whistled low. "She looks terrible."

"Her whole family turned their backs on her. They're too invested in believing Dane Fischer really killed Ellie. Jamie Simmons has been manipulating them all for twenty years. Grooming them to believe he's this hero. The guy who took control and pulled them out of their grief."

"Wow. That poor kid. I can't even imagine. She's solid though? She's not going to change her mind?"

"No. She sees her dad for who he is. I think Cutler's afraid of her."

I had the copy of Erin Luke's petition. I handed it to Kenya. She scanned it.

"She's seeking a restraining order against her own daughter? This is sick."

"I know. Cutler put her up to it just so he could ask Hayden about it on the stand."

"And you'll object and Judge Saul will sustain it."

"Probably," I agreed. "But Cutler's whole case will be painting Hayden as disturbed. I've got her in touch with the Silver Angels. They're looking out for her. She's in therapy and I think it's helping. But she needs someone else in her corner."

"You have someone in mind?"

I smiled. "You think you could find the time to take her on as a client? Handle the hearing on that petition for her?"

"It's gonna go nowhere," she said. "Has Hayden been in contact with her mother? Has she threatened her?"

"No."

"Then this is easy," Kenya said, waving the petition.

"You'll do it?"

"I'll do it."

"That's fantastic. I'll get word to her to expect a call from you."

"I assume you want me to do this pro bono?"

"I never assume with other people's money. I just know Hayden doesn't have much. She's been thrown out of her parents' house. She's living in an apartment the Silver Angels helped her find. They're helping her with her rent for now."

"It's okay," Kenya said. "I'm happy to do it. Sounds like this kid could use as many friends as she can."

"Thank you," I said. "That'll give her ... and me ... peace of mind."

"What about you?" she asked. "Are you ready for this?"

I looked at the whiteboard. "I don't know. I mean, of course I am. It's just ... this isn't a slam dunk. Not by any means. Simmons is a monster. Of that I'm sure. He kept souvenirs from the crime scene, from Ellie Luke's body."

"Then he married a souvenir," Kenya said, wrinkling her nose in disgust. "Lord, Erin Luke could have been her sister's twin."

"It's disturbing. But that alone doesn't prove murder. Everything I have is circumstantial. I don't have a confession. I don't have definitive physical evidence tying him to the actual killing."

Kenya smiled. "And I know you've gotten convictions on less. If anyone can pull this off, it's you. I for one can't wait to watch."

"You'll be there?" I asked.

Kenya put her hands on my shoulders. I hadn't realized how much I'd missed her strong presence in this office. It led me to another question. The big one. The county needed her ... I needed her ... to run for office again. To get back where she belonged in the corner office next to us.

"I'll be here if you need me," she said. "I'll be your good luck charm. And I'll back Hayden Simmons."

Relief flooded me. Stress I hadn't realized I'd been holding released. At the same time, I knew how big a battle I had in front of me. And Bennett Cutler may very well have more ammo.

15

Eight women. Four men. An English teacher. A preacher. An ironworker. A plumber. A stay-at-home dad. A stay-at-home mom. Two bank tellers. A retired therapist. A college student. A dog groomer. An accountant.

Educated people. Earnest people. They sat poised to listen as I took my spot at the lectern. Jamie Simmons leaned close to Bennett Cutler and whispered something to him. He wore a well-tailored blue suit with a brown monochromatic tie and matching brown leather shoes. Handsome. Not smiling, but not frowning, either. Just one member of Ellie's family was in the courtroom. George Luke sat against the back wall, glowering at me.

As I adjusted the microphone, I felt the weight of Ellie Luke's presence. The family she knew couldn't bring themselves to stand for her today. So I did.

"Good morning," I started. "Thank you for your patience and your honesty during voir dire. This won't be an easy trial to listen to. It won't be easy not to talk about. But I trust you. As I told you at the beginning of this, my name is Mara Brent and I represent the state of Ohio. I'd like to introduce you to Ellie Luke."

I stepped out from behind the lectern. It felt important to get as close to the jury as I dared. With each breath I took, it was as if Ellie herself filled me. I knew what had happened to her. What I could prove was something else. But while I delivered my opening statement, proof didn't matter. Only Ellie's voice did.

"Twenty-two years ago, Elizabeth Luke was a twenty-one-year-old nursing student. She had dreams. A calling. She wanted to help people. No. Not just people. She was hoping when she graduated she could go to work for a hospice organization providing end-of-life care to terminally ill patients. She liked the idea of getting to know her patients, being a part of their lives, their families.

"Ellie supported herself through school. She hadn't taken out a single loan. She worked for a home health agency. Her last assignment was working with an elderly woman, Hattie Corning, with dementia and congestive heart failure. She took care of her overnight so her husband could sleep. She read to her. Changed her. Helped her shower. Cooked for both her and her husband. She was paid ten dollars an hour for it. Enough to make her tuition payments. Plus, she could study in the quiet hours of the night before leaving at seven in the morning, getting a couple of precious hours of sleep, then heading to class in the afternoon.

"Ellie's friends will describe her as a serious, dedicated student. She helped them through anatomy class. Was the quiet voice of reason in their lives when they went through relationship drama or self-doubt about school. Everyone loved Ellie Luke. They wished they were more like her.

"Then, early one morning, as Ellie finished her shift at the Corning home, she got in her car and started toward home. She never made it there. What happened next would remain a mystery, a horrible nightmare for her family and friends for the next two decades.

"It might have remained a mystery if not for one very brave member of Ellie's family. Someone she never even had the privilege of meeting.

"What we know now, what the evidence will show, Ellie was the object of one man's obsession. An obsession that has spanned these twenty years and embedded itself into Ellie's grieving family. Jamie Simmons was supposed to be Ellie's friend. She thought so. He was a classmate. Someone who, in the beginning, seemed like a lot of fun. A goofy sidekick, if you will.

"Jamie Simmons wanted more from Ellie. He wanted to own her. Possess her. But she was never interested in him in that way. She was only interested in being his friend. A study partner. But by all accounts, she was kind to him. And that was all Jamie Simmons needed to allow his obsession to grow.

"There are things we don't know about the night Ellie Luke disappeared. Things we will never know. We don't know what Jamie Simmons said to her. What she said to him. Whether she fought for her life. Whether she was afraid. But in this trial, we will focus on what we do know. It is horrible enough.

"The evidence will show that Jamie Simmons knew Ellie Luke's schedule. On March 12th, Monday morning when Ellie tried to drive home, she got a flat tire. Her car was found with a puncture in the back right tire. We know someone picked Ellie Luke up that morning and drove away with her.

"Ellie Luke never came home. The hours ticked by and her parents started to worry. It wasn't like Ellie not to call if she was going to be late. By noon, they knew something was terribly wrong. They called her friends. Ellie hadn't shown up for classes either. That wasn't like her. She missed a midterm that morning. By one o'clock, George and Claudia Luke called the police.

"For seven months, nobody knew anything. Ellie vanished without a trace. Her friends organized search parties. Combed the woods surrounding campus. The river running behind the Cornings' house. All the while, Jamie Simmons became a constant presence in the Luke family's life. He helped organize the searches. For weeks after, as interest in Ellie's case waned, Jamie Simmons was there handing out flyers. Pounding on doors. Asking questions.

"Ellie's friends found it strange. They knew Ellie wasn't particularly fond of Jamie. None of them were, anymore. He was too eager. They'll say he had issues with boundaries. Didn't seem to understand the word no.

"Then, in October of that year, Ellie's remains were found by a hunter. Her skeleton was propped up against an oak tree. You'll hear how the police believed Ellie hadn't been killed there, but placed there. Posed there. You'll hear how certain items from her personal effects were missing. Her underwear. An earring. A lock of her hair cut from the back of her head. By all indications, someone wanted a trophy, a souvenir of Ellie Luke.

"You'll hear how even though so much time had passed, Ellie's remains told a grisly story of her final moments. The back of her skull was caved in.

"And you'll hear the story of a grieving family. The Lukes had a remaining daughter, Erin. Her resemblance to Ellie is remarkable. Most people thought they were twins. They still do. In the depths of their grief, Jamie Simmons took advantage of them. He endeared himself to Erin Luke. Married her. Had a daughter with her. And three months ago, that daughter, Hayden Simmons, found something in her father's possession that will haunt her until the day she dies.

"Jamie Simmons has a box of treasures. Ghoulish souvenirs from a crime scene no one was supposed to know about. Only the killer. Only the person so obsessed with Ellie Luke, he took over her family. One by one, you'll learn what he kept in that box. You'll learn how Jamie Simmons knew he could never have Ellie Luke in life. So he made sure no one else could ever have her. Then, one by one, he collected the things most important to her.

"Jamie Simmons killed Ellie Luke because he couldn't have her. He stalked her. Terrorized her. Murdered her. Posed her body in a place he thought no one would ever find it. He returned to her grave. Took things. Keepsakes. Mementos. Then he acquired the greatest prize of all. Ellie's lookalike sister. His own daughter.

"At the conclusion of this trial, I'm confident you'll return the only verdict you can. Jamie Simmons murdered Ellie Luke and hid her body from her family. He is guilty of aggravated murder. He stalked. Planned. Executed. Then he destroyed Ellie's family by making it his own."

The members of the jury never lost eye contact with me. Though I couldn't read their expressions, I knew the impact of the story I'd just told. I just didn't know if they'd believe it.

Bennett Cutler took a moment, then stepped up to the lectern. He seemed cool and confident. He folded his hands and never moved from behind the microphone.

"Good morning," he said. "That was something, wasn't it? That story Ms. Brent told ought to be a movie. I'd buy a ticket, that's for sure. Only ... she can't prove a word of it. That's the thing I need you to keep in mind.

"Proof. You'll get instructions from the judge on what that means. Proof. Has the state proven to you beyond a reasonable doubt that my client, Jamie Simmons, is guilty of murder? Murder. That's what he's charged with. That's the only thing you're being asked to decide. Can Mara Brent prove beyond a reasonable doubt that Jamie Simmons murdered poor Ellie Luke?

"I'll make it easy for you. She won't be able to. So what she'll do instead is try to draw your focus on other things. Sensational things, I'll give her that. But her case is the equivalent of clickbait. It seems interesting. Compelling. But there's nothing there of substance.

"Nobody saw Jamie Simmons with Ellie Luke the night she disappeared. She hasn't got a shred of physical evidence tying him to the crime. All she has is a story. Because Jamie didn't kill Ellie. The only thing he's guilty of is falling for Ellie's kid sister out of their shared grief over losing her. That's not a crime, folks, no matter how you feel about them. Unfortunately, this entire case stems from one disturbed girl seeking attention. That's the current tragedy. Mara Brent herself is responsible for that. That's what I'll prove to you, even though I have no obligation to prove anything at all."

Cutler shook his head. He stepped out from behind the lectern.

"You don't have to like Jamie Simmons. You're welcome to whatever opinion you have of him. You can judge him for how he's lived his life. Who he's loved. What kind of husband or parent he is. But none of those things make him a murderer. Not one. You can't condemn someone to death because you don't like his life choices.

"It doesn't matter how he felt about Ellie Luke. They were friends. Yes. He was gutted by her disappearance and murder. He grew close to her family. He married her sister and started his own family with her. So what? This thing has been a witch hunt since day one. Jamie Simmons is no murderer. He had nothing to do with what happened to Ellie. What you'll see instead is how this case was botched from the beginning by a detective who was in over his head. Who's still in over his head. But you won't see evidence of murder. Because there isn't any."

Cutler went back to the lectern and pounded his fist on it, earning him a stern look from Judge Saul. He shook his head as if he couldn't believe he'd been asked to even come here today. For his part, Jamie Simmons stayed stoic. When Cutler took his seat next to him, Jamie put an arm around him. Almost as if he were consoling him for having to waste his time.

"Ms. Brent?" Judge Saul said. "You may call your first witness."

16

Dr. Lois Palmieri wore the same suit in every trial I'd ever known her to testify in. I believed she had at least a dozen of them in her closet. It was navy blue, double-breasted with gold buttons. She wore a white blouse underneath and a blue-and-white-polka-dot scarf. She cut a trim figure in blue kitten heels and tan pantyhose. Her steel-gray hair was cropped short around her face. She took her oath and slipped her gold aviator glasses up the bridge of her nose.

"Good morning, Dr. Palmieri," I started. "Could you please explain to the jury what you do for a living?"

She adjusted the microphone. "Of course. I'm a criminal forensic scientist. I spent the better part of my career working for the Ohio Bureau of Criminal Investigations, conducting crime scene analysis."

Dr. Palmieri went through her credentials. She had a doctorate in forensic science. Had served as BCI's senior crime scene analyst for over twenty years before her semi-retirement. For the past eight years, she taught doctoral students in criminal forensics at Ohio State University. The woman was a legend among crime scene analysts all over the country.

"Do you still work as an analyst or are you exclusively in academia now?" I asked, already knowing the answer.

"Although I'm a full professor at OSU, I also consult with Ohio's BCI quite frequently. I've also been brought in to consult on different criminal cases throughout the country."

"I see," I said. "Can you tell me how you became involved with the Ellie Luke murder case?"

"Twenty-two years ago, I was the senior analyst with the northwest Ohio region of BCI based in Bowling Green. I was called in to process the scene out near what's now Homer Park where the victim's remains were discovered."

"It was your crime scene?" I asked.

"Well, Detective Gus Ritter with the Maumee County Sheriff's Department was the lead detective. I came out at his request. But yes, I was put in control of the scene."

Dr. Palmieri went through the background of how she came to the scene. Ritter called her almost immediately when suspected human remains were found. Palmieri's team took control and protected the scene. The jury maintained rapt attention as the doctor explained the steps she took to secure the area.

"Dr. Palmieri," I said. "Can you describe for me what you discovered and where?"

"Well, the area where the victim's remains were found was remote. There were old hiking trails out there, but the body wasn't along any of those. It was about a quarter of a mile northwest of what's now known as the S trail that runs past the Maumee River."

We'd entered an aerial satellite map into evidence. Dr. Palmieri marked off the site where two hunters found Ellie's bones.

"Is this public hunting land?" I asked.

"No, there's state land that abuts it, but this was outside the border of that. My understanding is that the two gentlemen who found the remains were actually tracking a deer one of them believed he nicked earlier in the morning."

"Okay. Please describe for me what you observed when you came on scene?"

"Of course. As I indicated, the area was rather remote and off the literal beaten trail here. There is thick underbrush and it's difficult to get to. But here, just over this ridge, there's a clearing. There's a large oak tree in front of an area I'd describe as a sort of grassy, mossy knoll. The victim's remains were found propped up against the trunk of the tree."

I marked the next photograph as an exhibit. Dr. Palmieri identified it as the scene as it appeared when she first arrived. Part of Ellie Luke's skeleton, her skull, rib cage and right arm could be seen leaning against the base of the tree. We went through a series of close-up photographs. Palmieri talked the jury through what they were seeing.

"The victim was lying against the base of the tree, her arms crossed in front of her at the wrists. Her legs splayed out in front, crossed at the ankles. The skull had partially detached from the neck. Although most of the flesh was gone except around the skull. Her hair was still pulled back in a ponytail."

"Was there anything remarkable to you about the way the body lay?" I asked.

"Well, it didn't appear to be lying in a natural position. As in, I immediately suspected the body had been posed in this fashion rather than falling this way."

"Why do you say that?"

"The hands crossed and linked together, in almost a prayer pose. The legs crossed at the ankles. Even the way the body was propped against the tree. She was partially under a foot of dirt from the torso to the upper thighs. Then, when we moved the body, I could see the defect in the back of the skull. It wasn't immediately visible the way the body was discovered against the tree like that."

I flipped to another photograph, a close-up of Ellie's skull with the large, jagged hole in the back.

"What are we looking at?" I asked.

"A large portion of the back of the victim's skull was caved in. When we moved the body, the missing piece was found underneath her."

"Why is that significant?"

"Well, for one, it represented the most likely cause of death. A wound like that would have most certainly been fatal."

"Objection," Cutler said in an almost nonchalant tone. "This witness isn't a medical doctor."

"This witness has already testified about her extensive experience with crime scene analysis, specifically murders. If ..."

"I'm going to sustain it," Judge Saul said. "Dr. Palmieri, please leave the medical conclusions to the medical doctors."

Palmieri seemed nonplussed by the judge's ruling. "Of course," she said. "May I finish my answer?"

"Please do," Saul said.

"Let me rephrase and say that the wound was the only sign of trauma I was able to observe. You asked me why that was significant. With the way the body was positioned, I believe that it was put there in that specific pose. It didn't fall that way naturally. The blow was to the back of the head. She was found leaning against the tree, face up, partially buried. It is my scientific opinion that the victim was probably already dead or at least unconscious when she was placed there."

"Okay," I said. "Thank you. Doctor, what else did you find at the scene?"

"The victim was wearing a blue polo-type shirt with a Lennox Caregiving logo above the right breast. Under that, she wore a white tank top. A pair of size 4 denim jeans were found folded next to the victim at the base of the tree."

"Folded?" I asked. I flipped to the next photograph. The jeans were there, loosely folded about a foot from Ellie Luke's skull.

"Yes. She was still wearing white tennis shoes. They were unlaced as if they'd been removed and put back on. Perhaps when the victim's jeans were removed. She wasn't wearing any undergarments other than the tank top."

"No underwear?"

"Correct."

"What else did you find?"

"There was a gold chain around the victim's neck. There was a blue pendant dangling from it. We also found an earring near the victim's skull in the dirt."

I flipped to the next photograph, a blow-up of the earring found at the scene.

"What can you tell me about this earring?" I asked.

"It's a flat, gold-colored circular hoop with a heart pattern cut into it. There is a blue stone inside one of the hearts."

"Did you have cause to analyze the properties of this earring?"

"Of course. The earring was made up of 92.5% sterling silver with other metals mixed in. The earring back was the same metal. The stone was made of Tanzanite. Detective Ritter had a photograph of the victim wearing the earrings. Her family reported that she'd been wearing them the day she disappeared."

"You found one earring, not its mate?" I asked.

"That's correct."

"Was there anything else significant about what you found at the scene?"

"There was no other jewelry. As I said, the victim's hair was still present and pulled back into a ponytail. She was wearing a blue satin scrunchie that roughly matched the color of her sweater. But it appeared a large chunk of hair had been cut."

I flipped to another photograph, a close-up of Ellie's ponytail. You could clearly see a large, uneven hank of it had been cut from the rest of the ponytail.

"Was there anything significant about the hair?"

"Well, it was dark brown in color. It had been bleached and the victim had lighter brown, artificial highlights. After speaking with her hair stylist and our chemical analysis, we identified the dye as Chestnut #7. The victim was definitively identified through dental records though. She had two crowns on her first molars as well as a permanent retainer in the upper palate. She had four fillings."

"All right. You indicated it's your opinion the victim wasn't killed as she lay?"

"No. I said I don't believe the victim was found in a natural position. There was no evidence of any other disturbances in the area around her that would indicate a struggle. Though I have to point out, the victim went missing in March of that year and wasn't discovered until October. With the advanced decomposition and the changing of seasons, I can't definitely state there wasn't a struggle at the site. I can only say we didn't find any evidence of such. No blood. No broken branches. We found overturned earth next to the body, likely what was used to partially bury her. But you have to understand, that's seven months out in the elements. There was evidence that animals had gotten to the body. Bite marks on hands and wrists. The flesh had either decayed or been eaten away."

A few members of the jury grimaced, but they were still with us.

"All right. So based on your thirty-plus years as a crime scene analyst, what conclusions were you able to draw about what happened to Ellie Luke?"

"Ms. Luke was likely killed somewhere else and placed at the base of that tree in those woods. I can't say for sure where she was killed, but I don't believe it was nearby. I also believe someone took time with the body."

"What do you mean?"

"To remove her jeans, put her shoes back on. Remove her panties. Someone cut a large hank of her hair. Also, the location of the body itself. It was protected. Away from where hikers would have naturally come upon it. And as I've indicated, partially buried. It was also unusual that we found Ms. Luke's complete skeleton. Over that amount of time, I would have expected animals to carry part of it off."

"Do you have any way of knowing how long the victim's remains were in that location?"

"Not precisely. But based on the vegetation and insect activity, it was consistent with the amount of time she'd been missing."

"So you're saying you believe the victim was lying under that tree since March of that year?"

"Mostly likely, yes."

"Thank you. Dr. Palmieri, have you had occasion to analyze any other artifacts in connection with this case?"

"Yes," she said.

"Can you tell me what those were?"

"Three months ago, items were sent to BCI and I was asked to conduct the analysis of them. They included an earring, a lock of hair, and a pair of underwear."

One by one, I introduced photographs of the items Dr. Palmieri described. Then, I took her through the chain of custody of the lock of hair. Hayden would testify later where it came from, but for now, Dr. Palmieri could drop the first bomb.

"Dr. Palmieri, were you able to form a scientific opinion about the lock of hair sent for your analysis?"

"I was. I compared the length and cut marks to those found on the victim under that tree. The hair dye. Though we weren't able to extract DNA from the locks sent in, we were able to match it to the victim."

"What do you mean?"

"I mean the hair sample sent to my lab on September 1st of this year belonged to Elizabeth Luke. It matched the lock cut from her head."

"Thank you," I said. "What about the underwear?"

"Two pubic hairs were combed from the underwear. We were able to extract DNA from the roots. They were a match for Elizabeth Luke."

"Okay, what about the earring?" The picture of the earring was up on screen. Dr. Palmieri authenticated it as being the earring she was sent from the Maumee County Sheriff's Department.

"We subjected the earring to the same analysis as the one found at the scene twenty-two years ago. The metals matched. The stone matched. The earring back matched. Additionally, the wear patterns at the front top of the earring matched."

"What's significant about that?"

"On both the earring we found at the scene twenty-two years ago, and the one sent for analysis this year ... there are distinct wear patterns at the top of the hoop. You can see it in Exhibits 25 and 39."

I put the photographs side by side on the monitor. Dr. Palmieri used a laser pointer to show two dull patches in the metal just below the stem that would have gone into Ellie's earlobe.

"Most likely, this is where the wearer would have grasped each earring before lining the stem up to go into the ear hole. It's a similar wear pattern on both."

"Which tells us what?"

"It tells us these are mated pairs. The earring sent to my lab this year is the mate to the one found on the victim's body twenty-two years ago. You can also see those same wear patterns in photographs taken of the victim wearing those same earrings."

I flipped to the photograph I'd admitted as Exhibit 12. It was Ellie Luke's high school senior photo. I zoomed in. Dr. Palmieri pointed out the same dullness in the metal at the top of the hoops.

"Thank you, Doctor," I said. "I have no further questions."

"Your witness, Mr. Cutler."

Bennett Cutler practically plowed through me to get to the lectern. I looked at the back of the courtroom. George Luke sat still as stone, his face unreadable. As far as I knew, that was the first time he'd actually seen what his granddaughter found in Jamie Simmons's horrible box.

※

"Dr. Palmieri, you don't know if Ellie Luke was murdered, do you?"

Lois Palmieri barely blinked when Bennett Cutler asked the question.

"My findings are that the victim met with foul play," she said.

"Foul play. Let me ask you again, you cannot say that Ellie Luke was murdered, isn't that right?"

"As you pointed out, I'm not a medical doctor. I won't testify about the specific cause of death. But Ms. Luke was most likely bludgeoned to death in the back of her head. It was not a self-inflicted wound."

"Could a fall have caused that kind of defect to the back of her head?"

"I won't testify to the cause of death in that way, Mr. Cutler."

"You don't even know whether the defect happened post mortem, do you?"

"That's beyond my expertise," she said.

"Dr. Palmieri, you were questioned about the things you found at Ellie Luke's gravesite. I want to make sure I understand what you didn't find."

"By all means."

"You didn't find blood?"

"I did not."

"You didn't find DNA belonging to anyone other than Ellie Luke."

"I did not."

"Didn't find skin or tissue samples under her nails or anything like that, right?"

"The victim didn't have fingernails by the time we found her, Mr. Cutler."

"Fine. So answer the question. You found no skin or tissue samples belonging to anyone but the victim. Isn't that right?"

"That is correct. The tissue samples we recovered, such as they were, came from the victim's scalp."

"Got it. So isn't it fair to say you found no physical evidence in terms of blood, hair, skin, or DNA belonging to anyone other than Ellie Luke, correct?"

"That is correct."

Cutler scratched his chin and paced in front of the jury box. "So there was no physical evidence tying anyone to that crime scene, let alone the defendant, right?"

"I didn't say that. There was physical evidence as I've described."

"Clothing. An earring. Is that right?"

"That's correct. Along with the victim's remains themselves."

"Got it. But none of the things you found. The earring. The clothing. The body itself ... you can't conclude Ellie Luke was murdered from your findings. That's not within your purview, is it?"

"Not as such," she said.

"Good. Thank you. Dr. Palmieri, you've been at this a long time. That was your testimony?"

"I've been a crime scene investigator for thirty-plus years, yes."

"You've worked on some relatively high-profile cases, haven't you?"

"I suppose so."

"You've written books about it too, haven't you?"

"I believe my curriculum vitae was entered into evidence, Mr. Cutler. Are you asking me to list my publications?"

"No, thank you. You said you've consulted with BCI since you began teaching full time. But they aren't the only organization you've consulted with, are they?"

"No."

"In fact, you've consulted on television shows and movies too, haven't you?"

"Once or twice, yes."

"Once or twice. I would assume those consultations are more lucrative than working for the government or a university, aren't they?"

"Objection, relevance," I said.

"Mr. Cutler?" Judge Saul said.

"Your Honor, it's proper cross for me to explore any biases this witness might have. I'm getting there."

"Please do," Saul said. "Overruled."

"You're aware this case has garnered national media attention, aren't you?"

"I can't say that I am," Palmieri said.

"You can't say that you are. Doctor, you've worked closely with an author by the name of Remy Redstone, haven't you?"

"I was hired as a consultant by Mr. Redstone's publisher, yes. Mr. Redstone and I exchanged some emails. He came to visit me on campus to interview me in person once, maybe five years ago."

"You're being modest though, aren't you? Isn't it true that Mr. Redstone has a character based on you in his latest series of crime thrillers? The Louise Palmer Mysteries. That's you, isn't it? Lois Palmieri, Louise Palmer."

"Objection! Your honor, we've gone way afield of relevance now."

"I agree. What's your point, Mr. Cutler?"

"I'll make it," he said. "Doctor, isn't it true that Remy Redstone has already approached you about your involvement in this particular case?"

"No. That is not true."

"You didn't take a phone call from Mr. Redstone in the last two weeks?"

"I received a call from Mr. Redstone. I didn't speak to him. And if I had, and he had asked me about my involvement in this case, I wouldn't have answered. I don't discuss active investigations with members of the media."

"But this one will make a pretty good book, don't you think?"

"Objection! Your Honor, Mr. Cutler is fishing without bait at this point."

"Sustained. Move on, Mr. Cutler."

Cutler smirked as he took his place behind the lectern. "Doctor. These items you analyzed this year, you don't know where they came from, do you?"

"They came from the Maumee County Sheriff's Department. I believe I've already testified about chain of custody."

"Sure," he said. "But you don't know where they came from before that, isn't that right?"

"I'm not privy to that. I was asked to analyze them. I did. My findings are in my report and I've already testified about them."

"Got it," he said. "And in your findings, you can't say who had access to them before they came into the Sheriff's Department's possession."

"I cannot."

"You didn't find anything in your analysis of the earring, the underwear, the lock of hair that would connect them to anyone other than Ellie Luke, isn't that right?"

"That's correct."

"No fingerprints. No DNA. No blood. Nothing like that on those items?"

"That isn't what I said. I said the hairs found in the underwear belonged to Ellie Luke. We made that determination from extracted DNA from the roots of those hairs."

"But you found no DNA belonging to anyone other than Ellie, right?"

"That's correct."

"Thank you. I'm finished with this witness."

"Ms. Brent?" the judge said.

He'd done all he could do. Lois Palmieri had tied the most damning items from Jamie Simmons's treasure box to Ellie

Luke's dead body. It would be up to Hayden to convince the jury who had possession of them all these years. If she could get through it. If she could stand up to Bennett Cutler, this case would be all but over.

"I have no further questions," I said.

"You may step down, Dr. Palmieri," the judge said. "Ms. Brent?"

"The state calls Hayden Simmons to the stand."

17

Before she even climbed into the witness box, I had to believe Bennett Cutler realized the problem he would have with Hayden Simmons. She was nineteen years old. She could have passed for about twelve that day. Thin, pretty, trembling as she raised her right hand and swore to tell the truth, Hayden had to be immediately reminded to speak up. She folded her hands in her lap to keep them from shaking. She fixed her gaze on me. She sat as straight in her seat as she could.

"Ms. Simmons," I started after letting her introduce herself to the jury. "How are you related to the defendant in this case?"

"He's my father," she said, her voice gaining a bit of volume. Look at me, I thought, hoping she could read my mind. Look only at me. Don't look at your father.

"How are you related to the victim in this case?"

"My mother is Erin Luke. She was Ellie Luke's younger sister. Ellie Luke is my aunt."

"Did you ever meet her?"

"No, ma'am. Ellie died almost three years before I was born."

I wanted Hayden to be able to tell her story in as conversational a tone as possible. Cutler would give me leeway to a point. Part of me wanted to push him. Let Hayden get used to the sound of his voice. The combative tone he'd take when objecting. She wasn't my client. But that didn't mean I wouldn't protect her.

"Hayden, when did you first learn your aunt had been murdered?"

"Objection," Cutler said, as I expected. "The state has yet to prove Ellie Luke was murdered."

"Your Honor ... we're going to be here a very long time if counsel for the defense intends to object to what amounts to semantics."

"I agree," she said. "The witness may answer."

"It wasn't until I was older. There were photographs on my grandparents' wall that I assumed were of my mother. They bear a strong resemblance. But once when I was ten or eleven, I asked my grandpa about one of the pictures and he told me it was actually my aunt."

"Did you know you had an aunt at that point?"

"No. I was young enough it hadn't even really occurred to me to ask about that. There was always just my mother and my grandparents on the Luke side of the family. My dad was an only child, too. His parents died when I was little. We're a really small family. I just didn't know any other way."

"All right," I said. "So, your father is the one who told you about the circumstances of your aunt's death?"

"No. I was playing over at a neighbor of my grandparents, and they told me …"

"Objection. The question calls for hearsay."

"The question isn't being asked to prove the matter asserted. Only to establish what this witness believed about the victim."

"I'll allow it," the judge said.

"The neighbor was the first one who ever used the word killed or murdered."

"How did you react?" I asked.

"I was just shocked. It felt like she was talking about some other family. Other people. I didn't understand why none of my family talked about it. It was this big thing that impacted all their lives."

"Did you confront either of your parents about it?"

"I asked my father. I was afraid to talk to my mom."

"Why is that?"

"I didn't want to upset her."

"What happened when you asked your father about your Aunt Ellie?"

"He was abrupt. He just said it happened a long time ago. That Aunt Ellie wasn't careful and that I should never walk home alone in the dark."

"He said your Aunt Ellie wasn't careful?"

"Something like that. He dismissed me pretty quickly. He didn't say I should never ask about it, but I felt strongly that it was a topic that shouldn't be brought up. That it would be too painful for either my grandparents or my mother. So at the time, I let it go."

"Did you ever ask your mother about her sister?"

"Not in those years, no. Like I said, I was pretty young. Ten or eleven. Still young enough, I kind of took whatever my parents said as the way things should be. It wasn't until I was older, maybe fifteen or sixteen, I started asking more questions."

"Who did you ask?"

"I tried to ask my mom. It was after I turned sixteen. I got my driver's license and she lectured me about being careful. She said something about not walking to my car alone after work. I worked at an ice cream parlor then. So I asked her if she was scared because of what happened to her sister. She just burst into tears. My dad stepped in and changed the subject. He gave me this angry look. I felt like I'd overstepped. And my mom was so upset. Crying. She had to go lie down. I felt terrible. So I just didn't bring it up with her again."

"Did you ever talk to your grandparents about Ellie?"

"No. Nothing substantive. I think I might have mentioned once or twice to Grandma that I knew the picture in the hall was of my Aunt Ellie. After seeing how upset Mom was, I was more careful. I wanted to give them the opportunity to talk about Ellie if they wanted to. But they never did."

"I see," I said. "So, how did you find out the details of what happened to your aunt?"

"Well, I was always curious. My father kept telling me to leave it alone. That it happened long before I was born. That my mom and her parents had moved on and we shouldn't upset them. Like I said, for a while, I accepted that. But as I got older, I just had so many questions. So I started looking online."

"What did you find?"

"I found news articles from when Ellie disappeared. It had been all over the local stations. There were search parties and everything. I didn't know any of that. I didn't know that she hadn't been found right away. I mean, until I started looking it up online, I didn't know whether she'd been stabbed or strangled or shot or raped or any of it. I just knew she'd been killed, that it happened before I was born, and that you don't talk about it with my family."

"Did you ever discuss what you found with anyone?" I asked.

"Not in person. No. But while I was searching for information about Ellie, I stumbled onto this website. An online forum about cold murder cases in Ohio. I discovered there was a whole sub-forum devoted just to Ellie's case."

It was here Hayden's nerves seemed to fall away. She took the jury through how she connected with amateur sleuths who had researched the case.

"Did you learn anything you didn't already know?" I asked.

"God. Yes. I learned everything. That she was found in the woods like that by hunters. One of these amateur sleuths had done some interviews on his own. He'd talked to a friend of my Aunt Ellie's who went to college with her. He posted photographs of her I'd never seen before. Although that wasn't hard to do. The only pictures I'd ever seen of her were the ones hanging in my grandparents' house."

"I'd like to direct your attention to what's been marked as State's Exhibit 49. Do you recognize it?"

"Yes."

"Can you describe it?"

"This is the picture my online friend showed me. It's Aunt Ellie with a group of her friends from nursing school."

I admitted the photo into evidence and displayed it on the overhead for the jury. "Did anything strike you about this picture?" I asked.

"That's my Aunt Ellie in the middle," she said. "I recognized her right away because she looks so much like Mom. For a second, I thought it was my mom. But the hair is different. Longer than my mom usually wore it. But that's my dad sitting on the end of the bench there."

Hayden pointed out her then twenty-four-year-old father. He sat on the edge in profile, looking straight at Ellie Luke. She seemed unaware of it, smiling at the camera like the rest of the young people in the photo.

"Your father," I said. "That surprised you?"

"I had no idea my dad and Aunt Ellie were friends. Were classmates. He didn't tell me. No one told me. It was unsettling for me to find this all out from strangers online."

"What did you do next?"

"I printed the picture out and took it to my dad. I asked him about it."

"What did he say?"

"He shut me down. Got really angry. He wanted to know where I found it. He said he'd never seen that picture before. I asked him over and over, were you friends with Ellie too? Did Mom know? He just refused to answer any of my questions. He snatched the photo out of my hands and took it. He told me to stop chasing ghosts. Told me I didn't understand what I was messing with. He was so angry. It scared me. So I just didn't bring it up to him again."

"Was that the end of it? Did you do what your father asked?"

"No. I just ... it bothered me how angry he got. He just exploded. I didn't know what to think. I mean, I guess I thought maybe he was trying to protect my mom. But I didn't understand why they wouldn't want to remember my aunt. Like they wanted to erase her. I felt ... I don't know. I felt like she deserved better."

"What did you do next?"

"A couple of weeks after Dad blew up at me, he started acting strange around me. Like he wouldn't talk to me. He just avoided me. He has a workshop in the basement. It's an old coal bin he turned into his own little man cave. He'd go down there and to be alone. I asked my mom if he was okay. She just shrugged and told me not to bother him. Well, I was worried. It just seemed out of character for my dad to be so moody and withdrawn like that. So I went down there. Two or three times I saw him sitting at his workbench looking at something in a box. When he heard me coming, he closed it so quickly and shoved it into a drawer. The first time, he snapped at me. Told me to stop sneaking up on him."

"Did you ever find out what was in the box?" I asked.

"Yes," she said.

"What happened, Hayden?"

"About two weeks after the first time I caught him down there, he left the door open. Dad was at work. I got home early from class and my mom was on a shopping trip. I was alone in the house. I don't know. I just decided to go down there. I went into Dad's man cave. I opened the drawer I saw him shove that box into. The drawer itself was open a little bit. So I pulled the box out."

"What did you find, Hayden?"

"There were pictures in it. Of my aunt. One she was sitting on a bus talking to someone. Whoever took the picture must have been sitting behind her. You could see her in profile. Another picture she was sitting at a picnic table eating lunch. It was a close-up of her face. And another one ... she was at my grandma's. I recognized the side of the house and the bushes she keeps outside. The picture was of my aunt sitting on her bed. It was taken through a window. She was naked."

One by one, I marked the photographs for identification. When I moved to admit them, Cutler objected.

"This witness can't authenticate these photographs. She didn't personally know Ellie Luke. She isn't claiming to be the photographer."

"She can testify that these photographs are the same ones she found in that box in her father's drawer," I said.

"Overruled," Saul said.

I admitted the photographs and displayed them on the overhead. The ones of Ellie Luke in her own bedroom were, of course, the most disturbing. She clearly had no idea she was being photographed. In one, she sat in nothing but her bra and panties rubbing lotion on her elbow. In the final one, she was naked, looking at herself in the mirror.

"Hayden," I said. "Do you recognize the item marked as Exhibit 16?"

"Yes. It's an earring. I found it in the box."

I admitted the earring. The one Dr. Palmieri had already testified was a mate to the one found near Ellie's body.

Then there was the lock of hair and the underwear. Hayden was strong, assured, confident as each item was admitted into evidence.

"What did you do next, Hayden?"

"I threw up," she said. "I was so upset. I couldn't believe what I was seeing."

"Did you tell anyone?"

"No. Not at first."

"Did you ask your father about the box?"

"No."

"What did you do with the box?"

"I took it. I just ... God. I knew it was bad. I knew I had to tell someone. I knew I had to get in touch with the police. My dad wasn't coming home until the next day so I knew if I didn't do something then and there ... if he knew I saw what I saw ... I was afraid he'd throw it all away or hide it where I couldn't find it. I knew ..."

"Knew what?"

"I recognized that earring. I saw Aunt Ellie wearing it in the photographs at my grandparents'. One of the articles I found online said they'd found it next to her body. Just the one. I was so confused. But I don't know. I just *felt* it all.

"Every online theory about her murder, they thought it had to be someone she knew who killed her because ..."

"Objection," Cutler said. "Again, this is hearsay testimony. The witness is trying to testify about what some random person said on the internet."

"Once again, this goes to the witness's state of mind," I said.

"I'll allow it to a point. The witness may answer in terms of what this information caused her to do. Not about random theories on the internet," Judge Saul said.

"They're not random," Hayden said, earning her a stern look from Judge Saul.

"Hayden, what did you think the items in the box meant?" I asked.

"He knew her. My dad knew her. The police said she was followed home from the lady she worked for. And all these things in that box. How else could he have gotten them? I just knew in my gut that I wouldn't get a straight answer. That this was important. That the police needed to see it.

"My dad had kept everything from me. My whole family had. And here was this thing ... things. Things that shouldn't be in the house. I didn't trust my parents anymore. I'm sorry. I just felt so lost and alone. So I took that box and I ran with it. I was going to go to the police. But I saw you and Sheriff Cruz sitting and eating lunch outside the building. So I came up to you and

Sheriff Cruz took me over to the Sheriff's Department. I gave the box to him."

"Have you spoken to your father? Your mother?"

"I tried to explain everything to my mom. She showed up at my friend's house where I was staying after I turned over the box. She blew up at me. My parents threw me out of the house. They think ... they think I'm making this all up. How could I do that? How could I make up something like that? I wasn't alive when this all happened?"

I had one more photograph I wanted the jury to see. "Hayden, do you recognize this photograph?"

"Yes," she said, a silent tear falling. I knew what the jury was thinking. She looked so much like her sister. They could be twins.

"Who is this, Hayden?"

"It's my mother," she said. "Erin Luke Simmons."

Four members of the jury gasped. They saw what we all saw. Jamie Simmons had married and impregnated a woman who looked exactly like the one I knew he had murdered. And before them sat Hayden. She, too, looked enough like her mother and aunt. She had their eyes. But she had her father's coloring. A perfect blend of the two of them. His final trophy.

"Thank you," I said. "I have no further questions."

18

Cutler stood at the lectern for a moment, rifling through notes I suspected he wasn't even reading. More likely, he wanted to build anticipation. Make Hayden even more nervous as she waited for his attack.

"Thanks for your patience," Cutler finally said. "I'd like to talk about this so-called box of yours for a minute. You say you found it in a drawer in the basement of the home you shared with who, again?"

"At the time, I lived with my mother and father. Erin and Jamie Simmons," she said.

"But they weren't the only ones with access to the house, isn't that right?"

"We're the ones who lived there. I don't know what you mean."

"Who is Willa Jennings?"

"Willa's my mom's cleaning lady."

"She comes once a month, isn't that right?"

"Yes."

"And she has the passcode to get into the front door, correct?"

"Yes."

"Last spring, isn't it true your parents hired contractors to do a kitchen remodel? Isn't that right?"

"Yes."

"How many workers were in and out of the house that you recall?"

"I ... what? I don't recall. It took them a couple of weeks, I think."

"Was it more than five workers?"

"I think so."

"More than ten?"

"I don't think more than ten."

"Willa works in the home by herself sometimes, doesn't she?"

"What do you mean?"

"I mean a lot of the time the house is empty when she's cleaning, right?"

"Um ... sure."

"Good. Okay. Thanks for clarifying that. And the coal bin. The space in the basement you say your father has converted to a workshop. Is there a lock on that door?"

"There's a latch on the outside of the door."

"A latch. So no key."

"No key, no."

"And it latches from the outside. Is there any way to lock that door from the inside?"

"I don't think so, no."

"So then anyone could unlatch that door and enter the room, correct? If they were in the house already, that is."

"I suppose so, yes. But nobody goes in that room but my dad. It's his space. My mom doesn't go in there. He gets mad at her if she does. I learned when I was little not to go in there."

"But you went in anyway, isn't that right?"

"No. I never went in that room."

"Right. Except when you claim you went in and took this box out of it when your dad wasn't home."

"I ... Yes. I went in there that time. Yes."

"Fine. Thank you. Ms. Simmons, you never asked your father about what he kept in his desk, did you?"

"No."

"And you never spoke to your mother about this so-called box or its contents either, did you?"

"I said I tried to. She confronted me in the driveway of my friend's house. But she wouldn't listen to me. She just kept screaming."

"So you've never given either of them a chance to explain or defend themselves. You just assumed you had everything all figured out."

"Objection, argumentative."

"Sustained, Mr. Cutler."

"Ms. Simmons, how would you describe your relationship with your parents today?"

"We don't ... we don't talk. I no longer have a relationship with them."

"I see. Not even your mother?"

"She won't return my calls. My father won't let her. He controls everything. He always has."

"Your Honor," Cutler said. "I'd like the last part of the witness's statement to be stricken as unresponsive."

"I'd say it's entirely responsive," I said. "Mr. Cutler may just not like the answer to his own question."

"I agree," Saul said. "Objection overruled."

"Let me ask this another way," Cutler said. "Isn't it true that your mother has since taken out a restraining order against you for harassment?"

"Objection!" I said. "Your Honor, may we approach?"

Saul waved us forward.

"Your Honor," I started. "This issue of Erin Luke's petition for a restraining order against her daughter is irrelevant and highly prejudicial. It's a stunt. No order has been granted. Counsel has manufactured this issue for the sole purpose of asking this witness about it."

"That's ridiculous," Cutler said. "I didn't file that petition. I had nothing to do with it. Hayden Simmons's mother filed it on her own."

"You expect me to believe that?" I said. "It's got your prints all over it, Bennett."

"Stop," Judge Saul said. "Counselor, are you planning to try to enter Mrs. Simmons's petition as an exhibit with this witness on the stand?"

"Yes, Your Honor."

"He can't," I said. "That petition is filled with hearsay."

"Court proceedings are an exception to the hearsay rule," Cutler said.

"And you cannot try to shroud Erin Luke's statements as an exception to the rule simply because they were written on a bogus petition filed for the sole purpose of trying to get around the hearsay rule. It's ridiculous."

"Here's what I'm going to do," Judge Saul said. "We're not going to get into the status of this other legal proceeding. If you want to call Erin Luke ..."

"Erin Simmons, Your Honor," Cutler interjected.

"Fine," she said. "Erin Simmons. If you want to put her on the stand and ask her about her relationship with her daughter, you certainly can. But I agree with Ms. Brent that you can't try to recharacterize her statements as non-hearsay because of the format they're in."

Judge Saul made a shooing gesture, directing us back to our ready positions. I went to my table. Cutler went back to the lectern. It took him a moment to regroup as the judge asked the jury to disregard Cutler's last question.

"Ms. Simmons," he said. "I'd like to ask you some questions

about your online activity. Can you remind me when you first joined the cold case crime forum you described on direct?"

"It was about a year ago, now."

"You claim you were just researching information about your aunt's alleged murder case?"

"That's correct."

"You understand that your phone records, computer usage, and online activity were submitted to me during the discovery phase of this trial?"

"I know I gave the police access to all of that," she said.

"I'd like to direct your attention to some screenshots, if I may." Cutler marked a series of screenshots from the cold case forum for identification. I'd already stipulated to the entry of many of them.

"Ms. Simmons, I just want to make sure I'm being accurate. Which of these posts are yours?"

Hayden pointed to a post on the screen. Cutler highlighted it.

"For the record," he said. "You're pointing to an entry authored by a Shimmer417. Is that your handle on the forum?"

"Yes."

"I'm curious. What's the significance of Shimmer417?"

"It's just ... Shimmer is kind of a mashup of my name. H for Hayden. Simmer is kind of like Simmons."

"And the number?"

"April 17th was my aunt's birthday."

"Got it. Clever. Do you recall how many times you logged on to this forum after you joined it last year?"

"Not off the top of my head, no."

"Well, do you at least recall how frequently you logged on once you found it?"

"I don't know specifically. I know it was a lot. Especially in the beginning."

"It was every day, multiple times a day, wasn't it?"

"Yes."

"In fact, you were spending upwards of eight hours a day in the forum, isn't that right?"

"I don't ... if you have the records and that's what it shows, I can't dispute that. But it's not accurate to say I was actively participating in the forum eight hours a day. Sometimes I'd just forget to log off. Forget to close my laptop."

"I see. Ms. Simmons, I'd like to direct your attention to a post from November 10th of last year. Do you recall this one? Shimmer417 posts, I'm new to researching the Ellie Luke case. This happened not far from where I grew up. I'd never heard of it before. Does anyone know whether there were any main suspects?"

"I recall posting that, yes," Hayden answered.

"But you weren't being truthful in that post, were you?"

"I don't think I was lying, no."

"To say you were new to researching the case, that's not accurate, is it? You'd been obsessing over the details for years, hadn't you?"

"Objection to the characterization," I said.

"Sustained."

"I don't think I was being inaccurate," Hayden said. "I was new to researching the case."

"Fine," he said. "But you weren't just someone who grew up in the area, were you?"

"I did grow up in the area."

"But you weren't forthright with the members of the forum about your relationship to the victim, were you?"

"I didn't lie," she said. "But no. I didn't tell anyone Ellie Luke was my aunt."

"So, isn't it true that you solicited information from these so-called amateur sleuths under false pretenses?"

"No. That's not true. They weren't false pretenses. There was no requirement that you couldn't be related to a victim to participate in the forum. If someone had asked me point-blank if Ellie was my aunt, I wouldn't have lied."

"The other members of the forum didn't know they were interacting with a family member of the victim, isn't that right?"

"I'm sure they didn't," she said.

Good job, I thought. Cutler had tried to paint Hayden as deceptive but she was smart enough not to let him.

"You gained their trust, didn't you?" he asked.

"I don't know what you mean."

"I mean ... you spent hours a day interacting with the other members of this sub-forum. Establishing a rapport with them.

Isn't it true that there can often be a culture of mistrust in forums like that?"

"I don't know what you mean."

"Let me put it this way. Members of this forum wouldn't have appreciated it if you'd been an undercover cop, isn't that right?"

"I don't know what they'd appreciate."

"But they never suspected you were related to the victim because you never told them."

"I can't speak to what they suspected. I never got the feeling they suspected or mistrusted me. It's true I never told them I was related to Ellie Luke. It's also true nobody ever asked."

Cutler sighed in frustration. I had to resist the urge to fist pump. Hayden was handling him brilliantly.

"You gained inside information into the investigation of your aunt's case from members of that forum, isn't that true?"

"I gained information. I don't know that I'd describe it as anything on the inside."

"Well, now you're not being forthright, are you? You testified another member of the forum produced photographs of your aunt you'd never seen, isn't that right?"

"That's true. How is that inside information though?"

"You learned about what had been found at the murder scene through this forum, didn't you?"

"Yes."

Cutler pulled up screenshots of the thread where the members discussed the crime scene and what had been publicly disseminated about it. One by one, he had Hayden tick off what she learned.

"You learned where your aunt had been found on November 18th last year, correct?"

"I learned that from reading a newspaper article. I don't know what date I read the article."

"You learned she'd been found partially clothed on December 2nd in the forum, correct?"

"Yes. I think that's right."

"But you had seen a photograph of your aunt wearing her gold hoop earrings, correct? That's the one you identified as hanging in the hallway at your grandparents' house?"

"Correct."

"So you knew what earrings your aunt was allegedly wearing the night she disappeared?"

"I didn't know she was wearing them the night she disappeared. I only knew she owned a pair that looked like that because I'd seen that picture."

"You didn't tell your parents you were frequenting this forum, did you?"

"No."

"You kept it a secret from them, didn't you?"

"I didn't tell them. That's not the same thing as keeping it a secret."

"Hayden, where was your mother when you allege you found your dad looking at this box you claim he kept in his workshop?"

"What? I don't know."

"She wasn't there, isn't that right?"

"Not right there, no."

"So nobody but you saw your father with this box, isn't that right?"

"I don't have any idea who else knew about the box. I only know he didn't want me in that room. I only know he didn't want my mother in that room and as far as I know, she never went down there. She respected his wishes because my mother always does whatever my dad says."

Cutler threw up his hands. "That's not what I asked you. I asked you if anyone besides you saw your father with this so-called box that day. Yes or no."

"I don't know."

"But nobody was there when *you* claim you saw him with it, correct?"

"Yes."

"And you never asked your father or your mother about it, did you?"

"No."

"No. You just magically appeared in front of Sheriff Cruz with the thing."

"Objection!"

"Sustained," Saul said. Cutler put his hands up in surrender.

"Ms. Simmons, in a nine-month period, you spent more than thirty hours a week on the cold case crime forum, didn't you?"

"I don't think so. I told you. Sometimes I just didn't log out. It doesn't mean I was sitting at the computer the whole time."

"You spent more time on the forum than you did at school. Or at your job, isn't that right?"

"I wouldn't say that, no."

"You wouldn't. But your login activity doesn't lie, does it? Can you read the number at the end of the activity report that's been entered as Exhibit 81?"

It was up on screen. The jury could already see it. Hayden sat back. "It says one thousand two hundred and thirty-one hours."

"One thousand two hundred and thirty-one hours," he repeated. "That's the equivalent of fifty-one solid days. I'd say that sounds like an obsession, wouldn't you?"

"Objection!" I shouted.

"Withdrawn," Cutler said. "I have no further questions."

"Ms. Brent?"

I was proud of her. She'd withstood Cutler's attempts to paint her as a liar. As a troubled girl. She was neither.

"I have no more questions," I said. I tried to lock eyes with Hayden. She did well. The hard part for her was over at least in terms of the trial. But as she left the witness box, I watched her walk through the gallery and toward the courtroom double doors. Against the back wall, George Luke sat. He looked like he was seeing a ghost. Anger filled his eyes. And for the first time, he was looking straight at Jamie Simmons.

19

"She did okay," Sam said. "From where I sat, I think the jury believed her."

"She has no reason to lie," I said. We sat in my office eating Hunan takeout. It was well past eight o'clock. Will was staying over at Kat and Bree's tonight. After the second full day of trial, I felt weary. "But Cutler got off some good rounds. He's right that many other people had access to Jamie's basement workshop over the years."

"You're thinking like a lawyer, not a juror," Sam said. "That was just dancing. Distraction. The bottom line, Simmons has relics from Ellie's body. Things that make it clear he knew where she was. Because he put her there. You'll drive that point home in closing."

"I know." I stabbed my chopsticks into my cardboard box and fished out the last of my sesame chicken. "But he's right about one thing. I haven't proved murder yet."

"Again, lawyer brain. Not common sense brain."

"Thanks," I said wryly, though I knew what he meant.

"What'd you make of George Luke?" he asked.

"You were watching him too?"

"I watched him pretty closely. Mara, it was a shock to him. I don't think the man had any idea what Simmons had in that house. The earring in particular. His whole body just shook."

"What in God's name has Jamie been telling that man?"

"I don't know if they've talked at all. Cutler's smart enough to counsel him not to talk to anybody. He knows you'll be able to put them on the stand."

"True," I said. "But he had to have told Erin something. I'd like to talk to her again."

"Will she take your calls?"

"No. She won't even take Hayden's."

"That poor kid. Jamie's trying to make her into some kind of villain in this. And they're buying it. Ellie's whole family."

"Maybe not," I said. "Maybe today was the first crack. I'd like to talk to George Luke alone. But I don't want to approach him. Maybe he'll come to me."

"He's slammed the door," Sam said. "Gus tried to go over there several times. The grip Simmons has over that family is tight."

"Until today," I said. "George was alone. I can't imagine Simmons wanted him in that courtroom today."

My desk phone rang. Sam and I exchanged a look. Nobody knew we were here. It was well past business hours.

I answered it, putting the caller on speaker. "This is Mara Brent."

"Ms. Brent," a female voice said. "I'm so glad you're in your office. I didn't think I'd catch you."

I looked at the caller ID. It was a 313 area code. That was near Detroit.

"Well, you caught me. But I was just leaving. What can I do for you?"

"I was ... I've been reading online about your trial. About that cold case murder? Ellie Luke?"

Sam rolled his eyes. The office took plenty of crackpot calls during high-profile trials. But most of those went to the main line. Whoever this was dialed into my extension.

"May I ask who's calling?"

The woman on the other end of the phone hesitated. "I debated calling at all. I didn't want to get involved. I have reasons to ... well ... stay far away. But my husband encouraged me. My name is Deena Landon. Well, it used to be Deena Price."

Sam looked puzzled. Neither name rang bells for either of us. I slid a legal pad closer to me and gestured to Sam. The cup I usually kept pens in was empty. They had a way of walking off by themselves. Sam took a pen out of his breast pocket and handed it to me.

"Ms. Landon," I said. "Forgive me. But it's pretty late. If you've been following the trial, then you know I've had a long day. If ..."

"I know Jamie Simmons," Deena blurted. "That is ... a long time ago ... we dated. It's been twenty-five years. We went to community college together for a year. Washtenaw County. Then he transferred to UT. We ... Ms. Brent, he was violent."

I jotted down her name and the number from the caller ID. Still, I was skeptical. As she'd said, the case had made its way into the news. Crackpot was still a possibility.

"Ms. Landon," I said. "I'm going to need specifics."

"I know," she said. "I would have come forward a long time ago. I had no idea Jamie would be involved in anything like this. But ... he's not a nice guy. I know that firsthand. He was sweet at first. Attentive. My parents liked him. But then he just got really possessive. Didn't want me hanging around my friends. He was isolating. Controlling. It got suffocating. He ... he got physically aggressive then. I tried to break things off and he hit me. Kicked me in the stomach."

"When was this?" I asked. "Did you go to a doctor?"

"Twenty-five years ago," she said. "And yes. I ended up in the ER with a couple of cracked ribs. I broke things off then. I didn't press charges but there was a cop who came and talked to me. I don't think there's a record of it."

Sam shook his head. He grabbed another legal pad and quickly wrote, "SIMMONS = NO CRIMINAL RECORD AT ALL."

"Okay," I said. "When's the last time you saw Jamie?"

"I left school after that. I was really afraid of Jamie. For a while, I was agoraphobic. I blocked Jamie's number. A few weeks went by and I reconnected with Doug. He was my brother's friend and he'd always kind of had a thing for me. Doug was a Marine at the time. We started dating. I wanna say it was about two or three months after I left WCCC. I was getting ready to re-enroll. Jamie showed up again out of the blue at my mom's house. He threatened me. Doug was there. He beat the living crap out of Jamie. I thought he was going to kill him."

"Were the police called then?" I asked.

"No. That was the end of it. Jamie was terrified. He left. I never saw him again. I've always felt like Doug saved my life that day. We got married about a year later."

"I'm glad he was there for you," I said.

"Me too. But ... I just ... I thought you should know. I didn't know that other girl, Ellie Luke. Whatever happened with her sounds like it was a couple of years after I last saw Jamie. God. Maybe if I'd pursued things with the police. I should have. I don't know."

"You can't blame yourself for any of it," I said.

"But he killed her? Were they dating? Did he ..."

"I can't discuss the particulars. I hope you can understand. But do you think you and Doug would be willing to come down to Waynetown and talk to me in more detail?"

"We'll do anything. I just wish I knew before all this. I only saw the story about this trial a few days ago. I swear I would have reached out."

"It's okay," I said. "We're talking now."

Sam was writing furiously on his pad. He turned it toward me. "Get her address. The husband's phone number. Dates of birth."

Nodding, I asked Deena for her information. She provided it willingly. I thanked her again and told her I'd be in touch. When I hung up the phone, sweat beaded my brow.

"What the hell was that?" I asked.

"Nothing," Sam said. "We found no record of any kind on Jamie Simmons. Nobody knew any old girlfriends or anything like that. I know Gus has never heard of Deena Price."

"It's too convenient," I said. "She could be seeking attention."

"I'll have Gus get into it," Sam said. "Run backgrounds on her and the husband. I'll talk to this Doug Landon myself."

"Even if every word she said was true, I don't know if I can use it. Prior bad acts aren't generally admissible."

"Maybe you don't need to call her," he said. "Maybe you just need Jamie Simmons and Bennett Cutler to think you're going to call her. Get her in the courtroom. Rattle him."

"Cutler's too smart for that."

"Still, you need to let me run this down."

"Absolutely. In the meantime, I'm putting Gus on the stand first thing in the morning. How's he holding up?"

Sam's face darkened for a second, then he quickly recovered and gave me a smile. "He's Gus. He's solid."

"He knows Cutler's going to come at him hard on cross."

"He can handle it."

"Okay," I said. "I'm counting on him."

"He knows."

Sam rose, leaned across the desk, and planted a kiss on my cheek. "Come on. Stay at my place tonight. It's closer. And I can make sure you eat breakfast before you leave for court in the morning."

It was in me to protest. There was a part of me that was afraid of getting too dependent on this man. But the warmth in his eyes melted me. It was okay to need him. He wasn't Jason. Will was taken care of for the night. It was okay to let someone else take care of me, too.

20

"It was a mistake," Gus said, his voice a low monotone. "I can admit that. At the time of my interview with the defendant, I wasn't thinking of him as a person of interest."

Jamie Simmons's face was frozen on the large screen in front of the jury. They had just finished watching the brief, videotaped interview Gus conducted with Simmons in the days after Ellie Luke disappeared.

"Twenty-two years ago," I said. "What changed, Detective?"

Gus pulled at his tie. I hadn't liked his color from the moment he took the witness box almost an hour ago.

"Hayden Simmons," he said. "Mr. Simmons's daughter came forward with new evidence. The box in the defendant's possession contained items that were connected to the crime scene, to Ellie Luke's body."

One by one, we reintroduced the contents of Simmons's box. I projected the earring on-screen.

"Detective," I said. "What's significant about this earring to your knowledge?"

"Its mate was found near Ellie Luke's body. Her parents identified it as belonging to her. They produced a photograph of Miss Luke wearing it. They had been a gift from her father on her sixteenth birthday. They were apparently her favorites."

I showed another picture previously admitted. Ellie Luke's senior portrait, both earrings on prominent display.

"Detective, who else knew Ellie Luke was wearing those earrings the night she disappeared?"

"I can't say for sure. Certainly anyone who saw her that night and the following morning. Her mother provided a description of the clothing she wore when she left for work that evening. She wore a top with the Lennox Caregiving company logo. That was her standard uniform. She wore a pair of jeans and sneakers. Mrs. Luke indicated Ellie had been wearing the earrings."

"Was it ever made public?"

"Yes. At the time of Ellie's disappearance, we disseminated a current photo of her along with a description of what she was wearing. But after her body was found several months later, we did not disclose to the public what was found with it."

"Meaning her clothing?"

"Her clothing, the earrings, the condition of the body ... none of those things were disclosed to the public. Only someone who'd seen how the body was found or was privy to the evidence collected would have known what items we had."

"Objection," Cutler said. "Calls for speculation. Detective Ritter is making assumptions here."

"Detective Ritter has firsthand knowledge of what was found at the scene and what was disseminated to the public," I said. "He's not speculating. He's stating the facts as he knows them."

"Overruled," Judge Saul said.

"Detective," I said. "Can you tell me about Ellie Luke's vehicle? Where was it found?"

"We found her car, a 1995 blue Ford Taurus, about a mile away from the Cornings' residence on Chalmers Road. The right rear tire was completely flat. We later determined that it had been slashed. There was a small cut in the tread."

"Was the car locked?"

"It was. Mr. Luke, Ellie's father, had a spare key so we used that to gain access."

"What evidence, if any, did you find inside Ellie's vehicle?"

"Well, there were some personal items. A makeup bag. A blood pressure cuff. Some empty fast food bags. Her insurance and registration cards were in the glove box under her father's name. The trunk had a snow scraper and an unmatched pair of gloves in it. But it was relatively clean. No traces of blood. We found hair on the floor belonging to Ellie Luke, but nobody else. The key was gone."

"Either she or someone else took the key. Is that what you're saying?"

"I'm only saying we never found the other key to Ellie's car. We also didn't find her purse, wallet, or anything like that. Mrs. Luke indicated she had her purse with her when she left for work. She would have also been wearing an ID badge clipped to her scrubs. But we never found any of that to this day."

"Okay. How did you first become aware of Jamie Simmons?"

"I spoke to Ellie's classmates. From them, I compiled a list of people in Ellie's social circle. The people she hung around with the most. Jamie Simmons's name popped up. I interviewed him along with several of her classmates at the time."

"Did you form a theory of the case after your investigation?"

"Yes. Based on the condition of Miss Luke's car and the statement of the last person known to have seen her, I believed that Ellie Luke either left with someone she knew and felt safe with, or she was taken from that vehicle at gunpoint or under threat."

"Why did you think that?"

"The last person to see her was Tracy Jones. She was another home health aide with Lennox. Ellie did the night shift with Mrs. Corning. Tracy relieved her at seven a.m. the next morning. Tracy had no indication that there was anything unusual about their exchange. She was in good spirits when she left Mrs. Corning's home. Ellie's car was found facing north on Chalmers Road. She appeared to be heading home as was her custom after that shift. Her tire was flat. She appeared to have pulled off to the side of the road. She had a flip phone but hadn't used it to call for roadside assistance or her parents. As I said, her purse wasn't in the car so she presumably had it with her when she exited the vehicle. There was no sign of a struggle. The car was locked. The windows were rolled up. All indications are that she exited that vehicle of her own volition with her purse. So, as I said, she either left voluntarily with someone she knew or someone coaxed her out of that vehicle under threat. There were no footprints leading away from the car. No other tire tracks. Unfortunately, we had a pretty good rain that started late that morning. Chalmers Road wasn't paved at the time. It was pretty mushy out there."

"Understood," I said. "Thank you, Detective. I have no further questions."

I smiled at Gus. He remained stoic. We both knew the worst was yet to come.

21

Cutler folded his hands and slammed them together on the lectern. It earned him a stern look from Judge Saul but it got the jury's attention. There was something about Gus's expression I didn't like. I'd seen him in action on the witness stand scores of times. He always kept his expression neutral. His delivery was gruff but straightforward. Defense attorneys never intimidated him. It's not that he looked scared now. He just looked ... haggard.

"Detective," Cutler started. "I just want to make sure I have certain facts clear. This was your case from the beginning, isn't that right?"

"I was assigned the Luke case at the outset. Yes. A pair of hunters called 911 after discovering what they believed to be human remains in the woods. Two deputies were dispatched to the scene. One of them, Deputy McBride, called for a detective. I was up on the rotation. I was working afternoons at the time."

Already he seemed off his game. Gus knew the cardinal rule of testifying. Only answer the question you're asked. He wasn't following it.

"Got it. And how many homicide cases had you handled at that point in your career?"

"Maybe a dozen."

"A dozen. When you say a dozen, you don't mean you handled those cases solo, do you?"

"No."

"But the Luke case, you'd never handled a murder case on your own before, had you?"

"I'm afraid I have to reject the premise of your question. Nobody ever handles a murder case on their own. We work in conjunction with the medical examiner's office, the Bureau of Criminal Investigations, and any number of other supportive personnel."

"Right," Cutler said. "Of course. But you're still the one directing the investigation. You're calling most of the shots, isn't that right?"

"I suppose that's true."

"You suppose. Okay. Again, I just want to make sure I have a clear picture of what you found. From your own report, from BCI's analysis, there was no blood at the scene where Ellie Luke was found."

"No. She had decomposed to the point there was very little soft tissue left on her remains. No blood."

"No DNA other than Ellie's?"

"That's correct."

"And that's true for her car as well, right? Because you searched that within a few hours of her disappearance."

"Is what true for her car?"

Better, I thought. Keep it together, Gus.

"No foreign DNA, blood samples, hair, fingerprints. Only Ellie's."

"Her car was clean of any of those things, that's correct."

"Okay. Thank you for clarifying that," Cutler said. "How many witnesses did you interview in this case?"

"Do you mean before or after Ellie Luke's body was found?"

"Either. In total."

Gus squared his shoulders. "I believe it was around a hundred."

"One hundred. It's one hundred and seven according to your report."

"That sounds right."

"One hundred and seven witnesses. Including Jamie Simmons, right?"

"Yes."

"Not one of them mentioned any concerns they had about Mr. Simmons, did they?"

"Objection to the extent Mr. Cutler's question calls for hearsay," I said.

"I'm not soliciting statements to prove the truth of the matters asserted. I am questioning this witness, the lead investigator in the case, about the trajectory of his investigation."

"I'll allow it," Judge Saul said. "The witness may answer."

"Detective, do you need me to repeat it?" Cutler asked.

"No," Gus said. "I do not recall asking any of the witnesses about their specific concerns regarding Jamie Simmons."

"That's not what I asked you. I asked you if any of your one hundred and seven witnesses said anything that would have raised your suspicions about Mr. Simmons's involvement in Ellie Luke's disappearance?"

"Well, that's not what you asked me. Which question would you like me to answer?"

I watched the jury. A few in the front row started to squirm. Gus was technically in the right, but if he played games, it could backfire. Juries do not like feeling as if their time is being wasted.

"Detective, isn't it true that not one of your one hundred and seven witnesses said anything that caused you to regard Jamie Simmons as a suspect in the disappearance of Ellie Luke?"

"His name didn't come up," Gus said.

"So that's a yes?"

"I was not suspicious of Jamie Simmons twenty-two years ago. That is correct."

"And you didn't find anything on Ellie Luke's phone that led you to suspect Jamie Simmons of any involvement, did you?"

"No, but cell phones weren't used then the way they are now. Ms. Luke had a very basic flip phone that she primarily used to send and receive calls. She did very little texting. She also kept the phone off when she wasn't using it. We couldn't and didn't use cell phone tracking the way we do today. Additionally, the phone she had was a family cell phone. Her father indicated that he shared it with her. He gave it to her when she worked nights so that she could call if she had an emergency or would be running late."

"To call if she had an emergency," Cutler said. "She didn't call her parents the night she disappeared, did she?"

"She did not, no. Additionally, her phone was never recovered. Neither was her purse."

"Got it. Detective, you indicated you didn't suspect Jamie Simmons twenty-two years ago. But you did suspect someone. Isn't that true?"

Gus looked at me. I felt every muscle in my body go rigid. But Cutler had asked an appropriate question.

"I eventually zeroed in on a person of interest, yes."

"A person of interest. And who was that person, Detective Ritter?"

Gus cleared his throat. "Dane Fischer."

"Dane Fischer. And how was he connected to Ellie Luke?"

"He was a second cousin. His mother was Claudia Luke's first cousin."

"And why did you first become suspicious of Mr. Fischer?"

"Well, naturally, in any murder investigation, it's standard practice to inquire whether there might be anyone who had animosity toward the victim."

"Animosity. Mr. Fischer had more than animosity toward Ellie Luke though, didn't he?"

"I can't speak to that. You'd have to ask him."

Cutler smiled. "Who told you about Dane Fischer?"

"Claudia Luke."

"Claudia Luke. Ellie's mother. Jamie Simmons's mother-in-law."

"That's correct."

"What exactly did she tell you?"

"Objection," I said. "Again, counsel is soliciting hearsay."

"And again, I am questioning this detective about the trajectory of his investigation. He has admitted that Dane Fischer was a person of interest. I should be allowed to explore how and why he became a person of interest."

"May we approach, Your Honor?" I said. Saul waved us forward.

Judge Saul leaned over the side of her bench and covered her microphone.

"What are you doing, Mr. Cutler?"

"Dane Fischer isn't on trial," I said. "I think it's patently obvious what Mr. Cutler is trying to do."

"I didn't manufacture Dane Fischer," Cutler spat. "I didn't bring him into this. Detective Ritter did. It is absolutely within my client's rights to explore whether there were any alternative suspects to the crime he's been accused of and what evidence there was against those alternative suspects."

"I'm inclined to agree with him, Ms. Brent," Judge Saul said. "Detective Ritter's investigation is fair game. It's part of this. But we aren't going to slander a man, Mr. Cutler. Ms. Brent is right. Dane Fischer isn't on trial."

"He should be," Cutler said, earning him a withering glance from the judge. We went back to our positions.

"Detective Ritter," Cutler said. "What caused you to view Dane Fischer as a person of interest?"

"Ellie Luke's mother indicated Mr. Fischer and her family had a complicated history. That he had some substance abuse issues. When Mrs. Luke's cousin threw him out of her home, the Lukes took him in for a brief period. Mrs. Luke later learned that Mr. Fischer may have stolen some things from the house."

"How did she learn that?"

"Ellie Luke brought it to her attention. I believe that was the source of the friction between the families at that point."

"Friction. But that's not really a strong enough word for what happened, is it? Isn't it true that Dane Fischer threatened to hurt Ellie Luke if she went to the police with what she knew?"

"I don't know if that's true. I know that's what Mrs. Luke believed."

"And you brought Dane Fischer in for questioning based on Mrs. Luke's belief, didn't you?"

"I questioned Dane Fischer, yes."

"You did more than question him, didn't you?"

"I don't know what you're implying?"

"I mean you asked him to submit to a polygraph, isn't that right?"

"Objection! Do I even have to explain?"

"No," Judge Saul said. "Mr. Cutler, you're on thin ice. Defense counsel's last question should be stricken. The witness is instructed not to answer."

"Your Honor, the results of any polygraph are inadmissible. I didn't ask about the results. I only asked if Detective Ritter asked Mr. Fischer to submit to one."

"Enough," Judge Saul said. "My ruling stands. Move on."

God. The smug bastard had done it. It didn't matter that the question was stricken. The jury heard it, just as Cutler intended. They would assume the rest of it, that Fischer had failed one. Gus's expression turned even more sour.

"You interrogated Dane Fischer about his whereabouts the night Ellie Luke went missing, didn't you?"

"Of course."

"Did Mr. Fischer's alibi check out?"

"No."

"No. According to your report, Mr. Fischer claimed he was at the Lakeside Bar in Rossford?"

"That's what he said, yes."

"But his alibi didn't check out, did it?"

"No."

"And why not?"

"The Lakeside Bar was closed due to a water main leak the entire week, including the night before Ellie went missing and all through the next day."

"So he lied about his alibi."

"That's what I believed at the time."

"You confronted him about that, didn't you? You interviewed him again?"

"Yes."

"Did he give you a different alibi?"

"Yes."

"What did he say?"

"Your Honor," I said. "Again, counsel is soliciting hearsay testimony."

"I agree," Judge Saul said. "You can't ask the man what Dane Fischer said."

Cutler huffed, but recalibrated his question.

"All right. Let me ask this, then. Were you able to exclude Mr. Fischer based on his second story about where he was the morning Ellie went missing?"

"No, I was not."

"It didn't check out? The new alibi?"

"No."

Cutler nodded, satisfied with himself. "So he threatened the victim. Lied about where he was the morning she disappeared ... twice. But that wasn't the only thing that had you suspicious of Dane Fischer, was it? Tell me what you found in Mr. Fischer's vehicle."

"There were drops of blood in the trunk of Mr. Fischer's car."

"Drops of blood. You were able to type those blood samples, weren't you?"

"Yes."

"They were B positive, isn't that right?"

"Yes."

"What was Ellie Luke's blood type?"

"Mr. Cutler, blood type isn't dispositive. The lab was unable to extract any DNA."

"That's isn't what I asked you. What was Ellie Luke's blood type?"

"B positive."

"Thank you. I have no further questions."

I traded places with Cutler at the lectern. "Detective Ritter, what was Dane Fischer's blood type?"

"B positive," Gus practically shouted his answer.

"You never arrested Dane Fischer in connection with Ellie Luke's case, did you?"

"No."

"And why not?"

"Because there wasn't enough evidence. The blood evidence was inconclusive. It was most likely his own blood. Although there were reports of animosity between Mr. Fischer and the victim, I had no proof he acted on it. There was no evidence they'd been in communication or that there was any ongoing feud. Then, after Ellie Luke's body was found, there was no physical evidence connecting Dane Fischer to the crime."

"Thank you. I have nothing further."

"The witness may step down," Saul said. Gus looked like he might actually be sick. I wanted to go to him. To console him, even though that wasn't my job.

"Ms. Brent, please call your next witness. I believe we have time for one more today."

I nodded. "The state calls Sabrina Wharton-Brent to the stand."

22

Bree walked in wearing purple scrubs, having just gotten off work. She smiled as the clerk swore her in.

"Ms. Wharton-Brent," I said. "I'd like to clear something up off the bat. Will you please tell the jury how you and I are related?"

"Technically, we're not," she said. "But my wife is Kathleen Wharton-Brent. Her brother is your former husband, Jason Brent. Your son is our nephew."

"Thank you. And how were you acquainted with the victim in this case?"

"Ellie was my classmate. We went to nursing school together. We were friends."

"So your connection to Ellie Luke predates you and I knowing each other."

"Oh yes. By quite a bit. I didn't know you back then. Kat and I have been married for just shy of two years. I've only known her and you for a little over four years. I met Ellie twenty-five years ago now."

"Okay. And have you and I talked about Ellie's case prior to today?"

"Yes. You were present when Detective Ritter interviewed me again a couple of months ago."

"Is that the first time Detective Ritter interviewed you regarding Ellie Luke?"

"No. I, along with most of our friend group, was interviewed after Ellie went missing."

"Thank you," I said, hoping that would satisfy the jury and head off any attempts by Bennett Cutler to make something out of our relationship that wasn't there.

"Sabrina, how well did you know Ellie?"

"We were close," she said. "I wouldn't say she was my best friend, you know, in life. But she was certainly one of my closest school friends."

"How often did you see each other?"

"During the school year? Almost every day. We were in a cohort together. Took the same classes. And we did a clinical rotation together at the same hospital. We were in a weekly study group together that we formed early on."

"Who else was in the study group?"

"Well, there were seven of us initially. We met freshman year. It was me, Ellie, Paul and Sarah Mansfield, Lisa Gorman, Shante Jones, and Jamie Simmons."

"Jamie Simmons," I repeated. "So you were also acquainted with the defendant?"

"We were. Initially."

Bree took me through the basic history of her college friends' group, how Ellie had always been the most serious and studious. How she was viewed as the most responsible. The mother of the group, in a way. She then described what she'd told me earlier about how Jamie began to make others in their original group uncomfortable.

"He started to cross a line," she said. "Jamie would make inappropriate comments. Come-ons."

"To you?"

"Yes. To me. He kind of burned through every female in the group. First, he'd start calling all the time. Wanting to meet up outside the study group. Then he'd start bringing gifts. Little trinkets. He tried to give me a necklace one time. Flowers another. He did the same thing to Shante and Lisa."

"How did you handle it?"

"I was polite at first. Jamie was just ... I don't know. He just didn't vibe well with the rest of the group. He was too intense somehow. When he started coming on to me, I told him I had a girlfriend. He backed off and things were sort of normal after that. But then he moved on to Shante. It got awkward in the group after that. We started making plans to meet without him. Shante wasn't comfortable around him. Neither was Lisa."

"What about Ellie?"

"Well, what I'm describing, how Jamie burned through the group. This happened over the course of about two years. Freshman to junior years. It wasn't all at once. It was gradual. That first year, we were all kind of joined at the hip. But by the time we were juniors, Jamie was really on the outside of it. I personally didn't see him much at all. Ellie still did."

"She did. Did Ellie know about your experience with him?"

"I told her," I said. "I know Shante and Lisa did too."

"Why did you tell her?"

"It was just kind of a known thing within the group. That Jamie was on the make. That we didn't feel like his friendship was genuine. That he was looking to hook up."

"How did Ellie feel about all this, if you know?"

"The thing with Ellie. She was just nice. She never had a bad word to say about anyone. She was one of those people who was always gonna take in a stray, you know? So I think she felt a little sorry for Jamie. As far as we knew, he didn't have any other friends. He just put people off. Came on too strong. Seemed to have an agenda. So of all of us, Ellie was the last one to maintain a friendship with Jamie."

"How would you describe Jamie and Ellie's relationship in the months before her disappearance?"

"Well, she went missing right around spring break our junior year. I know she was still communicating with Jamie that previous Christmas. Just before Christmas. She was going to meet him for coffee. She told me that and I remember having a reaction."

"What kind of reaction?"

"I just rolled my eyes, you know? I asked her why she was still giving him the time of day. She knew how the other women in our friend group felt. But Ellie felt sorry for him, I think. That she felt sorry for him because he didn't have any family and was going to be alone on the holiday. So he asked her to meet him for coffee. She didn't see the harm in that."

"Do you know how that meeting went?"

"I don't. But I know when we came back after break, Ellie was different."

"How so?"

"She was like the rest of us. Didn't want anything to do with Jamie."

"How do you know that?"

"We were sitting in class, just before class started. Jamie tried to call her on her cell phone. She saw the caller ID and got mad. She didn't answer. She just clicked it off. He called two or three more times right after. She seemed upset. And as far as I know, she never met with him again after that."

"Was there anything else you witnessed about Jamie and Ellie in those weeks before she disappeared?"

"No. But I never saw her with him. As far as I knew, they weren't talking. And I have to be honest, I didn't think much of it. Jamie was just kind of this annoying guy in our classes. We just all stopped hanging out with him. I can't say I thought much about him after that. The school year went on. Then Ellie disappeared and it was just all so awful."

"I can imagine. What did you tell the police when you were questioned?"

"There wasn't much I could tell them. I knew Ellie was working for that home health aide agency. During that time, I can't say I saw her much outside of class. We were all so busy with our studies and our jobs and gearing up for our senior year and finding placements after that. Ellie going missing just came as such a shock to all of us."

"Did you have any interactions with Jamie Simmons after Ellie went missing?"

"Yes. He was very involved in trying to organize search parties for her. He took her disappearance very hard."

"Did that surprise you?"

"Actually, no. Like I said. I knew Ellie, at least up until the couple of months before she went missing, kept up some kind of friendship with him. She ... I'm sorry to say it. But in my opinion, from what I observed, I felt like she had taken pity on him. She felt bad that he'd alienated everyone else in the group."

"Objection, witness is speculating."

"Ms. Wharton-Brent indicated it was her opinion based on her observations."

"Sustained," Judge Saul said. "The jury should disregard the witness's statement about Ellie Luke's feelings. She has no firsthand knowledge of those."

"Okay," I said. "Tell me about your interactions with Jamie Simmons after Ellie disappeared."

"Well, again, Jamie was just very involved in setting up search parties. Encouraging all of us to put time in whether it was actively searching or putting up flyers or attending vigils. It was like he made it his mission to ensure everyone in Ellie's class did something. He took her disappearance very hard. That was my observation."

"Did that seem strange to you?"

Bree shrugged. "Honestly? At the time? No. It was a confusing time. We were so rocked by what happened. Everybody had to deal with it in their own way. I just kind of assumed it was

Jamie's way of dealing with it. It was ... well ... he was abrasive, almost bullying about making sure we all did something. But I just ... I don't know ... we didn't give him trouble about it because again, I just figured it was how Jamie had to cope. I wasn't going to get in the way of someone else's grief process."

"I see. But you used the word bullying. Can you elaborate on that?"

"Jamie was very much in everyone's face ... in my face ... about what we were doing to help in the search. Like he'd ask for time at the beginning of classes to address the whole class. Tell us when and where to meet to help the police search. And if there was a vigil, and I remember two specifically, Jamie was always right up there wanting to be one of the ones to talk. Once, Sarah and Paul Mansfield mentioned they weren't going to be able to attend one of the vigils. They were going to be out of town. Well, we were all talking about it in the courtyard on campus. Jamie got angry with them."

"What do you mean?"

"He snapped at Paul and Sarah. Accused them of not caring enough about finding Ellie. That they owed it to her to show up. Jamie got in Sarah's face and Paul grabbed him by the arm. Pulled him back. It was just extremely awkward and inappropriate on Jamie's part. In my observation, anyway. And I heard later that he'd befriended Ellie's family."

"How did you feel about that?"

"I don't know. I remember thinking I hope he doesn't overstep. I hope he's bringing them comfort and not expecting them to take care of him. But I did recall thinking it was weird."

"Weird? Why weird?"

"Well, just ... I knew Ellie wasn't super close with Jamie in those last months. I knew she was actually trying to avoid his calls. I saw her do that. So it was another kind of eye roll for me. Like Jamie was glomming on to this poor family and I didn't think Ellie would have liked it."

"Thank you," I said. "I have no further questions."

"Your witness, Mr. Cutler," the judge said.

Cutler stormed up to the lectern. "Ms. Wharton-Brent, you have no real idea how Ellie Luke felt about Jamie Simmons, do you?"

"I think I've answered that. I saw her annoyance when Jamie kept calling her. I saw her specifically not answer the calls."

"You never went to the police about any concerns you had about Jamie Simmons when Ellie disappeared, did you?"

"No."

"You were questioned for nearly two hours by Detective Ritter, isn't that right?"

"I don't recall the time, but if you have some record that it was two hours, I wouldn't dispute that."

"And at no point in your interview did you raise a single concern about Jamie Simmons? In fact, you didn't even mention his name to Detective Ritter as being part of your school friend group, did you?"

"Because he wasn't part of it at that point."

"But again, you have no idea what Jamie's relationship with Ellie Luke was, do you?"

"I think I explained what I knew based on what I saw. I don't have another answer to give you, Mr. Cutler."

"Did you and your friends talk about Ellie Luke after she disappeared?"

"What? Of course we did. We were all pretty shook up and worried about her. As the weeks went on and we knew the worst had probably happened ... it devastated us. We leaned on each other for support as best we could."

"Leaned on each other ... but none of you said a word about Jamie Simmons, did you?"

"I don't recall."

"Nobody said ... huh ... we should talk to the police about Jamie Simmons, did you?"

"No."

"You weren't suspicious of him."

"For having something to do with what happened to Ellie? At that time, no. It was more that I thought it was weird he was so involved with her family after the fact."

"You don't know anyone from Ellie's family, do you?"

"Socially? No. I saw them at her funeral later. I knew who her parents were, but no, I didn't know them."

"So you're up there spewing theories about Jamie's involvement with them that have no basis in fact, isn't that right?"

"Objection to the characterization," I said.

"Sustained. Let's be civil, Mr. Cutler."

"Civil," he said. "Certainly. I just want to make sure I have this right, Ms. Wharton-Brent. You, in fact, hadn't spoken to Ellie Luke in over two weeks before she disappeared, isn't that right?"

"I don't remember."

"But that's what you told Detective Ritter in your interview twenty-two years ago. Do you remember that? Would it help if you reread your statement?"

He handed it to her. Bree looked it over. "It says I said I hadn't talked to Ellie on the phone in over two weeks. That we hadn't talked during spring break. Ellie went missing right after spring break. So yes. It makes sense that I would have said we hadn't talked much in those two weeks prior to her going missing."

"Right. So you really don't know what was going on in Ellie's life in those two weeks."

"That's not true. I knew where she was working. She was my friend. We may not have talked every single day when school was on break."

"Ms. Wharton-Brent, you were subjected to a background check when you got your nursing license and your job at U of M Hospital, weren't you?"

I looked up. Bree's eyes went wide.

"What? Yes."

"You had to fill out extensive forms detailing your work, education, and personal history. Isn't that right?"

"I'm sure I did," she said.

"Do you recognize this document?" Cutler handed a copy to

me, then one to Bree. It was a standard form from the Ohio Board of Nursing. It was dated twenty years ago.

"Sort of," Bree said. "I filled it out when I applied for my nursing license."

"I'd like to draw your attention to item seven. It asks whether you've ever been convicted of a crime. What did you write?"

"I said no," she said.

"You said no," Cutler repeated. "But you weren't being truthful, were you?"

"Objection," I said. "May we approach?"

Saul waved us forward.

"This is ridiculous," I said. "How far do you want me to go down the list? There's absolutely nothing relevant about this witness's twenty-year-old nursing license application."

"There is if she lied on it," Cutler said. "Her credibility is an issue. I'm within my rights to explore it."

"If she lied on the form," Judge Saul said, "I agree this is some straw grasping, but it's relevant to Mr. Cutler's point. Let's not turn this into something it doesn't need to be, okay?"

Cutler nodded. "I'll be brief."

With a pit in my stomach, I walked back to my table.

"What did you write on the form, Ms. Wharton-Brent?" Cutler asked.

"I said I hadn't been convicted of a crime because I haven't."

"You haven't. You realize you're under oath now?"

"Of course."

"Isn't it true that you were convicted of using and being in possession of a controlled substance twenty-seven years ago?"

Bree lost a little color. "That was ... I was a minor. That was expunged."

My blood heated.

"I asked you," Cutler said, "and the OBN asked you if you'd been convicted of a crime. Twice under oath now, you've lied. You were convicted of being a minor in possession of alcohol as well as possession of a controlled substance, isn't that right?"

"I was sixteen years old and got caught drinking and smoking pot at a party. I went to a diversion class like the judge told me. Two years later, when I turned eighteen, the thing was expunged."

"But you were convicted and you lied about it to me. And you lied about it to the nursing board."

"Objection," I said. "This has been asked and answered at least twice now."

"I agree," Saul said. "Move on, Mr. Cutler."

"Fine. Ms. Wharton-Brent, you didn't suspect Jamie Simmons of any involvement in what happened to Ellie Luke twenty-two years ago, did you?"

"I didn't know."

"Didn't know. Exactly. But you never saw fit to bring up any of this to the police all those years ago because it was nothing. It's a fabrication. An exaggeration that you're only now bringing up because your sister-in-law wants you to."

"Objection!" I shouted. "I don't even know where to start. To the extent that Mr. Cutler is now accusing me of anything improper..."

"Cool it," Judge Saul said. "Mr. Cutler? I'm warning you."

"Why didn't you bring Jamie Simmons's name up to the police when Ellie went missing?" he asked.

"Because it never occurred to me that I should," Bree said.

"Didn't occur to you. And you didn't bring it up seven months later when Ellie's body was found either, did you?"

"No."

"Because you didn't think of it?"

"Yes. No. I don't ... I thought they had the guy. Everyone was saying it was some cousin of Ellie's. That he'd threatened her for saying he stole from her parents. I just assumed that's who did it. I didn't know the police got it wrong."

"Thank you," Cutler said, smiling. "I have no further questions."

I wanted to smack the guy. And to be fair, I wanted to throttle Bree. All Cutler had really succeeded in doing was upsetting Bree. But she'd said what I needed her to say. I just hoped the jury was smart enough to see past Cutler's stunt.

23

By the time I left the courthouse, I felt like I'd been hit by a Mack truck. My head pounded. My feet hurt. It was just past four so at least I'd be able to have a normal dinner with Will. I missed him. The trial had taken over my life. He was experiencing the first few weeks of high school with a basically absent mother.

My phone rang as I walked up the steps to the City-County Building. It was Bree. I never even got a chance to say hello.

"Mara, I'm so sorry," she said, crying. "I didn't know he was going to get into some stupid thing that I did when I was a kid. Did I ruin it?"

"No," I said. The truth was, I wished she'd have told me. But I honestly hadn't anticipated Cutler would bring up an expunged MIP charge. So that part was on me.

"You did all right," I said. "Don't let any of this upset you. You're not the one who hurt Ellie. Don't forget that."

"But if this gets screwed up because of me ..."

"It won't."

"I'm still sorry," she said.

"I know. I am too. I should have thought to prepare you for something like that. Nobody's perfect, okay? It's fine."

"Okay. Thanks."

"I'll see you soon," I said.

I clicked off. Caro waved to me as I walked into my office. She had her phone in her ear. Hojo was down the street at a meeting with the county commissioners. We'd sent the interns home for the day. I welcomed the peace and quiet as I intended to finish up a few things before finally heading home.

I made it two steps into my office before Gus Ritter's gruff voice hit me from behind.

"Why'd you just let him do that?" Gus said.

I turned. He stood there in his weather-beaten tan trench coat, his tie crooked as if he'd tried to wrench it free.

"I'm sorry?" I said.

"You let Cutler walk all over you in there. You let him basically tell that jury that Dane Fischer killed that girl."

I peeled off my own overcoat and tossed it on a chair. The pounding in my head got worse.

"Gus, that's not what happened. I lost a ruling. A ruling I knew I'd lose. There was no way I could keep Dane Fischer's name out of this. But you got to say what you had to. There wasn't enough evidence to convict him."

"You think that's going to matter? All Cutler needs is reasonable doubt. If he gives them a plausible alternative suspect, they'll acquit."

"You really want to lecture me on burdens of proof, Gus? I know what I'm doing."

"Do you? You're off your game, Mara."

"Gus!"

Sam filled the doorway just behind Gus. He looked winded, like he'd run all the way over here from his office. It occurred to me he probably had. He was trying to save Gus from himself, maybe.

"I don't want to hear it," Gus snapped. "Not from either one of you. If Jamie Simmons walks because you didn't do your job, there won't be a do-over. I'll spare you the lecture on double jeopardy."

"Gus," I said through gritted teeth. "You're upset. You're overworked. This isn't you. You're hanging on way too tight."

"And you're not hanging on tight enough."

"I'm doing the best I can with what I have," I said, then instantly regretted it. I hadn't meant it as a dig at Gus, but knew he could take it that way.

"What's that supposed to mean?" he snarled.

I was tired. I should have taken the high road. I should have just ignored him. But I didn't. My own insecurities came roaring to the surface.

"It means this case is weak. It's always been weak. I have a box. That's it. That's my evidence. I have nothing connecting Jamie

Simmons to the actual murder of Ellie Luke. At best, I can prove he's a creep. Or that he mishandled a corpse. The rest is going to take a leap of faith from all twelve members of that jury and right now, I don't have a lot of faith in them."

"I gave you a solid case. If you can't get a conviction on it, that's on you."

"Stop it!" Sam said. "Gus, go back to the office. Or better yet, go home."

"Or what?" Gus said. Sam's eyes widened as Gus turned on him. This was the Gus Ritter most other people knew. But it wasn't the Gus Sam and I knew. I took a breath and a literal step back.

"Gus," Sam said, his voice low and threatening. "Go home. That's an order. Get some sleep. Take tomorrow off. You need it."

"Or. What?"

"You really wanna push me right now?" Sam said, almost shouting.

"Yeah. I think maybe I do. I think somebody should push both of you. I think I'm watching this whole case fall apart right in front of my eyes and I'm the only one who seems to want to do anything about it."

"I'm doing everything I can," I shouted. "I got handed a turd, Gus. If they acquit, this isn't all on me!"

I felt like I was coming unglued. I wasn't a yeller. I didn't lose my temper. Not like this. Not like ... Gus.

"Mom?"

My heart dropped. Sam turned. Will was in the hallway right behind him. He had his backpack slung over his shoulder

Gus squeezed his eyes shut. His hard expression softened. He looked at me, his eyes pleading. But he didn't apologize. Neither did I. I waited a beat, then took a step toward him, reaching out. But Gus went stiff. He put a hand up, shook his head, then brushed past Sam and Will and walked out of my office.

I sank slowly into my chair.

"Hey, Will," Sam said, squeezing my son's shoulder. Will was only a couple of inches shorter than Sam now.

"They gave us a tour of the City-County Building," he said. "For my government class. We just got out. I thought I could ride home with you, Mom."

I'd completely forgotten that was today. "Of course," I said.

"Is Uncle Gus okay?" he asked.

I met Sam's eyes. "No," I said. "He's upset. This case is ... well ... it's upsetting. Hey, kiddo. You mind hanging out with Caro for a few minutes? Let me just finish a few things up and we'll head home. We can stop and grab some shakes or something from the Scoop Factory on the way."

"Ice cream before dinner?" Will asked.

I smiled. "Yeah. It feels like an ice-cream-before-dinner kind of day."

"Cool," Will said. He gave Sam a knuckle knock as he headed over to Caro's desk. She'd probably load him up with candy, too. Today, I didn't care.

"You okay?" Sam asked.

"I'm fine."

"That was ... look ... I'll talk to Gus when he cools down. He's just ... this thing has him rattled like I've never seen him. He didn't mean any of that."

"Really? Because I think he meant all of it. If I'm being honest, so did I."

I buried my face in my hands. I really needed something more potent than ice cream.

"He blames himself," Sam said. "That's guilt you're hearing. He thinks he overlooked something about Jamie Simmons all those years ago. That he focused too hard on Dane Fischer."

"Sam, he's not wrong. And I don't mean I think this was his fault. The mistakes he made were normal ones. Human ones. And to be honest, relatively small ones. But sure, they added up."

"I wouldn't have conducted that investigation any different than Gus did," Sam said.

"I know. But I did mean what I said. There's a giant hole in this case. And it isn't even about Dane Fischer. It's that I can't prove Jamie Simmons did anything other than pick over Ellie Luke's bones. Which is disturbing enough. And criminal. I can make obstruction of justice, evidence tampering. But aggravated murder? I should have pushed back on the charging document. That was a mistake."

"He did it. You know he did it."

"Of course he did. I just ... Sam, I'm sorry. I was pushed into this. Trying this case. It wasn't ready. We needed more. We shouldn't have charged as soon as we did. I should have pushed back. I just wish ..."

"What?"

It felt disloyal for saying it. But I was ragged. I had no energy to filter my words. And right now, even though he sat there in full uniform, I didn't need Sam the Sheriff. I just needed Sam.

"Kenya wouldn't have allowed this," I said. "She would have fought harder to hold off."

"What good would that have done? The evidence you have is all the evidence we're gonna get. We don't have an eyewitness. It's a miracle Hayden Simmons found that box when she did. If Simmons won't take the stand, then there's no logical explanation for him to have those things from Ellie's body unless he's the one who killed her. And frankly, if you're pissed this thing moved forward when it did, you have to be pissed at me, too."

"Sam ..."

"It was my call to arrest Simmons. Gus works for me, remember? And I'd do it again exactly how it played out."

There was truth in what he said. And yet Gus had rattled me enough I couldn't fully hear it.

"Do you think he's right?" I asked.

"About an acquittal? Who knows? Even if we had Simmons's DNA at the scene, it wouldn't be a guarantee they'd convict. Juries do what juries do. You know that."

"No," I said. "Do you think he's right about me? Am I off my game?"

"No."

"You can tell me. God. I wish Kenya were here. She'd give it to me straight."

"So do I. And no. You're doing the best you can. I've told you this before. There's nobody I'd rather have at that table in there. But I do think you're letting Cutler get under your skin more than you should. Gus was wrong in thinking you could have kept the Fischer stuff out. Even he knows that. But everyone seems to be forgetting common sense in this one. Jamie Simmons has a box with things he took from Ellie's body. Her dead body. And the only person who could have known where she was is the guy who put her there. Don't forget. She was lying there for seven months! Nobody had a clue where she was. Except Simmons."

I heaved a sigh. "Yeah. But like you said. Juries do what juries do."

"Who do you have left to call?"

I squeezed the bridge of my nose. "Deena Landon's up first thing in the morning."

"Simmons's ex-girlfriend?"

"Yep. But Cutler's going to object to her entire testimony. It's going to be a crapshoot whether Saul will sustain it. If she does, I don't have a lot of ammo left."

"My money's on you," Sam said. "Vivian Saul has about had it with Cutler."

"It won't matter."

"Come on," he said. "Will's waiting for you. Do what you promised him. Ice cream for dinner sounds like a damn good idea. I'd invite myself along if I didn't have to get back to the office."

He rose and came around the desk. He kissed me. I touched his cheek. He made me feel better, like a true partner should. It had been so long since I'd had that. I realized then maybe I never had. So much of my life with Jason had been focused on serving his ambitions. The moment I thought it, I forced Jason out of my mind. He didn't deserve space there. Not at this moment.

"Call me later tonight," Sam whispered.

"Okay. Thank you."

Sam grabbed my coat and held it out for me as I slipped my arms into it. I leaned back against his chest. His tall, solid strength fueled me. I could see Will was still at Caro's desk. She was laughing at something my son said. A small smile crept across his face as it gave him pleasure to make her happy.

For the rest of the evening, I would fight to keep the Ellie Luke case out of my mind. It would work for a while. Until I laid my head down on the pillow and knew my first witness tomorrow would be a Hail Mary.

24

George Luke sat on the bench outside the courtroom when I arrived at eight the next morning. Still as a statue, his eyes cut through me. Claudia Luke hadn't come. Neither had Erin. Only George sat vigil for the entire week.

"Good morning, Mr. Luke," I said, just as I had every morning. And just as he had every morning, he gave me a cold stare and said nothing.

My witness, Deena Landon, sat on the opposite bench. Her husband, Doug, had his arm around her. I turned from George Luke and walked over to the Landons.

"How was your drive?" I asked.

"Fine," Deena said. "I just want to get this over with."

"I understand. You'll be first up. And there's nothing to worry about. Promise."

Doug Landon stared at me with about as much contempt as George Luke had. The specter of Jamie Simmons. These people didn't seem to realize I was on their side. In George's case, Jamie had been poisoning that family's mind for over two decades. For the Landons, they saw Jamie Simmons clearly and I was the one forcing them back into his world.

Steeling myself for the onslaught I knew would come on the other side of those double doors, I made my way into the courtroom.

A moment later, Jamie Simmons was brought in from a side door. He seemed jovial, smiling and laughing with Bennett Cutler as the deputies led him in. He held his wrists out as they uncuffed him. I gathered my notes at the table and waited for Judge Saul to take the bench. The courtroom doors opened behind me. I looked over my shoulder. Gus came in and took a seat against the back wall. He didn't look my way. I was getting damn tired of everyone seeing me as their enemy.

"All rise!"

Judge Saul took the bench. Then the jury filed in.

"Ms. Brent?" the judge said.

"The state calls Deena Landon," I said in a loud, clear voice. I chanced a look at Jamie Simmons. He kept his posture rigid, his face neutral. Deena walked up the aisle and climbed into the witness box.

She was petite, not quite five feet tall. She had dark hair, maybe dyed now, but she bore a casual resemblance to Ellie Luke. I hoped the jury noticed.

Deena took her oath and stared straight at me. She hadn't once looked at Jamie, but she trembled a bit as she adjusted the microphone.

"Ms. Landon," I started. "Will you explain how you're acquainted with Jamie Simmons?"

"I'm not," she said. "Not anymore. But Jamie and I dated a long time ago."

"How long ago?"

"I want to say we met twenty-five years ago. We were both students at Washtenaw Community College. I was nineteen. He was twenty or twenty-one."

"How did your relationship start?"

"We just had a couple of classes together. One was a human sexuality course. It was a small class. Only like twelve students. Jamie was the only male in it. We did a group project together so we ended up spending a lot of time one on one. The other members of the group didn't really pull their weight so it was Jamie and me doing the bulk of the work. He was nice. I thought he was funny. And cute. Toward the end of that term, I asked him out."

"You asked him out?"

"Yes. Well, it was more, my roommates were having a party. We lived in an off-campus apartment. I invited Jamie to come. He did. That night, we just hit it off. Everything grew from there."

"You began dating?"

"Yes. I can't remember now exactly how that all played out. Like if we went out the next night or the next weekend. But heading into that winter break, we saw each other a few times. Then, moving into the next semester, we were exclusive."

"By that you mean ..."

"I mean we weren't dating other people. At least not as far as I know. At least not as far as I was concerned."

"Jamie was your boyfriend? You considered him that way?"

"Yes."

"How would you describe your relationship at that time?"

"It was good. Jamie was great. I'd dated my share of losers up until that point. Jamie was different. He was thoughtful. He asked me about my family. He seemed secure with who he was, you know?"

"How long did you end up dating?"

"It was over a year."

"You described things as going great. Did that change?"

"Oh yes. And I mean it *really* changed."

"What do you mean?"

"Well, I wanna say things were good all that term and through most of that summer. But as we moved into the next school year, I don't know. Jamie became really controlling."

"In what way?"

"He just ... he was always asking me where I was going. Like wanting my schedule. I had a cell phone at the time. An old clunky flip phone my dad wanted me to carry. If I had a call, Jamie always wanted to know who it was. I just started getting a bad vibe."

"Did you talk to Jamie about that?"

"I did. I wasn't happy. If I went out with other friends, Jamie would call me constantly. Like every hour, wanting to keep tabs on me. Then he'd just show up in places. Once I went to a strip mall to buy new clothes for this job interview I had lined up. Jamie was in the parking lot. He acted like it was a coincidence, but I knew it wasn't."

"Objection," Cutler said. "Calls for speculation."

"Sustained," Judge Saul said. "Please disregard the witness's last statement about whether Mr. Simmons's appearance was a coincidence or not."

"Ms. Landon," I said. "How did your relationship with Mr. Simmons end?"

In the course of telling her story, Deena Landon gained more confidence. She sat straighter in her chair. Her voice became more clear. And she looked right at Jamie before answering my question.

"I ended it," she said. "I told Jamie I wasn't comfortable with how jealous he was becoming. I felt smothered. He didn't take it well. He got ... we got into a fight. He ..."

"Objection! Your Honor, may we approach?"

I expected this. In truth, I was surprised Cutler waited this long for this particular battle. As I gathered my notes and walked up to the bench, I prepared for the worst.

"Your Honor," Cutler said. "I think we're going to need to argue this one outside the jury's presence. I need everything on the record."

Judge Saul nodded. She instructed her bailiff to send the jury out of the courtroom. I took my position back behind the prosecution table.

"Your Honor," Cutler started. "Ms. Brent's entire line of questioning is improper under Rule 404(B). She is attempting to introduce the defendant's alleged prior bad acts."

"Ms. Brent?"

"Your honor, this witness can testify about the defendant's habits. His behavior with the victim in this case fits a pattern of conduct that is relevant to the issues here."

"Is this witness going to talk about domestic violence?" Judge Saul asked.

"I believe she is."

"She's lying!" Jamie shouted. It was the first peep I'd heard out of him during the whole trial.

"You're the liar!" Deena shouted back. "How can you sit there and pretend I don't know who you are, you piece of ..."

"Enough!" Judge Saul banged her gavel.

"Your Honor," I said. "Again, Jamie Simmons's behavior with this witness establishes a pattern of conduct that he has repeated time and again. They are similar to the current crime he's charged with. As such, we fall under the exception to the rule and this witness's testimony should be allowed. She has been on my witness list that was duly filed with the defense. Her testimony isn't a surprise."

"That's not the standard," Cutler said. "It's well-settled law that evidence of any other crime, wrong, or act is not admissible to prove a person's character in order to show that on a particular occasion the person acted in accordance with that character. Additionally, Mr. Simmons has been charged with murder. Whatever this witness thinks she experienced, it's not similar to the current charge. The state's argument doesn't fall within any recognized exception. Frankly, I'd ask that Ms. Landon's entire testimony up until this point be stricken. The jury shouldn't have even heard from her at all."

"You didn't object to her being called," Judge Saul said.

"I couldn't predict what she'd say," Cutler said. "Now that I have, now that Ms. Brent has made clear where she's going with this, it falls squarely within the prohibitions of Rule 404(B)."

"Ms. Brent," Judge Saul said. "I'm afraid I agree. To me this is a classic application of the prior bad acts rule. I will sustain Mr. Cutler's objection. The witness is not permitted to testify about any prior domestic abuse committed by the defendant."

Cutler sank my battleship. Straight up. It wasn't unexpected. It didn't make it less of a blow. I knew I was taking a risk putting Deena on the stand.

"And I'd also ask that her testimony up to this point be stricken," Cutler said.

"I'm not going to go that far," Judge Saul said. "Ms. Brent, does this witness have anything to say about the events of this case directly?"

Deena's eyes welled with tears. "He's going to get away with it? You're going to let him get away with it?"

"That's not what this is about," Judge Saul told her.

"No, Your Honor," I said. "Ms. Landon's testimony is centered on her relationship with Mr. Simmons."

"All right," Judge Saul said. "Will you continue?"

"No," I said.

"You are, of course permitted to cross-examine this witness based on her testimony thus far," she said to Cutler. He smirked.

"No, Your Honor," Cutler said. "I'm fine with the witness being dismissed."

I could just bet he was. The jury would file back in and see Deena Landon abruptly removed from the witness box.

"Fine," she said. "Here's what we're going to do. We're going to take a one-hour recess. Ms. Brent, will that be enough time for you to gather your next witness?"

"Yes," I said.

"So ordered." Judge Saul banged her gavel again. Deena rose from the witness box. I'd have just enough time to walk her out and see that she and Doug were safely escorted from the building.

She followed me out into the hallway.

"I don't understand," she said. "Why won't she let me talk? They have to know who Jamie is."

"I know," I said. "I'm sorry. This was a risk we took putting you on the stand."

"They have to know what I was going to say," she said.

"I hope so," I said, though the jury would be instructed not to make any inferences from her testimony so far.

Doug Landon reappeared. He put a protective arm around his wife.

"Should we leave?" Deena said. "Are you going to call Doug?

He can tell them what happened. The things Jamie said to him. His threats."

"We'll run into the same problem," I said.

"Ms. Brent?" A gravelly voice came from my left. Startled, I turned to see George Luke. His eyes darted from me to Deena Landon.

"You knew him," he said to Deena. "You knew my son-in-law?"

"Deena," I said. "This is George Luke. Ellie Luke was his daughter. Mr. Luke, if you would ..."

"I want to hear what she has to say," George said. I looked over my shoulder. The courtroom doors remained shut. Cutler and Jamie Simmons were inside, out of earshot for now.

"Is there someplace we can talk?" George asked. The courtroom doors opened. My heart skipped. But it was just Gus. His eyes narrowed when he saw George standing next to Deena and Doug.

"There's an empty jury room down the hall," I said. "We can go there." I eyed Gus, gesturing with my chin for him to follow. George caught it.

"No," he said. "Not him. I don't want him anywhere near me."

Gus froze. Something went through his eyes, but he didn't respond to George's insult. I mouthed an "I'm sorry" to Gus then led the Landons and George Luke out of sight and into the open jury room.

Deena stayed glued to her husband's side. I pulled out a chair for George but he refused it, preferring to stand against the wall.

"What would you have said in there?" George asked. "I'd like to know what happened between you and Jamie."

"He's a monster," Doug answered for his wife. "If you care about your other daughter, you'd get her away from him."

"I'm asking her," George said.

"It's okay, Deena," I said. "We're not in a courtroom now. You can say whatever you'd like."

"Jamie was ... he's good at pretending to be someone he's not," she said. "You think he's kind. Caring. But it turns. He ... it's little things at first. Just how he always seems to disagree. Has a better answer for everything. And he sounds right. He makes sense. But then, little by little, you realize you're doing everything he wants you to do. It was almost a year. But my world got so small. He didn't like my best friend, Lacey. He convinced me she was saying all this stuff behind my back. That she was jealous of me. I stopped talking to her."

"Everyone loved Ellie," George whispered.

"He takes over," Deena continued. "And it feels like such a relief at first. When Jamie and I started out, my parents were going through a divorce. My mom caught my dad cheating on her with her best friend. It was just a mess. Constant turmoil. Jamie just started handling things. She threw my dad out and Jamie would do things around the house for her. Cut the grass. Fix the furnace. Just all the stuff my mom relied on my dad for. We didn't know how my mom would have survived that first year without Jamie's help."

George Luke blinked. He didn't say it, but I could imagine how Jamie had taken over when the Lukes were in their deepest grief.

"You tried to break it off," I said.

"Yeah," Deena answered. Doug put his hands on his wife's shoulders and she leaned back against him for support.

"What happened, Deena?" I asked her the question I wanted the jury to hear.

"My mom had a weekly bridge game. Actually, that was Jamie's idea too. He encouraged her to get out of the house. It was this divorcee support group he got her to join. Looking back, it's like he knew when the house would be empty. I came home from work and Jamie was just there. He was in the house. He knew where Mom kept the spare key. We got into a huge fight. I'd told him two days before that it was over. Jamie was just dark that day. So angry. He pushed me against a wall. Knocked me down. He kicked me in the stomach. I think ... I don't know what would have happened. But I'd ordered a pizza before I left work. The delivery guy showed up. The front door was open so the kid could see through the screen. Jamie got spooked and he left. Then, for a while, he was just gone. I thought it was finally over. I moved on with my life. Doug and I started dating. Then ... out of the blue, Jamie showed up again. Later on, I heard he'd found out I was going out with Doug. He showed up at the house. Barged his way in. But this time, Doug was there."

Deena finished the story she'd already told me. How Doug intervened, beat Jamie up and scared him off. I wondered right along with her what might have happened if Doug weren't in her life.

George Luke slid down the wall. He ended up on his knees, his face buried in his hands.

"George," I said, rushing to him. Doug got there when I did.

Together, we lifted the man off the floor and got him into a chair.

"What have I done? What have I done?" he cried.

"Nothing," I said. The man clung to me, wrapping his arms around my waist. He cried into my stomach.

"You've done nothing," I said. He looked up at me with pleading eyes.

"Did he do this? Tell me! Did he kill my Ellie?"

I met Deena and Doug's eyes over George Luke's head. I found myself smoothing George's hair back, trying to comfort him like I did my own son. He'd asked me that question before. I told him the answer months ago. But today, George Luke was ready to hear it.

"Yes," I said. "I believe Jamie Simmons murdered your daughter, George. We wouldn't be here if I didn't."

"He did this," George said, turning to Deena. He reached out a hand. She grabbed it. "Just like you said. With your mother. He was just there. Doing things. Taking care of us. I let it happen. I didn't mean to. I swear I didn't mean to. Oh God. Oh God."

I wanted to tell him it was okay. But I couldn't promise it would be. It came down to what Sam had said. If the jury could remember their common sense, Jamie would go to prison. If Bennett Cutler succeeded in confusing the issues, he would walk free.

"What can I do?" he asked. "Tell me? What can I do?"

I stepped away from him. "You can pick yourself up," I said, my voice going flat. "You can dry your tears. And you can go into that courtroom and tell the truth."

25

Bennett Cutler and Jamie Simmons practically melded their foreheads together as George Luke took the stand. My heart dropped for a moment as George stumbled on the last step up to the witness box. The bailiff was right there and caught him by the elbow, but as George turned and waved off further help, his skin had turned ashen.

"Are you all right, Mr. Luke?" the judge asked.

George put a hand up. He coughed for a moment, reached for the water bottle in front of him with a shaky hand, but answered the judge in a clear, strong voice. "I'm perfectly fine. Just old."

But he was more than old. In the hour since Deena Landon took the stand and George heard her story in the jury room, it seemed to put twenty years on him. I worried about what the next hour would do. But George gave me a determined stare and the slightest nod. He was ready. So was I.

"Mr. Luke," I said. "For the record, will you explain your relationship to the victim in this case?"

"Ellie was my daughter," he said. "My firstborn. My baby girl."

"You have another daughter," I said.

"Yes. Erin. She's three years younger than Ellie was."

"Thank you. Mr. Luke, I want to make sure you're okay. If at any time you need to take a break, do you promise to let me know?"

George was defiant, rod straight in his chair. "I will not need a break, Ms. Brent. I will not need anything. Ask your questions."

"All right. Mr. Luke, I'd like to take you back to the year Ellie went missing. Where was she living at the time?"

"She lived with her mother, me, and Erin. Ellie was saving money to move out but she was a full-time student. She was paying her own way. And I mean paying her own way. She didn't take any loans out. She worked to pay for her tuition. So we let her live with us rent free."

"You must have been very proud of her."

"I was. I still am. Ellie was a go-getter. Never any drama with her like we had with her younger sister before everything happened. Ellie was serious. Driven. Polite. Respectful. Everybody always says teenage girls can be a nightmare. Not my Ellie. She was just a smart, sensible, hard-working kid. Always got straight As. Earned her own money from the time she was old enough to babysit at twelve years old. And before that, she helped around the house. Never had to remind her to do her chores."

"I see," I said. "She sounds like a very special young woman. Mr. Luke, we've heard testimony that Ellie was a junior in college, pursuing a nursing degree at the time she went missing. Is that accurate?"

"It is. She was gonna graduate early that December." George's voice broke a little, but he quickly recovered.

"Mr. Luke, how familiar were you with Ellie's routine, her friends, at the time she disappeared?"

"Well, she was twenty-one. A proper young lady, you know? She didn't have a curfew or anything. And she had her own car that she paid for. Insurance too. So I didn't require her to report to me like I did her younger sister. Erin was just eighteen at the time. Still in high school."

He was rambling a bit. It would be tricky to strike the right balance. I wanted George to feel comfortable telling Ellie's story. But I had to keep him focused as much as I could.

"Did you know her routine? When she had class, her work schedule? Things like that."

"Oh, for sure. See I was semi-retired at the time. I worked as a sales rep for a flooring company. I got laid up for a while after I was in a car accident and hurt my back. So around the time we lost Ellie, I was only working out of the home two days a week. Ellie's mother, Claudia, was working part time as a bank teller. Anyway, Ellie and I had lunch together a couple of days a week. She worked nights as a home health aide for this elderly woman over in Pine Ridge. The lady had dementia and a heart condition. She required twenty-four-hour care. Ellie worked there from eleven to seven five nights a week. She had class in the afternoons. She'd come home. Sleep for a few hours. My wife or I would make sure she was up by twelve-thirty. We'd have lunch together. Then Ellie would go to class from two to eight a few afternoons a week."

"Thank you," I said. "That's helpful. Was Ellie dating anyone that you knew?"

"Not that I knew. No. She said she didn't have time for boys. I mean, she'd go on dates here and there. But nobody serious. I don't think she'd had a date in several months before we lost her."

"What about her friends? Did you know any of them?"

"Sure, Ellie had friends from high school she kept in touch with. But she mostly hung around kids in her nursing classes. There were three girls in particular that I knew she was close with. Sabrina, Lisa, and Shante. I met Lisa and Shante a few times. Real nice girls."

"Okay. What about Jamie Simmons? Was he one of your daughter's friends?"

"I didn't meet Jamie until after Ellie went missing."

"How did that come about? Your meeting him?"

"He came to the house. I wanna clarify. That time ... those weeks. It's kind of a fog for me. So I don't remember the first time I met him."

"Fair enough. But let me ask this another way. You mentioned you knew three women Ellie was close with from her nursing classes. Sabrina, Lisa, and Shante. Did you know about Jamie Simmons as well?"

"No. Ellie didn't talk about Jamie. I didn't know him until after. I'm sure of that."

"Okay. So let's talk about after. How did Jamie Simmons become part of your life?"

"It was a bad time. A very bad time. I was ... I'm ashamed to admit this now ... but I wasn't a very good husband or a very good father after Ellie went missing and everything that we learned after that. I couldn't cope. Could barely get out of bed. I blamed myself."

"For what?"

"Well, a father is supposed to protect his daughter. They said Ellie had a flat tire. I should have checked her car. I should have made sure. I should have been there when she needed me so she wasn't alone on some country road in the dark like that where anything could happen."

"I understand. And I'm sorry for your loss, Mr. Luke. But back to Jamie Simmons ..."

"Right. You asked me how he became part of our family. The best I can tell you is that he was just there. I think he came to the house once offering to help out. Mow the lawn. Claudia had him fixing a part of the fence in the backyard. Like I told you, I was checked out that whole summer. It got even worse after they found Ellie. After we knew she was really gone. And that it was as awful as we feared. By then, Jamie was a fixture. He came over almost every day. He brought me lunch a few times. Claudia invited him over for dinner."

"Did you find that strange?"

George shook his head. "No. I didn't have any opinion of anything at the time. I was just going through the motions. And ... it got very dark, Ms. Brent. That Christmas, a couple of months after Ellie was found, I tried to take my own life."

"I didn't know that," I said.

"Jamie was there even more after that. Claudia called him. They were afraid to leave me alone. It took a very long time for me to walk out of the woods, Ms. Brent. By then, Jamie was pretty much part of the family. He just ... took over. Claudia and I had a pretty conventional, old-fashioned kind of marriage. I paid the bills. Did everything around the house. Maintained the cars. Claudia cooked and cleaned. Jamie just stepped in and started doing for us what I couldn't do. At the time, I was so grateful for it. Now ... I see what was really going on."

"What do you think was going on?" I asked.

"It's like he was grooming us," George said.

"Objection!" Cutler said. "Your Honor, this has gone on long enough. While I am, of course, sympathetic to Mr. Luke's plight, I fail to see the relevance of this line of questioning. Not to mention the witness is wholly unresponsive. Ms. Brent and the court are allowing him to ramble."

"Your Honor, Mr. Simmons's obsession with the victim and, by extension, her family is absolutely relevant in this case."

"This entire narrative is about events that took place after Ellie Luke went missing," Cutler said. "This is a murder trial."

"Overruled, Mr. Cutler," Judge Saul said, surprising me. "Mr. Simmons's relationship with the victim and her family is relevant. You'll be free to argue to what extent when the time comes. Proceed, Ms. Brent."

"Mr. Luke," I said. "You described Mr. Simmons's relationship with your family as grooming. What did you mean by that?"

"I mean Jamie took over. We were vulnerable. In deep grief. I took everything Jamie said at face value. Claudia and I could barely function. We couldn't be there for each other. For ourselves. For Erin. But Jamie was. Looking back, I can see now it wasn't normal."

"What wasn't normal?"

"Jamie practically moved in. He was there almost every day. He cooked for us. Cleaned. Took my checkbook and wrote everything out for our monthly bills. He told me it's what Ellie would want. He told me he'd promised her he'd take care of us if anything happened to her."

"He said that?"

"Yes. And I believed him."

"But you're also saying that until Ellie went missing, you'd never met Jamie Simmons?"

"No. I mean, yes. I'm saying I never met him."

"Ellie never mentioned him to you?"

"No, ma'am."

"But you believed him that he and Ellie were close enough that she'd want him looking in on you if something happened to her?"

"That's what he told me. And he was just so ... competent. I was in such a bad state. It just felt easier to let Jamie take over. Claudia loved him. She said he was like the son she never had. I can see now she transferred feelings. It wasn't healthy. But it was easy."

"What about Erin?" I asked.

"Time went on. I didn't know Jamie and Erin were getting close. I thought it was kind of a brother/sister thing. But I'd say a little over a year after Ellie went missing, it was clear Erin was smitten with Jamie. They were inseparable. Erin didn't make a move without Jamie."

"How did you feel about that?"

"I don't know. I was still so numb. Erin seemed happy. I ... God. This is hard to admit. But when you lose a child. It blows up your world. Your heart. Sometimes it seems better not to feel at all. I don't want to say I didn't care. But I just didn't have the mental strength to think anything of it. Erin was over eighteen. I thought Jamie was a little old for her. But Claudia thought it seemed natural. They were both grieving Ellie. So it was easy to think their love grew from that. But ... things started to happen."

"What things?"

"Erin was a different person. She'd always been my wild child. My troublemaker. After Ellie, she got quiet. Withdrawn. Jamie became dominant over her. He had opinions about everything. What she wore. Her haircut. Erin was going to go to college but then she never did. Before we knew it, she found out she was pregnant and Jamie married her."

"How did you feel about that?"

"By then, I had nothing to say about it. Erin was almost twenty. Jamie had a good job and could provide for her. And on we went. Whatever Jamie says goes. Every time I've tried to speak up when I saw something I didn't like, Erin would get so upset."

"What things didn't you like?"

"Erin is ... her world is small. I never thought that would happen to her. I thought it was because of what happened to Ellie. Erin became agoraphobic. Didn't want to leave the house. And it's like her personality changed. She's meek. Afraid. Looks to Jamie for everything. God. I should have said something. I should have gotten her into counseling or something. And then when I started seeing bruises …"

"Objection!"

"Approach the bench," Judge Saul said.

"We're right back here," Cutler said. "Ms. Brent is trying to do through George Luke what this court wouldn't allow her to do with Deena Landon. If she's trying to paint some picture that my client is a domestic abuser, it's impermissible as a prior bad act."

"I'm inclined to agree," Judge Saul said.

"Your Honor, this witness can establish a pattern of abuse going back decades. His obsession and control over this family is at the heart of this case."

"And like I told Mr. Cutler, you're free to argue that in closing."

"There is no record of any abuse," Cutler said.

"My witness is competent to testify about what he saw," I said.

"He can say he saw bruises on his daughter," Judge Saul said. "But she's not the one who was murdered, Ms. Brent. Let's not forget that. The objection is sustained. Wrap it up."

She hadn't ruled that George Luke's testimony be stricken. The jury had just heard he'd seen bruises on Erin Luke. Would it be enough?

I went back to the table. I brought up two photographs that had been previously entered into evidence. One was Erin Luke, the other her lookalike sister, Ellie.

"Mr. Luke," I said. "Can you tell me who these photographs depict?"

"Those are my girls," he said. "That's Ellie on the left. Erin on the right. Everyone used to think they were twins."

"The resemblance is remarkable," I said. "Mr. Luke, are you aware of what your granddaughter, Hayden, found in your son-in-law's basement?"

"Yes," George said through gritted teeth.

"Did you speak to Hayden about it?"

"No."

"Why not?"

"He told us ... Jamie swore to us we shouldn't believe it."

"You shouldn't believe your own granddaughter?"

"Yes. He said she was disturbed. He said ... God. I'm sorry. I'm so so sorry. But this is what he does. He makes you think he has all the answers. Makes you doubt yourself. Preys on your vulnerabilities. God. Did he do that to Ellie? Did she trust him too?"

"Mr. Luke, did your son-in-law tell you not to talk to the police after he was arrested?"

"Yes. He said this was all made up. He said you and Sheriff Cruz were telling Hayden what to say."

"Did he tell you not to talk to me?"

"He didn't say don't talk to you. He said not to trust you. He said this was all Dane Fischer. And that's what we'd believed for so many years. But now ... now that I know what he had. After I saw it with my own eyes. I can't go along with this. I can't. I just can't."

"Thank you," I said. "I have no further questions."

George shifted in his chair as Cutler stepped forward. The tips of Cutler's ears turned purple, but I could sense no other outward sign of his mood.

"Mr. Luke," Cutler said. "I want to be clear about something. You said Ellie was living with you at the time she went missing."

"Yes."

"She had her own bedroom?"

"Yes."

"Her clothes, her jewelry, she kept them in the bedroom at your home?"

"Yes. Of course."

"Okay. After Ellie went missing, did you go into her bedroom?"

"What? I don't know. I'm sure I did. Passed by it at least."

"Did you remove Ellie's things from the house after she went missing?"

"No. God. No. It was her room. We held out hope that she'd come back."

"Did you remove Ellie's things from her room after you found out she was dead?"

George looked down. "Not for a long time, no."

"So you left Ellie's room, which contained her clothing, her underwear, her jewelry, her hairbrushes, all of it remained undisturbed for how long after she died?"

"I don't know. A while."

"More than a year?"

"I think so."

"More than two years?"

"Maybe two years. Finally, Jamie convinced us it was time to clean everything out."

"Jamie convinced you. Did Jamie help you and your wife clean out Ellie's room?"

"I don't know. He might have. But I think it was mostly Claudia. She wanted to do it."

"The police went through Ellie's room after she went missing, didn't they?"

"Yes. We let them."

"And you had other people in that house in those two years, didn't you? In fact, you held a wake at the house after Ellie's funeral, didn't you?"

"We did, yes."

"How many people were in the house that day?"

"Objection," I said. "Relevance."

"Your Honor, the prosecution's entire case rests on a box of what is alleged to be Ellie Luke's belongings. I think it's highly relevant to establish who might have had access to them over the years."

"Sustained," the judge said.

"How many people were in the house for Ellie's wake?" Cutler repeated.

"I don't know. I ... I went to my room that day."

"You didn't come out," Cutler said.

"No."

"It was dozens and dozens of people, wasn't it?"

"It might have been."

"And they traipsed through your home and you can't even say where they went in the home because you didn't come out of bed, isn't that right?"

"I don't know if I'd say traipsed. But we had people in the house, yes."

"Okay. Mr. Luke, you've hit your daughters, haven't you?"

"Objection!"

"Your Honor, Ms. Brent was allowed to make the salacious implication that Erin Luke had bruises on her. I'm allowed to inquire whether this witness ever hit her."

"Overruled," Judge Saul said.

"Did you hit your daughters, Mr. Luke?"

"I resent your implication, sir. Sure. I spanked my girls when they were little. Not often. But if you're suggesting I hurt them, well, then you can go to hell."

"You have a temper, don't you, Mr. Luke?"

George Luke turned white. He rose from his chair. "You son of a bitch. You killed her. You lied to us for twenty years. You killed her. You beat her until she was dead because she knew what a creep you are. You had the rest of us snowed, but not Ellie. Ellie knew exactly who you are!"

"Your Honor!" Cutler shouted.

I rose from my chair. Judge Saul banged her gavel. Something came over George Luke's face. His entire body shook with rage. He started to move. Then, he vaulted over the side of the witness box and lunged for Jamie Simmons. Simmons remained stoic, almost smirking in his seat. Two bailiffs wrestled George Luke to the ground.

"He killed her!" George shouted, spit flying from his mouth. "He killed her! He killed my little girl!"

"Your Honor," Cutler practically screamed. "I demand an immediate mistrial!"

The deputies hauled George out of the courtroom. Judge Saul buried her face in her hands. Adrenaline shot through me. I couldn't believe what had just happened.

"Please escort the jury from the courtroom," Judge Saul instructed her bailiff.

The deputies made it halfway up the aisle with George before the man passed out.

26

I could still hear George Luke railing out in the hallway. Muted voices beneath his told me several of the deputies were still trying to calm him down and get him out of the building. Doug and Deena Landon stayed in the courtroom, determined to see how this played out.

Jamie Simmons remained remarkably stoic through it all. I knew he was guilty. Believed it in my bone marrow. But his chilling gaze forward cut through me. The man was a master manipulator. It occurred to me he wasn't afraid. It occurred to me that even from behind the defense table, he had manipulated George into action with his smug expression while the man bared his soul in public for the first time.

"Your Honor," Cutler started. He was sweating, his face flushed. If his client hadn't been upset by the events of the last fifteen minutes, Cutler certainly was. "The conduct of the prosecution's case has been a farce since the beginning. Ms. Brent has been allowed a parade of witnesses with nothing relevant to testify about. George Luke is merely the latest stunt.

After that unchecked outburst, I don't believe there is any way a fair verdict can be rendered in this case."

"Unchecked?" I said. "Mr. Luke was dragged out of this courtroom by two armed deputies. He is a grieving father. If we declared mistrials anytime a family member of a murder victim got upset in court, there'd be no justice at all."

"Mr. Cutler," Judge Saul said. "If you're bringing a motion for a mistrial, you're going to have to do better than personal attacks against the prosecution."

"George Luke's entire testimony was irrelevant and highly prejudicial," Cutler said. "It does not matter what his relationship with the defendant is. It does not matter what Jamie Simmons's relationship with his wife is, or his father-in-law's perception of it. I raised objections to that effect repeatedly and got shot down. Well, now we've seen exactly why he shouldn't have even been allowed to take the stand."

When I spoke, I had to make a real effort not to shout. To keep my cool. "Mr. Luke testified about how Jamie Simmons exerted undue influence on his family. How he essentially lied to Ellie's family about their relationship. His behavior around the time of Ellie's disappearance and the discovery of her body is extremely relevant. The physical evidence in this case was found in Jamie Simmons's home. In his possession. He collected souvenirs from his victim, including her whole family."

Vivian Saul squeezed her eyes shut and rubbed the bridge of her nose. "Mr. Cutler, I'm inclined to agree with Ms. Brent. As I've said repeatedly, you are free to argue the relevancy of Mr. Luke's testimony in your closing arguments. But your client's conduct with the Luke family, especially within the time frame of the victim's disappearance and the discovery of her body, is relevant."

"My client is on trial for murder," Cutler shouted. "The critical issue of this case is whether the state can meet its burden of proof that Jamie Simmons caused the death of Elizabeth Luke. Everything George Luke said pertained to events that happened after Ellie Luke's disappearance and death. Everyone in this room but me seems to want to conveniently forget that. Mr. Simmons isn't on trial for the kind of son-in-law he is. Or the kind of friend he was to Ellie Luke. And his outburst just now? You can't ask the jury to disregard it. Well, you can, but it's not reasonable to expect that they will."

"I have more faith in the jury than you do," Judge Saul said. "Your motion for mistrial is denied, Mr. Cutler. However, I will strongly admonish the jury to disregard Mr. Luke's emotional outburst at the conclusion of his testimony. I don't know how many ways I can say this, but closing arguments will be your opportunity to argue to them whether the state has met its burden."

"Your Honor ..." Cutler began to raise his voice again. Judge Saul's withering gaze looked like she could have melted him with it.

"That's my ruling," she said. "Your objections have been sufficiently preserved for appeal. We will proceed. It's late enough in the day now that we'll restart in the morning. I'm going to have the jury brought back in. I will do what I said I was going to do. They'll be instructed to disregard Mr. Luke's behavior. We're back here first thing in the morning. Will you be ready to call your next witness at that time, Ms. Brent?"

"Of course," I said.

"Good." Judge Saul directed her bailiff to bring the jury back in. I stayed on my feet while she told them to pay no attention to George Luke's emotional outburst. She explained it was not evidence and should not be given weight as such. Once again, Cutler raised an objection, asking for Luke's entire testimony to be stricken. Once again, he was overruled. Then Saul banged her gavel to dismiss us for the day.

Jamie Simmons rose to his feet. Saul's bailiff approached the bench. From where I stood, I could read his lips. The deputies had made sure to remove George Luke from the courthouse. There was no chance he would run into Jamie Simmons on the way out. The entire time, Simmons stared straight at me as he turned toward the deputies ready to be led back to his holding cell. He winked at me.

Hojo stood at the door to my office as I walked in. "What the hell happened in there?" he asked.

"George Luke finally woke up," I said. "He all but accused Jamie Simmons of murder right in front of the jury. Right before he jumped over the witness box ready to strangle Simmons with his bare hands."

"Geez. How'd Cutler handle it?"

"Not well. But Saul wouldn't give him his mistrial."

"Thank God." Hojo sank into one of the chairs in front of my desk. I took the other.

"I don't know," I said. "Cutler got a few clean shots in."

"Like what?"

"He was able to establish that Ellie Luke's bedroom was kept untouched for up to two years after she went missing. That any number of people, including Jamie Simmons, would have had access to it."

Hojo rubbed his chin. "He's gonna try to argue whatever Simmons had in that box. He collected it after she went missing?"

"That's crap!" I startled, not having heard Sam walk up. He stood in the doorway, his campaign hat in his hand. I waved him in.

"It might be reasonable doubt," I said.

"Mara, fine. Maybe that theory works for the underwear. But Ellie was wearing those earrings when she disappeared. He took one off her dead body. Agent Palmieri established that the lock of hair was cut straight from her head."

"And that's my counterargument," I said. "But the problem I have is the same one I've had since day one. I can prove he's a creep beyond a reasonable doubt. Murder is something else. I just wish ... we needed more time."

"We didn't have it," Hojo said.

I was exhausted. George Luke had unsettled me. So had Deena Landon. But as I sat there, I had to bite back the retort bubbling up in me. Kenya Spaulding would never have filed charges in this case when we did. She'd have given me more time to work on the Luke family.

"I'm worried about Claudia Luke," I said. "George went rogue today. That's why Cutler was so unhinged. He tightly controlled that family at Jamie's behest. I need to talk to

Hayden. Fill her in on what happened. I have no idea how this is going to shake out for her."

"Mara," Sam said. "I know how invested you are in this thing. But you're not responsible for the Lukes. It's not your job to play social worker for them. Hayden's got support. She's been provided resources through the Silver Angels."

"What's next?" Hojo asked. "Who do you have left to call?"

"I honestly don't know," I said. "George Luke left an impact. I said Cutler got off some hits. But George basically laid out what Simmons has done to the entire family. If the theory of this case is an obsession, Ellie's father painted the picture I needed. And the bottom line ... I don't have anything stronger than Jamie Simmons's box of souvenirs."

It was a dig. Both Sam and Hojo knew it. I felt guilty for a moment. The outcome of this case impacted their careers more than mine. They were trusting me to do my best. I hoped I had.

"Call it a day," Hojo said. "Go home, Mara. Get some rest. Come back fresh in the morning. If you rest, Cutler's going to come on strong. Who do you expect he'll call?"

"I don't know. He may feel he's gotten his best case in during cross."

"You think he'll put Simmons on the stand?" Sam asked.

"He'd be crazy to," I said. "But I suppose that depends on how much control Cutler has over him."

"If Jamie Simmons wants to testify," Hojo said. "He'll testify."

"He's not stupid," Sam said. "He's disturbed. A psychopath. But he's no fool. He won't take the stand."

Hojo rose to his feet. "Well, my advice stands. Get a good night's sleep, Mara."

He passed an awkward look to Sam. Then Hojo patted me on the shoulder and left.

"He's not wrong," Sam said. "You look beat."

"It was a lot," I said. "I said George Luke woke up today. That's what it felt like. He listened to Deena Landon. Her experience with Simmons was like the pregame to what happened to Ellie and her family. God. Sam. In some ways, it feels like Ellie's murder was the least awful thing Jamie Simmons did. George used the term grooming. He's right. Simmons worked his way in when the Lukes were at their most vulnerable. He took over. He made them think they couldn't survive without him. Ellie ended up being the strong one. Maybe the only one who saw Jamie for what he was."

"He didn't protect her," Sam said. He stared in the distance.

"George said that. He blamed himself for not protecting Ellie."

"No," Sam said. "I mean he didn't protect Erin. Simmons molded her into what he wanted her to be. His."

"Yeah. The thing he couldn't do with Ellie."

"So he killed her for it. Maybe Erin isn't as asleep as you think she is. Maybe she just figured out how to survive him."

"God, Sam," I said. "What if she never believes it? Even if I get a conviction. What if Erin stays loyal to him?"

Sam came to me. "You can't worry about that. You can't let it into your head. It's not your job to save the Lukes. It's only your job to convince that jury."

The jury. I couldn't read them. Were they as asleep as the Luke family?

"But if he walks, Sam," I said. "Then Erin isn't safe."

"Come on," he said. "Let me take you to dinner. Let's try to put the Luke case out of our minds just for tonight. Hojo's right about that. Come at it fresh in the morning."

I took his hand and walked out with him. But I couldn't shake the feeling that Erin Simmons would never be free of her nightmare.

27

"Your Honor, at this time, the prosecution rests."

Judge Saul didn't look surprised. The jury did. Beside me, Bennett Cutler did what all defense lawyers do at this stage of the trial. He moved for a directed verdict in his client's favor. He argued I had not met my burden of proof as a matter of law.

Judge Saul did what most judges do at this stage of a jury trial. She denied Cutler's motion. After ruling on several other procedural items, Saul dismissed us for the day. We would be back here first thing Monday morning where Bennett Cutler would call his first witness for the defense. I tried not to, but I couldn't stop myself from looking over at Jamie Simmons. Without the jury present, he kept a smug look on his face. If he was scared or nervous, he would never let me see it.

I collected my notes, stuffed them in my briefcase, and left the courthouse. A handful of reporters tried to get me to comment as I made my way to my car.

"No comment," I said. "You know I'm not going to talk about an ongoing trial."

They let me go with relatively little protest. Cutler had just walked out of the building. They knew he might be more than willing to throw them a few quotable scraps.

I didn't want to go back to the office. I didn't want to go home. With no real plans as to where I was headed, fifteen minutes later, I found myself pulling into Kenya Spaulding's driveway. I hadn't called ahead. Hadn't texted her I was coming. And yet, when I stepped out of my car, Kenya stood in her front door as if she'd been expecting me.

She held a tumbler in one hand, filled with what looked like a mimosa.

"Is it late for that?" I asked. "Or early?"

"Does it matter?" she said, handing it to me. She wore a bright-red kimono, her hair hung long, almost to her waist. If it was possible, the woman looked like she'd grown younger in the year and a half since she left the prosecutor's office.

I took the drink from her. It tasted perfect, as usual. I followed Kenya out to her solarium at the back of the house. She had a new roommate. A tuxedo cat eyed me from the back of a chair, swishing her tail.

"That's Ramona," she said. "She showed up a couple of weeks ago and decided to stay."

I reached for Ramona and scratched her between the ears. She purred, then leapt off the chair and darted under a potted plant.

"She likes you," Kenya said.

"I miss you," I said. "When are you going to cut this out and come back to work?"

Kenya smiled. She draped herself over her chaise lounge, looking like every inch the queen she was.

"When are you going to stop asking me that?"

"We're a mess, Kenya. I love Hojo. He's trying his best. But things are falling through the cracks. I'm chasing my tail. And this case? We weren't ready to go to trial and next week everyone's going to see why."

Kenya arched a brow. "Since when have you questioned your own skills like that?"

"It's not about my skills. I just don't have enough to get past reasonable doubt."

"You're letting Cutler get under your skin. That's not like you. What's really going on?"

"I told you. I want you back. So far nobody else has thrown their hat in the ring to run for prosecutor. Hojo doesn't want it long term."

"You sure about that?" she asked, sipping her own drink.

"I'm sure. This thing is buckling him. He's not cut out for it. You are."

Kenya laughed softly. "Mara, when are you going to cut the crap?"

Her remark startled me. She leveled a hard stare at me. "What are you talking about?"

"I'm talking about you. Coming over here. Thinking you're going to bully me into taking a job I haven't decided I want anymore. Thinking it's because the county needs me."

"We do need you. Plus, it wasn't fair how things went down in your last election."

"My last defeat," she said.

"Water under the bridge. The electorate knows they made a mistake. I told you. You'll be unopposed. We can just go back to the way things are supposed to be."

Kenya put her glass down. "Mara, I've known you a long time. When are you going to stop lying to yourself?"

"Kenya …"

"You want me to tell you I'm going to run because then it'll make things easier for you."

"Easier, yes. But also because you were good at it. You're the best at it. We need you. I need you. If you'd been in the corner office, the Luke case could have ripened like it was supposed to. My hand wouldn't have been forced. And I wouldn't be on the verge of losing what might be the biggest, most important murder case this county has ever seen."

Kenya gave me that laser stare of hers. The kind that cuts through you. Only the tiniest lift to the corner of her mouth indicated what she was thinking. Then she hit me with it. Both barrels.

"Bullshit," she said.

"What?"

"Bullshit. If I were in the corner office, I'd have had you take that case to trial now, too."

"No, you wouldn't. Not if …"

"Stop. There wasn't going to be any better evidence against Jamie Simmons. This is as good as it's going to get. And it's damn good. You know he killed that girl. I know it. He knows it. And nobody delivers a killer closing argument like you do. I'm not worried about Bennett Cutler. What I haven't been able to figure out is why you are. Until now."

"What are you talking about? I'm not afraid of Cutler."

"Yes, you are. Well, not so much Cutler. But you're afraid of losing."

"Kenya ..."

"You never lose."

"I lose plenty."

"If you lose this one, then it wasn't winnable in the first place. No matter who prosecuted it."

I grumbled. "I *hate* losing."

"There she is." Kenya smiled. "So don't. But I do have one question."

"Fire away."

"Are you absolutely sure you don't want to run for prosecutor?"

"I wish people would stop asking me that. Yes. I'm sure. I like the job I have."

"You promise it's not because of Sam?"

"What? No. It's not because of Sam."

"Because some people might not like the sheriff dating the prosecutor. Some people might hold it against him at the polls."

"I know. But I swear, that's not why I don't want to run. I really don't want the job, Kenya." I put a hand up. "I'm tired of having this conversation. Between my mother, Sam, now you, it's getting old."

"Maybe we're all right. First there was Jason. He was always running for something. It made sense you wouldn't want to. Then there was Will. And granted, he did need more of you than most kids. But he's almost fifteen years old. He's out there, Mara. In the world. Making his way. To a large extent, your work with him is done. He'll always need you. But it's okay for you to want something more now."

"I like what I'm doing," I said.

"So keep doing it. Nobody ever said you had to stop trying cases if you took the top spot. You don't have to run the office like I did. And you shouldn't. But it's time for you to put your wants and ambitions first."

I sat back. "I have. I'll swear it on anything you'd like. I'm where I'm supposed to be. And I'm happy there. It's your job, Kenya. You belong there. So what, you're gonna sit here with your cat and your cocktails in the afternoon forever?"

She smiled. "It's not a bad gig."

"If you want me to be honest with myself, then you have to do it too."

She took the last sip of her drink then set the glass on the table next to her. "You're right."

"I am?"

"You are. I'm not ready to ride off into the sunset just yet. I just wanted to make sure you really, really don't want the job."

Ramona came back. She hopped up on the chaise and settled herself in Kenya's lap.

"You're going to run!" I shouted. "You've been jerking me around this whole time?"

"Not at all. I wanted to be sure what you wanted."

"Just tell me what I can do."

"Well, you can endorse me."

My head spun a little. I didn't know if it was the strength of Kenya's pour or her news.

"And you can tell that boyfriend of yours, I expect his endorsement." She smiled.

"You sly boots," I said. "When were you going to tell me all this?"

"Now. You've been busy."

I put my drink down and threw my arms around her. "Thank God."

"Just do me a favor and keep it to yourself for now."

She got up, went to the kitchen, and came back with a fresh pitcher of mimosas. She refilled my glass and then her own. She raised her glass and clinked it with mine.

"To new beginnings in the new year. For both of us," she said.

"That's worth drinking to."

"You really think the jury is going to buy Bennett Cutler's shtick? How's he planning on explaining the fact his client had trinkets from the crime scene in his possession?"

"He's going to argue someone else could have collected them. Or at the very worst, his client is a weirdo who collected them after the fact but didn't actually murder that girl."

"And her family has closed ranks around that creep," Kenya said. "You know I'm going to court with Hayden next week on that bogus restraining order her mother filed."

"I'm thankful for that. This has been horrific for Hayden. But ... her grandfather at least seems to be willing to support her."

Kenya shook her head. "She called here right before you got here. He's tried to contact her. She's not ready. Hayden feels pretty traumatized by all of them. She may never trust her family again."

"That's understandable. She has to do what feels safe for her right now."

"I suppose telling you this won't help the pressure you feel. But Hayden's terrified about what happens if Simmons gets acquitted. She's making plans to leave town."

I nodded. "That poor kid. I just wish someone could get through to her mother. She won't take my calls."

"Mine either. I tried," Kenya said. "She blocked my number."

"Jamie Simmons," I said. "The gift that keeps on giving. Even from jail."

"Who do you think Cutler's going to call first?" she asked. "Do you think he'll put Simmons on the stand?"

"I hope so," I said, feeling a rush of adrenaline. "I'd like to tear him to pieces on cross."

"That's the Mara I know and love." Kenya smiled. "You've got this. I still like your side of this thing a heck of a lot better than Cutler's."

"Thanks," I said, not realizing how much I needed her to say it. Whether it was the booze or the pep talk, I was feeling more myself. A little jolt of adrenaline went through me as I thought about getting Kenya back where she belonged. What we could do. With me trying cases, Sam as sheriff, and Kenya back in the big office.

But first, I'd have to tear Bennett Cutler and Jamie Simmons apart.

28

"The defense calls Claudia Luke to the stand."

Hojo sat beside me at the prosecution's table this morning. We were down to bare bones in the office with the fall interns having completed their semester. I wanted his eyes on the jury and in the back of my head. I still had no idea whether Cutler planned to put Jamie himself on the stand. Calling Claudia was a surprise, but not entirely unexpected. He knew I couldn't rip into her on cross without making myself into a villain.

What was unexpected was the waifish figure who floated into the courtroom along with Claudia. Erin Simmons was here. She sat two rows back from her husband, her skin pale. Her eyes were downcast. But she was here. Her dark hair curled under her chin. She'd cut it and changed the part. But it wasn't enough to alter her striking resemblance to her murdered sister.

"They're looking." Hojo wrote me a note.

Claudia wore a navy-blue knit dress with white piping around the collar. She had more confidence in her step than her husband had when he took the stand. Claudia's hand was steady as she raised it to swear her oath. She lifted her chin in defiance and looked straight at her son-in-law as Cutler began.

"Mrs. Luke, for the record, will you explain to the court how you're related to the victim in this case and the defendant?"

"Ellie was my firstborn," she said. "My daughter. Jamie Simmons is my son-in-law. He's married to my youngest daughter, Erin."

"Thank you. And to be clear, George Luke is your husband?"

"Yes."

"Have you communicated with your husband about his testimony in this trial?"

"Yes."

"Were you aware that he was going to take the stand for the prosecution?"

"Absolutely not."

"He didn't tell you he was going to do that?"

"He most certainly did not."

"Okay. Mrs. Luke, I'd like to take you back to twenty-two years ago, when your daughter went missing. I know these are difficult memories so I apologize for that. But you were the one who initially called the police to report your daughter missing. Is that right?"

"It is," she said. "Ellie worked until seven in the morning as a caregiver. She was usually home no later than eight. And that was if there was something keeping her over. Like if the aide scheduled after her was late. Or if Ellie got involved in doing something for Mrs. Corning like giving her a shower and things ran long. But again, Ellie was never home past eight."

"Is that what initially raised your suspicions?"

"Yes. Usually I would wake up when I heard Ellie coming in from the garage. Then I'd start my day. Ask her about her night. See if she wanted me to pack any kind of lunch for her if it was one of my days off. That day, I was off. But during the week, she would have to leave the house again by about one thirty. I wanted her to just go straight to bed and sleep as long as she could."

"Of course. So, can you take me through that last morning?"

"I woke up late. After eight thirty. I went to go look and Ellie wasn't home. Her car wasn't in the driveway. I tried to call her but it went to voicemail. I was concerned right away. She was never that late. Not without letting me know."

"So, what did you do?"

"I waited. Tried not to panic. Erin, my younger daughter, was already gone. She was a senior in high school at the time. She left by six thirty. I'm not that early of a riser so I didn't hear her go. But the house was quiet. I just knew something was wrong. I woke George up, but he just told me I was overreacting. Time ticked by. It got to be nine. Nine thirty. I called the agency where Ellie worked. They told me Ellie had already called in and given her nightly report on Mrs. Corning. The day shift aide had already relieved Ellie. That's when I knew something was really, really wrong."

"What did you do then?"

"I started calling a few of Ellie's friends. Only one answered.

Shante Jones. She didn't have class that morning. She said she hadn't seen Ellie or talked to her since the week before."

Claudia remained mostly stoic through her recounting. How she finally called the police at noon. Her frustration at the perceived slowness of the response from the sheriff's office. But by four o'clock that afternoon, Ellie's car had been found abandoned just under two miles from Hattie Corning's home.

"Mrs. Luke," Cutler said. "Did you have any idea what might have happened to your daughter?"

"No. Not at first. I was just in shock. We all were. But Ellie's friends were always so helpful. They just showed up. Helped search. Brought us meals."

"That's wonderful. Do you remember which friends?"

"There was Shante, of course. And Lisa ... you know I can't remember her last name just now. And even some of Ellie's friends from high school that I hadn't seen for a while."

"They all came to the house?"

"Oh yes."

"What about Jamie Simmons?"

"He came too. If you're going to ask me the first time, well, I can't remember that. I just remember him being part of a group of Ellie's friends that just came and made sure we had everything we needed."

"I don't mean to be redundant, but so I'm clear with what you're saying. These friends of Ellie's. From college. From high school. They were all in your home during those initial weeks when Ellie went missing?"

"Yes. Yes, they were."

"Okay. I'm going to come back to that. But I want to focus on your communication with the police. Did you ever tell them if you knew of anyone who wanted to hurt your daughter?"

"Here we go," Hojo wrote on the pad in front of us.

"Yes," Claudia said. "I told them there was only one person I knew of who would want anything bad to happen to my Ellie."

"And who was that?"

"My nephew ... well ... I suppose he's not technically my nephew. He's my cousin's son. Dane Fischer."

"Why did you think Dane Fischer wanted to hurt Ellie?"

"Because he said he did."

"He threatened her?"

"Yes. Dane said ..."

"Objection," I said. "Calls for hearsay. We've been over this, Your Honor."

"Your Honor, Mr. Fischer's statement isn't being offered for the truth of it. It's being offered to show Mrs. Luke's state of mind. She was responding to being questioned by the police."

"I'll allow it," Judge Saul said.

"Go ahead, Mrs. Luke."

"Ellie told me that Dane said he wanted to smash her head in for what he thought she'd done to him."

"Objection!" I rose. "Your Honor, now we have double hearsay. I'd ask that the witness's answer be stricken."

"Sustained. The jury will disregard the last answer, Mr. Cutler."

Cutler seemed unfazed. We could admonish the jury all we wanted. They'd heard the answer.

"Mrs. Luke, why did you think Dane Fischer was a threat to your daughter?"

"Because he was an addict. His behavior was unpredictable. I'd opened my home to him because I wanted to help. He betrayed my trust. He stole things to pay for his drug habit. Ellie was the one who figured that out. She told us about it. And she gave a statement to the police. So Dane blamed Ellie for us kicking him out of the house. It wasn't her fault. But he blamed her. And Dane was dangerous. When he was on drugs, he could be violent. He punched a hole in the wall right next to Ellie's head the last day he was in the house."

"He punched the wall right next to her head?" Cutler repeated, as if he were surprised by the revelation.

"That's right. And he shoved George."

"Okay. How would you characterize your relationship with your son-in-law?"

"Today?"

"Today, historically. All of it."

"I love Jamie. He's like a son to me. He's the one bright spot that happened amidst all that tragedy."

"What do you mean?"

"When Jamie started coming around, he was just so competent. So helpful. My husband has struggled with mental health issues. They flared up terribly after Ellie went missing and all the rest of it. He couldn't get out of bed. So when Jamie was over, I asked him if he'd help me with a few things. Getting the riding lawn mower started. Later, pulling the snowblower off the hooks in the garage."

"You asked him?"

"Yes. Absolutely. I know I relied on him more than I should have. We weren't his family then. He was just being nice. But I needed help and George wasn't in a position to provide it."

"Because of his mental health issues, as you described them?"

"Yes. George wasn't even capable of getting out of bed. Then later ... he tried to take his own life. He ... he went out to the garage and sat in his car with it running. Erin and I were out. We were supposed to be gone all day shopping. A girls' day out. Only my sciatica started acting up. So we came home early and found George slumped over the wheel. He spent some time in a clinic after that. It saved his life."

"I see," Cutler said. "So ... if your husband described Jamie Simmons's behavior as grooming, would you agree with that?"

"That's ridiculous. I already told you. I'm the one who asked Jamie for help. It was at my urging that he helped take over some of the things George couldn't handle. He was a godsend. He's the rock of our family. I don't know how we would have pulled through all of that without Jamie. Then, as time went on, he and Erin grew closer. It was natural and I thank God every day that Jamie was there for us. My husband has a disturbed view of things. It's not the first time."

"Okay. Thank you. I just want to touch on one last thing you said. Regarding Ellie's friends who came to the house to help.

Was Ellie's room locked when people would come into the house?"

"No."

"Your husband testified that Ellie's things were left mostly undisturbed after she disappeared. Is that your memory?"

"Yes. I couldn't bring myself to do it. It felt so final. I'd say it took me about two years before I could deal with Ellie's belongings. We kept her room as it was. Then, after Erin got pregnant ... the Lord blessed us. I decided to convert Ellie's room to a nursery for when my granddaughter would stay over."

"Two years," Cutler repeated. "Thank you. I have nothing further."

"Ms. Brent?" Judge Saul said.

"Mrs. Luke," I started. "You were also the one to give a description of Ellie to the police when you reported her missing, weren't you?"

"Yes."

"You described to them in detail what she was wearing, didn't you?"

"I told them everything I could think of, yes."

"Do you recall telling them what jewelry she had on?"

"I do, yes."

"Do you recall it now?"

"Yes. Ellie had a flat gold necklace she wore And a pair of earrings her father got her."

I directed Claudia's attention to the photograph we'd entered of Ellie wearing her infamous gold hoop earrings.

"You're certain she was wearing these earrings the morning she disappeared?"

"She had them on when she left the house, yes. Ellie wore them all the time. She sometimes slept in them, even. I was always telling her not to. I was afraid they'd snag on her pillow and rip her ear off. But they were her favorites."

"Mrs. Luke, are you aware of what items were found in your son-in-law's home by your granddaughter?"

"Hayden has issues like my husband. She's mentally ill."

"I'd like the witness's answer to be stricken as unresponsive."

"Sustained," the judge said. "Mrs. Luke, please answer the questions as asked."

"I'll repeat it. Mrs. Luke, are you aware of what was found in a box delivered to the police earlier this year?"

"Not all of it, no. But whatever Hayden ..."

"I'm not asking you about Hayden. Let me ask you this. When Ellie's remains were found, you were shown the items found along with her, weren't you?"

"Yes."

"What were they?"

"She ... some of her clothing. Her necklace. Her earrings."

"Earrings. But it was only one of the earrings, isn't that right?"

"I think so."

"You think so."

"Yes. One earring. Yes."

"You even remarked on that to Detective Ritter, didn't you? You asked him where the other earring was because it was important to you to get them back, wasn't it?"

"Yes. They were her favorites."

"Do you recall what Detective Ritter told you?"

"He said it was evidence. That they couldn't release it until the case was closed. Until after they made an arrest."

"Mrs. Luke, you understand the mate of Ellie's earring was found in a box in your son-in-law's possession, don't you?"

She shook her head almost violently. "No. Don't you dare. I know what you've done. You've poisoned my granddaughter's mind. She's disturbed. Just like my husband. Just like Jamie said."

My heart thundered. "Like Jamie said? Jamie Simmons told you not to believe Hayden, didn't he?"

"Of course."

"And he told you not to talk to the police, or to me, didn't he?"

"You're twisting everything. I knew you would."

"Did Jamie Simmons tell you not to talk to the police or to me?"

"I didn't ... that wasn't ... you're making it sound like ..."

"I'm not making it sound like anything. I'm asking you a question. Did Jamie Simmons ask you not to talk to me or the police in connection with this case?"

"He told me not to believe everything people were saying. I knew my granddaughter had an unhealthy obsession with what happened to Ellie. And I know my husband is having some of the same issues he had when Ellie went missing. That's all."

She wasn't going to budge. But she'd all but admitted Jamie had exerted influence over her.

"I have no further questions," I said. Cutler deferred rebuttal.

"You may call your next witness," Judge Saul instructed him.

Without missing a beat, Bennett Cutler squared his shoulders and spoke with a booming voice. "The defense calls Dane Fischer to the stand."

29

Dane Fischer looked different from the last time I saw him. He'd gotten leaner. His dark expression cut through me. It wasn't hard to understand how he saw the world. How he saw me, every deputy in the room, Bennett Cutler, Jamie Simmons. Even Erin Simmons as she sat meekly two rows behind her husband.

We were Dane's enemies. We were the people who he had to believe kept him from the life he wanted to live. He was another one of Jamie Simmons's victims and Claudia Luke had just pilloried him again in her direct testimony.

"Your Honor," Cutler began. "I would like permission to treat this witness as hostile. He was compelled here by subpoena and has made no secret of his animosity toward the family of the victim."

"He's the defense's witness," I said. "And this witness's family is his family as well."

"Be that as it may," Judge Saul said. "From the argument presented in defense counsel's written brief on this matter, I will grant his request to treat the witness as hostile. You may proceed, Mr. Cutler."

"Thank you," Cutler said. "Mr. Fischer, for clarification, will you remind the court how you are related to the victim in this case, Ellie Luke?"

Fischer's cold stare didn't soften. If anything, the question seemed to make him angrier. "She's a cousin. My mother and Ellie's mother are first cousins. They had the same maternal grandparents. My mom's mother and Claudia's mother were sisters."

"They were close, your mother and Claudia?"

"They were about the same age. My mom always thought of Claudia as one of her best friends when they were growing up."

"Are they still in touch?" Cutler asked.

"I wouldn't know."

"And why is that?"

"I don't have contact with my mother. And I'm not in contact with Claudia."

"You harbor ill feelings toward Claudia and her family, don't you?"

"I don't harbor any feelings at all toward them," Fischer said.

"Are you sure about that?"

"You asked me the question. I gave you an answer. I haven't communicated with Claudia or that side of the family in over twenty years. And as you said, I'm not here voluntarily. You forced me to be here."

"Be that as it may, Ellie Luke was your cousin. Or second cousin. However that works. You were close with the Lukes at one point, weren't you?"

"I don't know what you mean by close."

"Well, I mean you had a relationship with them. Didn't you?"

"I suppose you could call it that, yes."

"You lived with them for a time, didn't you?"

"For about three months when I was twenty years old. That was twenty-four years ago."

"Okay," Cutler said. "So you were twenty. How old was Ellie Luke at the time?"

"Eighteen or nineteen."

"Why did you come to live with the Lukes?"

"I was going through a hard time. I'm an addict, Mr. Cutler. I know that's what you're getting at with all of this. You think I'm ashamed of it? I'm not. When I was fifteen years old, some things happened in my life that aren't any of your business. I fell in with a group of kids who didn't have my best interests in mind. I started using. It took over my life. My parents kicked me out when I was nineteen. I stopped using but my parents weren't interested in letting me back in. I was out of a job, out of money, and trying really hard to start over. So Claudia agreed to let me stay at her place for a summer while I tried to get back on my feet. That's it. That's the whole story."

Cutler smiled. "It isn't really the whole story now, is it?"

"I'm done," Fischer said. He stood up.

"Mr. Fischer," the judge said. "You are not free to leave the witness box. You are here under subpoena. Mr. Cutler will let you know when he's finished with his questions. Then Ms. Brent will have an opportunity to cross-examine you. Please sit down."

He glared at her, but slowly sank back into his chair.

"Mr. Fischer, can you please explain the circumstances as to why you left Claudia Luke's home?"

"I'd rather not."

"You started using again, didn't you?"

"I had a relapse, yes."

"Your Honor," I said. "This has gone on long enough. Mr. Fischer's relationship with his family is irrelevant. This is a sideshow not related to the issues in the case."

Cutler let out a haughty laugh. "And Ms. Brent knows better. Detective Ritter admitted on the stand and in his report that Dane Fischer was the main suspect in Ellie Luke's disappearance. It is entirely relevant to explore how that came to be."

"Are we going to go down every single investigative lead?" I asked.

"If we have to!" Cutler shouted.

"Enough," Judge Saul intervened. "Mr. Cutler, get to your point. Ms. Brent, I've already ruled on the relevancy of this witness when Detective Ritter was on the stand. I haven't changed my mind. Proceed."

"Mr. Fischer, isn't it true that you threatened Ellie Luke with physical harm on more than one occasion?"

Fischer's eyes went red. His whole body shook with rage. "I refuse to answer that question on the advice of counsel. I'm invoking my Fifth Amendment rights."

A murmur went through the gallery. Several members of the jury sat straighter in their seats. Beside me, Hojo quietly whispered a single word.

"Shit."

"You refuse to answer?" Cutler asked.

"That's right."

"Mr. Fischer, isn't it true that you blamed Ellie Luke for getting thrown out of the Luke home?"

"I plead the Fifth."

"You were questioned by the police in connection with Ellie's disappearance, weren't you?"

"Yes. I was questioned."

"And when you were asked to account for your whereabouts on the night Ellie went missing, you lied, didn't you?"

"I plead the Fifth."

"At first, was it your statement to the police at the time that you were at a bar the morning Ellie went missing?"

"I plead the Fifth."

"And when that story didn't check out and Detective Ritter questioned you again, you lied again, didn't you? You said you were home the whole night and into the next day."

"I plead the Fifth."

"Only that was a lie because Detective Ritter checked. Your roommate said he hadn't seen you in two days."

"Your Honor," I said. "Counsel is testifying. And he's trying to introduce hearsay through a backdoor. I request his question be stricken and the jury instructed to disregard it."

"Sustained. So ordered. Move on, Mr. Cutler."

"The Lukes filed a police report against you, didn't they?" Cutler asked Fischer.

"I refuse to answer any more questions on the grounds that it might incriminate me. I plead the Fifth."

"Mara ..." Hojo started. I rose to my feet.

"Mr. Fischer, you threatened to kill Ellie Luke, didn't you?" Cutler shouted.

"I plead the Fifth!"

"Your Honor!" I said. "If we could ..."

"You wanted her dead. Ellie Luke ruined your life again in your mind, didn't she?"

"I plead the Fifth!"

"What is he doing?" Hojo said.

Judge Saul banged her gavel. "Enough," she said. "Mr. Fischer, is it your intention to invoke your Fifth Amendment privileges to all further questioning by Mr. Cutler?"

"It is," he said. "I will not answer any questions about Ellie Luke."

"Mr. Cutler?" the judge said.

"You knew where she worked. You knew when she worked," Cutler said. "Ellie Luke was working the same job, the same schedule when you were living in the home with her. You were well aware of her comings and goings."

"I plead the Fifth," Fischer said.

"Christ," Hojo whispered. "He's doing this on purpose. Cutler knew he was going to do this."

"You killed her," Cutler shouted.

"Objection! Your Honor, this is exactly what I've been objecting to all along. Mr. Cutler is playing games with this witness. His testimony is entirely irrelevant and highly prejudicial. I move that Mr. Fischer's entire testimony be stricken."

"Not on your life," Cutler said. "Mr. Fischer is refusing to answer questions that are germane to every issue in this case."

"Overruled, Ms. Brent," Judge Saul said. "Mr. Cutler? What do you want to do here?"

Cutler took a step back from the podium and crossed his arms. He made a great show out of pretending he was actually considering his options. Then he stepped forward and leaned in close to the microphone. "I have no further questions for this witness."

"Ms. Brent?" Judge Saul said.

I couldn't even ask the question and give Dane Fischer the opportunity to deny killing Ellie. If I asked and he pleaded the Fifth again, it could be viewed as good as an admission to the jury. Bennett Cutler had painted me into a corner and he knew it.

"Mr. Fischer," I said. "When was the last time you saw Ellie Luke?"

His expression softened. I could almost see Fischer's wheels turning. He was innocent. I knew this. He knew it. Hell, even Cutler probably knew it. And I'd just asked him an innocent question. Not where he was when she disappeared. My question had nothing to do with lies he'd told the police. Or threats he'd made against Ellie.

"I don't ... I plead the Fifth."

"Had you spoken to her at all in the months before she went missing?"

"I plead the Fifth."

His voice had gone quiet. I could barely hear him. From the corner of my eye, I could see Jamie Simmons with a satisfied smile on his face.

An idea formed in my mind. A last hope. But I knew if I were going to salvage this case, Bennett Cutler had forced me into the position of proving Dane Fischer's innocence as much as I had to prove Jamie Simmons's guilt. It was a nightmare scenario.

"Your Honor," I said. "May we approach?"

She waved Cutler and me forward. "Your Honor," I started. "This witness has invoked his Fifth Amendment privilege against self-incrimination. I'm going to give Mr. Cutler the benefit of the doubt that he was unaware that he would."

"Are you accusing me of something?" Cutler said.

"I believe I'm doing the opposite of that. I said I was giving you the benefit of the doubt."

"Make your point, Ms. Brent," the judge said.

"If Mr. Fischer is concerned about criminal prosecution relating to any part of his testimony in connection with this case, I'd like the opportunity to assuage his fears. I can offer him immunity. May we have a one-hour recess so that I can confer with Mr. Fischer on this matter?"

"This is ridiculous," Cutler said. "And I insist on being present for any discussions with Mr. Fischer."

"You're not his lawyer." Judge Saul and I said it in unison.

"All right," Judge Saul said. "One hour. But if you can't work it out, then I believe we're done with Mr. Fischer."

"Thank you, Your Honor," Cutler said with a confidence that made me livid.

Cutler went back to his client. The judge dismissed the jury and ordered us into recess.

"Mr. Fischer, please," I said as he tried to brush past me. "We can help each other. I'm just asking for an hour of your time. I know you didn't kill Ellie Luke. The cops know it too. Please. Just one hour."

He watched as Cutler and Simmons left the courtroom. They were jovial with each other. Laughing. A wave of anger went through Dane Fischer. He looked back at me.

"I'll give you ten minutes."

30

Gus was waiting in the hallway when we walked out. I didn't know if he'd been in the courtroom, but word of Dane Fischer's testimony had undoubtedly already spread.

"Good," I said to him. "I'm going to need you for this."

"No," Dane said. "Hell, no. I don't want him anywhere near me."

I whirled around and snapped at him. "Like it or not, he's your best shot at fixing this mess. Now get in here before you have a reporter in your face."

Dane's jaw dropped. Whatever he was expecting me to say, it wasn't that. To be fair, I hadn't expected to say it either. But my own rage started to bubble up.

Gus opened the door to the empty jury room to Judge Ivey's courtroom. He was on vacation this week.

"Sit," I ordered Dane. He took a chair at the long table in the center of the room. Gus stayed back, leaning against the door he'd just closed.

"What are you doing?" I asked Dane. "You had an opportunity to get your side of the story out. On the record. In open court. In front of members of the Luke family. Your family."

Dane looked from me to Gus. "I know what this is. I know what it's always been. You want me to think you're on my side?"

"No," I said. "I'm not on your side. I'm on Ellie Luke's side. I'm on Hayden Simmons's side."

"You think I killed her?" Dane said, but he wasn't talking to me. He looked straight at Gus. "You ruined my life."

Gus flinched. "I don't think that anymore," he said quietly. "But yes. Twenty-two years ago ... hell ... six months ago. I thought you killed her. I thought I knew it. I was wrong."

"It's too late," Dane said.

"Dane," I said. "I need you to understand what's happening. You went in there and pleaded the Fifth. Fine. It's your right. And if you want a lawyer in here while we talk, call one. I'll help you find one if you want. But right now, there's a good chance enough members of that jury are going to think the same thing Gus did. And let's not pretend he didn't have good reasons."

Dane crossed his arms in front of himself. He looked out the window.

"I know you didn't kill her," I said. "Gus knows it. George Luke knows it."

"I want to hear it from him," Dane said.

Gus stepped forward. He put his hands flat on the table and got in Dane's face. "I know you didn't kill Ellie. But I also know you're a liar. You don't have to like me. I sure don't have to like you. But if you made it harder for Mara to convince that jury Jamie Simmons did this, then that's on your head. So you better decide if you can live with that."

"I don't owe her anything," Dane said. "I don't owe you anything. I have to look out for myself. If you think that makes me a bad person, I don't care. When I say you ruined my life, I mean you ruined my life. I lost my job. I lost one side of my family. My own mother doesn't speak to me. I've been sober for over twenty years. But they're lost to me anyway because they believe I killed Ellie."

"So why don't you take this chance to convince them you didn't?" I said. "Dane, you lied to Gus about your alibi twenty-two years ago. We know you didn't kill Ellie. Jamie did. You're not in danger of prosecution."

"I don't believe you," he said.

"I'm the prosecutor! Gus is the detective on this case. We're the ones telling you you're not in jeopardy here. If you want it in writing, I'll put it in writing. Full immunity. But you have to tell the truth. Jamie's lawyer has used you to raise reasonable doubt. He only has to make one member of that jury think maybe you're the one who killed her. Then Jamie walks. And this whole thing starts all over again for you. Not from us. We know the truth. But everyone else will believe you're a murderer forever."

"Take the deal and do the right thing, Fischer," Gus said.

"I don't trust you!" Dane shouted. Spit flew from the corner of his mouth. Gus stayed right where he was, in Dane's face. "I don't trust your deal. And I don't owe you anything. I did what I had to do. The only one who can look out for me is me. I'm not signing anything. I know my rights. I'm not going back into that courtroom."

I sat back hard in my seat. Time was running out. Soon, there'd be a knock on the door when Judge Saul was ready to retake the bench.

"Dane," I said, softening my tone. "Okay. I get it. I really do. You've gotten a raw deal. It isn't fair. The Lukes were wrong about you."

"So was I," Gus said. "Is that what you need me to say? I was wrong. And it's killing me to know that. I wish I could go back in time and change things. You want an apology? You have it. I'm sorry."

"It's worthless," he said.

"Who else are you protecting?" I asked. It was almost a throwaway question. But as I said it, something clicked. Dane's eyes widened. I knew that look. I knew I'd hit on something.

"Your alibi," I said. "You told Gus two different stories about where you were and both of them were lies. But you weren't anywhere near Ellie Luke. We all know that. So why not come clean now? You've never told the truth about where you were. That's why you failed the poly. But we know you *had* an alibi because we know Jamie's the one who killed Ellie. Why do you think you can't tell us the truth now?"

"We're done," he said. "I told you ten minutes. We're well past that."

"Is there somebody who can vouch for where you were the night Ellie went missing?" I asked. "Dane, for god's sake. Tell me. Let me go in there and prove your innocence. If I don't, this cloud of suspicion will be over you the rest of your life. This is really your one chance, your last chance to take back some of what you lost."

He said nothing, but he didn't have to. A shudder went through him. Dane's eyes went red.

"I'm right," I said. "Aren't I? You lied because you were protecting someone. Who? Whatever it is, does it still matter after twenty years?"

He buried his face in his hands. Gus caught my eye across the table.

"Everything," Dane whispered. "I lost everything."

"Who did you lose?" I asked. "Who got scared away when Gus zeroed in on you as the prime suspect?"

It wasn't his family, I knew. They'd already turned against him at Ellie Luke's word two years before her death. So it had to be someone else he loved.

"Who was she?" I asked. Dane's head snapped up and he looked at me.

"You loved her," I said. "But you didn't want to drag her into all of this. Is that it?"

"You don't know what you're talking about," he whispered.

"I think she does," Gus said. "Who was she, Dane? Why didn't you want anyone to know you were with her?"

"The hell with both of you," Dane said, but I knew the fight had gone out of him. Love. It was the only thing I could think of that might make Dane Fischer hold on to his secret.

"Maybe she'd want to help you?" I said. "Does she know she could make it so the whole world knows you're innocent?

Finally. After all this time. If she cared about you at all, wouldn't she want that for you?"

"She doesn't deserve this," he said. "She never did. You had no idea what I put her through. I made a lot of promises I didn't end up keeping. But I kept this one."

"She wasn't supposed to be with you that morning, is that it?" Gus asked. "It would have cost her something if people knew."

Dane nodded.

A thought popped into my head. "Dane," I asked. "Did she have another boyfriend? A husband?"

"A husband," he whispered.

"Christ," Gus said.

"You were involved with a married woman," I said. "If she came forward and told Gus you were with her, then her husband was going to find out? Is that it?"

Dane nodded. I felt a wave of both relief and guilt. I knew Gus felt the same. It was so simple. Dane took a breath. I think he was relieved too. Because when he started talking again, it was as if a dam burst inside of him. His story came flooding out.

"I loved her," Dane said. "I got sober for her. Then when all this crap went down with Ellie ... she got scared. We both got scared. Then ... she found out she was pregnant. We were at her place that night. Her husband was out of town. She was gonna tell him. But then there was the baby. And we were pretty sure it was his, not mine. It all just got so messy."

"And you became the main suspect in a murder investigation," I said. "Oh Dane. That's why you lied? Why you failed your poly?"

"She was gonna come forward," he said. "If you'd arrested me, she was gonna come forward."

"But one lie wasn't enough for probable cause," Gus said bitterly. "So she didn't have to."

"Yeah," Dane said.

"Will you give us a name?" I asked. "Dane, please. Give her a chance to do the right thing. After twenty-two years, surely it doesn't matter anymore. Her baby is grown. Is she still married to her husband?"

Dane shook his head. "I don't know. She left Waynetown. Her husband took some job in Dayton or somewhere."

"Why in God's name didn't you just say that on the stand, Dane?" I asked.

"You've never believed anything I had to say," he answered, staring at Gus.

"I believe you now," Gus answered.

"I can put you back on the stand," I said. "You can tell your story."

"No," Dane said. "You think any of this makes me trust either of you? Plus, Jamie's lawyer will find a way to twist my words. He won't quit."

"You could have told me back then," Gus said. "You could have let me talk to her. If she was credible, this would have ended things. It would have been over."

"Yeah?" Dane asked. "Bullshit. You gonna sit there and lie to me now? You had your mind made up. I wasn't gonna drag her into this and ruin her life, too."

Gus had no answer for him. I knew Dane was right. Gus knew he was right. Twenty-two years ago, Gus probably wouldn't have believed him.

"Let us talk to her now," I said. "She might feel differently. Her life might be different. Please. I know you don't want Jamie Simmons to walk. You were mad at Ellie Luke. But you didn't want her dead. I know you didn't."

Dane squeezed his eyes shut.

"She ... I don't know."

"Yes," I said. "You do. It's time to close the book on this. It's time everyone knew the truth. It wasn't you. You didn't kill Ellie. Let me prove it for you. If your girlfriend back then really loved you, she'd want the same for you."

"She said that," he said, letting out a bitter laugh. "But I wouldn't let her. When I knew you weren't going to arrest me, I let her go."

"Who is she, Dane?" I asked.

"Holly," he whispered in a voice so low I almost didn't hear it. "Holly Logue. And I have nothing more to say to you." He rose from his chair. Gus moved away from the door and let him pass. As Dane opened the door, Judge Saul's bailiff stood there, ready to call me back in.

"Five minutes," I told him.

"You have two," the bailiff warned me, then left Gus and me alone.

"Gus," I said.

"Christ," he muttered. "What a damn waste. If he'd have just told me, I could have cleared him."

"Gus," I repeated. "I need you, okay? Whatever happened twenty-two years ago doesn't matter. I need you now. You have to find Holly Logue and convince her to testify. What I told Dane was the truth. If this trial ends right now, Jamie Simmons is going to walk. They're going to think Dane's guilty."

"Because of me," he said.

"Enough. You made a mistake. An honest one. A legitimate one. Dane *did* lie. He acted like a guilty man. Even today. He's been in his own way since the beginning. But we're out of time. I'm going to try to stall, but when I go back into that courtroom. I can almost guarantee you Bennett Cutler's going to rest. I have to convince Saul to give me until tomorrow morning to call my rebuttal witnesses. Get me Holly Logue. Can you do that?"

Gus straightened. His expression hardened. "I'll find her," he promised me. I prayed he could. But she could be anywhere. She could even be dead.

"I'll find her," Gus repeated. We both knew Jamie Simmons's fate would depend on it.

31

"Mom."

I felt weighed down. Peaceful. I opened one eye and the world seemed upside down.

"Mom!"

I blinked, taking a second to orient myself in the pitch dark. I was on the living room couch, face down, lying on top of my legal pad and notes.

I sat bolt upright. "What time is it?"

"It's early," Will said. He was still wearing pajama pants and a tee shirt. My eyes adjusted. Stars shone from the bay window in front of me. He looked so much like his father in the dim light.

"It's almost five thirty," he said. "You were talking in your sleep."

"You heard me from upstairs?" I asked, wiping the drool from the corner of my mouth. Five thirty. I patted the couch with my hands, searching for my phone.

"Here," Will said. He had my phone in his hand. I took it from him and quickly unlocked it.

Nothing. No missed calls. No texts from Gus. It was going on sixteen hours since we left the courthouse. Since he'd been on the hunt for Holly Logue. No news was bad news.

"I started the coffee," Will said. "I figured you'd want to head into the office early. Are you going to rest your case today?"

I rose. The smell of the brewing coffee hit me. Manna from heaven.

"Probably," I said. "I'm waiting for a call from Uncle Gus."

"Bo's mom is going to pick me up today," he said. "I figured that'd be easier for you."

My heart sank. My sweet boy. "That was thoughtful of you. I'm sure Aunt Kat wouldn't mind ..."

"No," Will said. "Aunt Bree's off this week. Aunt Kat didn't want to say, but she's having a hard time. Nervous about whether you're going to win this case."

"She was good friends with the girl who died," I said. I checked my phone again, making sure the ringer was on. Gus should have called me. In three hours, I'd have to tell the judge something. Either I had an alibi witness I could call on rebuttal, or I'd have to send this case to the jury with a big, fat hole in the shape of Dane Fischer.

Will followed me to the kitchen. I poured a cup of coffee and practically inhaled it.

"Do you think they'll decide today?" he asked.

"No. I don't know. I have one more witness. Then closing arguments if the defense doesn't call anyone else. So maybe tomorrow or over the weekend."

Worry lines creased his face. This had been an ongoing issue. My son got too invested in some of the cases I tried, especially the murders.

"You sure you're okay if I head in early?" I asked.

"What happens if Uncle Gus can't find this witness you need?"

I poured another cup of coffee. "I don't know, buddy. Hopefully, it won't matter either way. Hopefully, they'll see there's nothing else that could have happened."

"Hopefully," he said, those frown lines still deep. I reached for him. Will wasn't an affectionate kid, but he had a keen sense of when I needed it. I kissed him on the cheek. He gave me a rigid hug.

"It's okay," he said. "Bo's mom's a good driver. She'll be here in an hour. If something happens ... you'll text me?"

"Of course," I said.

He turned and headed back up the stairs. If I squinted, he almost looked like a grown man. My baby. I hoped I could make the world just a little safer today. I hoped Gus could, too.

"Anything?"

Hojo and Caro were already in the office when I walked in an hour later.

"He hasn't called here?" I asked.

Hojo's face fell. "No. I called Gus's office phone. Went straight to voicemail. You should call Sam."

"You two should calm down," Caro said. "So what if he can't find this woman? Dane Fischer's not the one who collected souvenirs from that poor girl's dead body."

"They need a reason to believe Fischer's innocent," Hojo said. "I was watching them. Fischer's testimony made them uncomfortable. I'm telling you. Juror number seven in particular. The retired plumber. He was staring right through Fischer. Pure hatred."

"Stop it," Caro said. "How does that help Mara? Don't you have some paperwork you have to file?" Hojo looked sufficiently chastised.

"It's okay," I said.

"You'll kill him on closing," Caro said. "No matter what Gus brings to the table today."

I didn't like this. I didn't like having to walk into the courtroom not knowing which version of my closing I'd have to give. If Dane Fischer's possible guilt hung over this thing, Jamie Simmons would likely be acquitted. I couldn't believe I was even thinking that to myself.

"You'll be great," Hojo said. Then he took Caro's advice and went down to his office.

"Ignore him," Caro said. "I mean, not the part about you being great. The rest of it. If Gus comes through, it'll just be icing on the cake."

"Thanks," I said. "I'm going to try calling Sam."

"Good idea." Then Caro's face grew serious. "Mara. This may not be the best time. But ... I know you met with Kenya the other day. She's not coming back, is she? Please tell me you are."

"Coming back?"

"Taking that office," she said, pointing down the hall where Hojo had just disappeared.

"Did Kenya talk to you about it?"

Caro's face betrayed nothing. But that alone told me what I needed to know. If anything, Caro had been the one to urge Kenya to put pressure on me to run. It meant Kenya hadn't told her about her true plans. There had to be a reason for that. But I knew it wasn't my place to share it.

"You'll have to talk to Kenya about it," I said. "But right now, I need to focus on the next couple of days."

My phone buzzed in my pocket. I jumped, hoping to see Gus's caller ID. But it was Sam. Caro discreetly went back to her desk so I could take the call in private.

"Hey, Sam. Do you know anything?"

He sighed. "I was about to ask you the same question. Gus isn't returning my calls or texts. I haven't seen him since last night."

"Dammit. Sam ..."

"He's got time."

"He's got an hour," I said. "I'm about to head over to the courthouse now. And even if he walked through my door right now with that witness, I'd barely have time to prep. I'll have to put her on the stand cold. I don't like that. I have no idea what she'll say."

"Is there someone else you can put on the stand?" he asked. "Stall. Vamp. Work your magic?"

"I'm out of ideas. If Gus can't bring Holly Logue today, I'm going to have to rest."

"Got it. I'll keep trying to get a hold of Gus."

"This isn't like him," I said. "Not to check in. Not even with you. Do you think he's okay?"

I wish Sam were in front of me. I could have read his face. Known for sure what he was thinking. Instead, he gave me what amounted to a party line.

"Gus is good at what he does. If he can't find this woman, it means she's unfindable. Either way, I trust him."

"Okay. But don't you think he should at least call one of us and tell us that?"

Sam let out a huge sigh. I knew he agreed with me. But he'd never say anything against Gus.

"Mara, my gut's telling me it's because he's found her. We have to trust him."

"He should call," I insisted, letting my frustration get the better of me. I clicked off. I had to prepare for what I'd do if I had to rest my case as is. As the minutes ticked away, I felt my options shrinking. And it was time to head to court.

"I'M SORRY, SHE WANTS WHAT?" BENNETT CUTLER WAS enjoying this. He stood at the lectern beside me. I wanted to knock the smug smile right off his face. Behind him, Jamie Simmons looked as relaxed as if he were sitting in his living room, not in a courtroom on trial for his life.

"I just need a bit more time," I said. "My witness has had some traffic issues."

"And I will renew my objection to her being able to call this witness at all," Cutler said. "Holly Logue wasn't on her witness list."

"And I'll renew my response. It's proper rebuttal. Mr. Cutler has been repeatedly allowed to enter testimony about Dane Fischer's relationship with the victim. His stunt yesterday opened the door. Ms. Logue has relevant information about the time period Ellie Luke went missing as it pertains to Dane Fischer."

"Be that as it may," Judge Saul said. "The elusive Ms. Logue isn't here. We cannot wait indefinitely. I'm going to ask you point blank, Ms. Brent. Do you know where your witness is?"

I couldn't lie. But the truth would end this here and now. Where the hell was Gus? I had at least a dozen unanswered calls to him. Never mind how many Sam had placed. Every unspoken doubt I'd had came bubbling to the surface.

This case had changed him. Thrown him off his game. Gotten too far under his skin. I was worried. I prayed he wasn't at the bottom of a bottle somewhere. Or worse.

"Ms. Brent?" the judge repeated. "Do you or do you not know where your witness is?"

"Detective Ritter is working on getting her here. As I said ..."

"Working on it?" Cutler shouted. "Your Honor, enough is enough. Ms. Brent either needs to put up or shut up. She's stalling for time. She's wasting the jury's time as well as everyone else's in this room."

"I'm afraid I agree," Judge Saul said. "I'm sorry. Your witness is either here or she's not. If she's not, then we must proceed. Call your next witness, Ms. Brent."

My knees turned to water. I hadn't felt like that in a courtroom since I tried my very first case. Unprepared.

There was nobody left to call. So be it. I looked behind me. Sam sat in the back of the courtroom, his face stoic. He gave me the slightest raise of his brow. He had no news for me either. Gus was AWOL.

"Your Honor," I said. "At this time, the prosecution ..."

Sam let out a loud cough that echoed through the courtroom. The door had just opened. Gus walked through, coated in sweat, his face flushed. He held the door open and a tall woman walked through behind him. Gus gave me just the slightest nod.

Holly Logue.

"Your Honor," I said. "My witness is here. If I could just have thirty minutes to confer ..."

"You may not," Judge Saul said. "You've had eighteen hours. Call your witness or rest, Ms. Brent."

I wished for the gift of telepathy. What had she told Gus? What would she say on the stand? I stared hard at Gus. He nodded again, then mouthed two words. *Trust me.*

This would have to do.

"I'm ready for the jury to be brought back in," I said.

Judge Saul motioned to her bailiff. I felt sweat running down my back as the jury filed in and took their seats.

32

"The prosecution calls Holly Logue to the stand," I said.

Cutler made another objection, but even he knew it was futile.

Holly Logue looked to be in her mid-forties. She was pretty, with short dark hair. She wore a loose white tunic and leggings. She politely swore her oath and climbed into the witness box. I gave her as warm a smile as I could, hoping my expression conveyed whatever encouragement she needed. If she could have read my mind, I would have told her we could get through this together.

"Will you please state your name for the record?"

"Holly Laverne Logue."

"Is that your married name or your maiden name?" I asked.

"It's my married name. I was Holly Peterson. But that was a long time ago."

"Are you still married to Mr. Logue?" I asked. Lord. I was flying blind here. I wanted to equally kill and kiss Gus Ritter.

"I am," she said.

"Ms. Logue, will you please explain how you know Dane Fischer?"

"I met him a very long time ago. Maybe twenty-five years."

"What was your relationship with him?"

"We met in rehab. I had an addiction to prescription medication. Xanax. Dane was using street drugs. We became close. Friends. And eventually, we dated."

"I realize this might not be something you're comfortable talking about. But were you married to Mr. Logue at the time?"

"Objection," Cutler said. "This is beyond the scope of the issues in this case. It's irrelevant."

"Your Honor, I believe I'm about three questions from getting there."

"You better be," Judge Saul said. "Overruled."

"Mrs. Logue, were you married at the time you began a relationship with Dane Fischer?"

"I was," she said. "I'm not proud of that. It was a complicated time in my life. My husband and I were in a rough patch. And I take the blame for that. My addiction made things very difficult for the people who loved me. Dane was ... at the time, I felt like Dane really saw me in a way my husband didn't. We became romantically involved for a while."

"Mrs. Logue, were you and Dane Fischer romantically involved in March of 2001?"

"Yes."

"Specifically, do you recall what you were doing on March 12th of that year?"

"I do."

"And what was it?"

"My husband had gone away on a business trip. I was feeling pretty vulnerable. Trying to decide what I wanted. I invited Dane to come stay with me. I wish I hadn't. But things were very ... confusing for me at the time. I thought I wanted a divorce. Dane came over the night of the 9th of March. That was a Friday. And he stayed until the morning of Wednesday the 14th."

"You were together from the 9th to the 14th of March?"

"Yes, ma'am."

"What about the morning of the 12th, specifically, do you remember it?"

"I do. Dane and I drove to Ann Arbor. That's about a forty-five minute drive from my house. We went to breakfast. It was my idea. I didn't want anyone I knew to see us together. I was cheating on my husband. As I said, I'm not proud of it."

"Mrs. Logue, we're talking about a random Monday morning in March, almost twenty-three years ago. How can you be so specific about where you were?"

"Because a few days after that, Dane was brought in for questioning about the murder of his cousin. And I knew he didn't do it. I knew he wasn't even in town that weekend, because he was with me."

A murmur went through the courtroom. Bennett Cutler was on his feet.

"You were aware that Dane Fischer became a suspect in Ellie Luke's murder?" I asked.

"Yes. I became aware of that, yes."

"How did you become aware of it?"

"Dane told me. And it was in the news. There was a search. The whole county was on high alert. I knew about Dane's troubled history with that side of his family."

"If you were aware that Dane was a person of interest, why didn't you come forward then? If you knew you could provide him an alibi?"

"Dane loved me," she said. "I loved him too. But I had decided I was going to try to make it work with my husband. With Brad."

"Brad didn't know you were having an affair?" I asked.

"No. Not at that time. No. And a couple of weeks after that, I found out I was pregnant with our first child. My son. Brad Jr."

"Did you discuss any of this with Dane Fischer?"

"Yes," she said, dabbing her eyes with a tissue. "Yes. Dane wanted to protect me. He didn't ... we knew he didn't kill that girl. Neither of us thought it would go as far as it did. I begged Dane not to tell anyone where he was. I regret that now. This thing has cost him so much. I was selfish."

"You're aware Dane gave false information to the police about his whereabouts the morning Ellie Luke went missing?"

"Yes. But he was protecting me."

"Did you ever talk to the police yourself?"

"No. They didn't know about me. Dane did what he promised. He kept my name out of it."

"What would you have done if Dane had been arrested?"

She shook her head. "I don't know. But it never came to that. I was terrified. And I was pregnant. I was scared about what might happen if Brad found out about Dane and me. I made every wrong choice. I know that. I know what people will probably think. But things just died down. Dane wasn't arrested. Time just ... moved on. I had my son. Brad and I managed to make things work for a while."

"Does your husband know now?"

She nodded. "Yes. Years later. After our daughter was born. I had a relapse. Postpartum depression. I went into treatment again. I decided I had to make amends. To come clean. I told Brad about what had happened and somehow, he forgave me. For the last fifteen years ... well ... the last twenty-two, I guess. I've been working to earn that forgiveness. To be worthy of it."

"Have you spoken to Dane since you ended your relationship with him twenty-two years ago?" I asked.

"No," she whispered. Then louder. "No."

"You didn't know this case had come to trial?"

"No. And I didn't know how badly Dane's family had treated him over the years. I didn't know they blamed him for killing that poor girl. He didn't tell me. If he had ... maybe I could have helped him. I don't know. But I'm telling you now, Dane wasn't in Waynetown on March 12th, 2001. He was with me. In Ann Arbor."

"Thank you," I said. "I have no further questions."

Bennett came to the lectern. "Mrs. Logue, just so I'm clear. You said you were addicted to Xanax twenty-two years ago?"

"I'll always be an addict. But I've been in recovery for twenty-three years. In 2001 I was sober."

"So you say," he said. "Twenty-two years. You admit Ellie Luke's case was on your radar. You knew about it."

"Yes."

"It made the news."

"Yes."

"And someone you cared about was directly involved with it. You knew that, right?"

"No. I'm telling you Dane had no involvement in it."

"He was cousins with the victim. You knew that?"

"Later, yes."

"And yet you failed to come forward until this very day. Out of the blue?"

"I didn't know this was going on. I didn't know people still thought Dane had something to do with it. When that detective over there came to my house and told me ... I'm sorry. I don't know what you mean by out of the blue. Nobody asked me, okay? If the police had asked me twenty-two years ago, I would have told them the truth."

"The truth," Cutler said. "Right. How convenient."

"Objection!"

"Sustained, Mr. Cutler."

Cutler had one hand on the lectern, the other in his pocket. He shook his head in disbelief. A show for the jury. Would they buy it?

"And we're just supposed to take your word for it, is that it?"

"I don't expect you to do anything. I was asked under oath to tell the truth about what I knew of Dane's whereabouts that weekend. I've done that. I can't control what people believe."

"You were asked. Mrs. Logue, have you ever been arrested?"

"Yes."

"What was the charge?"

"I have a DUI from 1998."

Cutler was baffled. He'd lost control. I could almost see his wheels turning as he scrambled for what to do.

"Dane put you up to this, didn't he?" Cutler asked.

"I believe I just said I haven't talked to Dane in over twenty years. I didn't know about this case. I live out in the country outside of Dayton. I make a point of not coming back to this area. It's not good for me. I have too many bad memories. I'm not on social media. Detective Ritter showed up at my house at six o'clock this morning. It scared the crap out of me. I thought something happened to one of my kids. But he explained what was happening with Dane. He asked me if I could verify where Dane was that weekend. If I remembered. Of course I could. Detective Ritter brought me here and here I am."

"Detective Ritter told you what to say."

"No, sir. We barely talked at all on the drive. All I've been asked to do is tell the truth, and I have."

Cutler paced in front of the lectern for a moment.

"I'm sorry," he said. "But I'm through with this witness."

Holly Logue left the stand. I wouldn't have time to talk to her. I could only hope that I'd done enough with her.

"Ms. Brent?" Judge Saul said.

I raised my chin and faced the judge. "Your Honor, I have nothing further. We rest."

33

I took a moment as I stood at the lectern and scanned the spectators in the gallery. George Luke was here. He sat just behind my table. Hojo sat beside him, comforting him. Quietly whispering to him what to expect. On the other side of Hojo sat Hayden Simmons. She had stayed mostly away for the last two days of trial. But today, she and her grandfather shared the same bench. Not side by side. Not yet. But it was something.

Erin Simmons sat with her mother, clutching her hand two rows behind Jamie Simmons. The divide between Hayden's side and Jamie's side had never seemed wider. Between them, in the ether somewhere, was Ellie Luke herself. I felt her today. More than I ever had since the moment this case came to me.

"Ladies and gentlemen," I started. "I thank you for your patience and attention over the last two weeks. I know you must be anxious to take control of this case. To fulfill the oath you all swore when you were seated on that jury.

"Two weeks of trial after twenty-two years. That's how long Ellie Luke has been waiting for justice. How long the story of the worst day of her life has taken to come out. And it was hiding in plain sight for all that time.

"This is my last chance to talk to you. To try to be Ellie Luke's voice. Soon that will be your role. To sift through the evidence you saw and decide the truth. And it's staring you in the face. It is irrefutable. It is logical. It is common sense.

"Twenty-two years ago, Ellie Luke was a bright, ambitious, caring woman who wanted to help people. Who brought comfort to the most vulnerable members of our community. Who would have dedicated her life to that pursuit. We are all less for having lost her. For having her taken away.

"And that is the evil that touched Ellie Luke. Because she befriended someone who wanted to take more from her than she was willing to give. So he did the next best thing. He took her away from the rest of us and kept her for himself.

"Here is what we know. And I want you to really hear me when I say that. What we know. We know that Ellie had tried to distance herself from Jamie Simmons. Her friends told you that. That he'd burned his way through their social group. Became too familiar. Crossed boundaries. Was always on the make. Ellie tried to be kind to him because that was her nature. And when she rebuffed him, when she could no longer tolerate his behavior, we know Jamie Simmons decided to take action.

"On March 12th, twenty-two years ago, Jamie leveraged his friendship with Ellie Luke. He knew her schedule. Knew the route she took home from Hattie Corning's house. So he waited. Slashed her tire. Just enough so that about a mile and a half from leaving Mrs. Corning's residence, Ellie had to pull over.

"We know that Ellie Luke left her vehicle of her own free will.

Because whoever stopped to help her was someone she didn't think to be afraid of. She knew Jamie Simmons.

"What happened immediately after that is something we will never know for sure. Did Jamie make advances? Was she afraid? I can't tell you that. But what we do know is chilling enough. Ellie Luke was beaten. Her skull was caved in. It was a violent death perpetrated by someone who wanted to snuff Ellie out.

"We know Jamie Simmons took her to the woods. He carried her through the deep underbrush. He laid her beneath a tree. Posed her. Crossed her hands over her chest as if she was in a casket. And then he spent time with her. He removed some of her clothing. Clipped a lock of her hair. Took an earring from her ear. Her underwear. Souvenirs. And for weeks. Months. Jamie Simmons was the only person on the planet who knew where Ellie Luke's body was.

"Think about that. Jamie had succeeded in taking what he'd been after all along. Ownership of Ellie Luke. In those seven months, from the time Ellie went missing to when she was found, Jamie owned her. He owned the knowledge of where she was. He taunted police and Ellie's own grieving family. He inserted himself into their lives.

"Let's talk about that for a moment. Jamie showed up on George Luke's doorstep pretending to be Ellie's friend. They'd never heard of him before. Ellie never talked to them about him. Never introduced him. But in their deep grief, Jamie took control. He'd done it before. Deena Landon told you that. This was his MO. He embedded himself in a vulnerable family and took over. To the Lukes he seemed like a welcome savior. Someone who loved Ellie. A connection to her. But it was a lie. George Luke has finally come to understand the manipulation. That he was being groomed.

"But it started long before Ellie died. You've seen the photographs Jamie took of Ellie when she wasn't aware. He invaded her privacy. It was all practice, like a gateway drug to what was to come."

I paused, displaying the photographs in Jamie Simmons's treasure box for the jury again. Ellie from a distance, sitting at a picnic table. Ellie in her car, adjusting her makeup in the rearview mirror. Ellie through her bedroom window in nothing but her underwear.

"But then Jamie Simmons found a way to have the real thing. Ellie was his doll. Something he collected. Treasured. And when that was finally taken from him, he realized he could have something else. The next best thing. He could have a replica of Ellie in the form of her living sister."

I put up the pictures of Ellie and Erin Luke side by side. Even I had to take a moment to make sure I knew which girl was which.

"Jamie Simmons collected souvenirs from Ellie's gravesite. From her person. Her earring. Her underwear. A lock of her hair. But then he encountered something else of Ellie's. Something more precious. An even bigger treasure. He took Ellie's sister, Erin, and collected her too."

The jury looked. Erin shrunk against her mother. Hayden cried silent tears. George Luke reached over Hojo's lap and clasped hands with his granddaughter.

"Jamie's lawyer is going to tell you how none of that is a crime. That Jamie Simmons's conduct after Ellie went missing didn't break the law. No. There was no crime in him marrying Erin Luke. Or manipulating the Luke family the way he did. The way he still is. Even now, his hold over Erin and Claudia Luke seems absolute. So much so they were willing to cut ties with their daughter and granddaughter over it.

"Hayden Simmons is a victim in this case, too. Another part of Ellie Luke that Jamie Simmons tried to collect. But she is brave. Powerful. And she did the right thing. Hayden Simmons had her eyes open. She saw what her father collected. How he encouraged the Luke family not to talk about Ellie. How he suppressed her memory to suit his own ends. But Hayden told you the truth. She found the thing her father had been hiding in that basement annex. She knew what it was. She showed courage in bringing it to the police and telling what she knew. Even though it cost her her relationship with her mother. Her grandmother. She could have stayed quiet. But she knew she was her Aunt Ellie's voice now too.

"No one but the person who killed Ellie Luke could have that earring she was wearing the morning she died. Agent Palmieri told you the lock of hair in that box matched the clipping taken from Ellie Luke's lifeless body. Only her killer could have that in his possession. Mr. Cutler is going to try to make you suspend logic. He's going to try to convince you that at worst, Jamie Simmons is disturbed. That being a creep isn't a crime.

"Don't believe him. Don't let him convince you to suspend your common sense. Jamie Simmons had those souvenirs from Ellie Luke's gravesite because he's the one who put her there. He's the one who killed her. And everything he's done since that day only proves the obsession that led him to kill.

"Mr. Cutler wants you to think someone else could have committed this crime. But there is no evidence of that. Dane Fischer had an alibi. There's a reason he was never arrested for this crime and Jamie Simmons was. Because Jamie Simmons was obsessed with Ellie Luke and decided to take her. He planned. He slashed her tire while she was inside Hattie Corning's house. He followed her until she had to pull over. He took her. He killed her. He hid her body. He posed her. Collected souvenirs from her. Then he went to her family and collected them, too.

"He wanted to own Ellie Luke. For twenty-two years, he has. Don't let him have her for another day. Jamie Simmons and only Jamie Simmons is guilty of the murder of Ellie Luke. It is logical, sensible, and beyond a reasonable doubt. Thank you."

Bennett Cutler was already on his feet. He waited until I'd taken my seat again before making his way to the lectern. Then he stood there for a moment. He had no notes in front of him, but he stared at the lectern, perhaps seeing his closing take shape in his mind. Finally, he lifted his chin and addressed the jury.

"It's a good story," he said. "Compelling. Could be a movie of the week for those of you old enough to remember those days. Only Ms. Brent can't prove any of it.

"No. That's not true. She did prove a couple of things. And I'll admit, they're upsetting. It might make you not like Jamie Simmons. That's okay. You're entitled to your opinions of him. Even if they're unfavorable. But none of that makes him a murderer.

"Let's just count down the things Ms. Brent could prove."

He stepped out from behind the lectern and silently counted on his fingers. Then he put his hands in his pocket.

"Honestly? She's proven that Jamie Simmons knew Ellie Luke. And that later he married Ellie's sister, Erin. Oh, and that Ellie and Erin look a lot alike. That's about it.

"Let's talk about the box, shall we? That's the Great Big Thing in this trial. The clickbait. The headline. Niece of murder victim finds grisly souvenir in her own basement. I mean, I'd pick up that book. Watch that movie.

"But here's the thing. Here's what Mara Brent has to prove. Premeditation. That the murder was planned in advance. Malice. That the murder was committed with the intention to kill. That the murder was committed by violent means.

"She can't even prove murder. We don't even know how Ellie died. The coroner just had a theory. The body was so decomposed a thorough autopsy couldn't be done. She had a fractured skull. Is it reasonable to assume she could have fallen? Tripped? Hit her head on a rock or the hard ground? We don't know. And because we don't know you are legally required to give the benefit of that doubt to Jamie Simmons.

"Malice. The intention to kill. There is not one shred of evidence that Jamie Simmons had a plan to kill Ellie Luke.

"Ms. Brent keeps telling you Jamie slashed Ellie's tire. That he lied in wait for her to get off work. Good theory. Only she has no proof of it. She's just making up a story. Nobody saw Jamie Simmons do any of that. There were no tire tracks other than Ellie's on the side of the road that night. Nothing.

"There was no DNA found at the scene where Ellie's body was discovered. No blood, skin, hair, or other tissue that could have connected Jamie Simmons or anyone else to the crime.

"Ms. Brent also likes her version of the story that Jamie Simmons wasn't well liked by his other classmates. Sure. Fine. Maybe that's true. But none of those witnesses bothered to mention it twenty-two years ago when their memories were fresher. When the police were actively trying to solve what they decided was murder. It wasn't important enough to Sabrina Wharton to bring it up in the two hours she was questioned by Detective Ritter twenty-two years ago.

"Ms. Brent wants to make something out of the Luke family's reticence to talk about Ellie after she was found dead. That's not a crime. It's not even abnormal. They were allowed to process their grief in the way they saw fit. How dare Mara Brent or anyone else try to judge them for that?

"But I digress. It's the box you're curious about. The mysterious box Ms. Brent claims is the bombshell in this case. That broke it wide open. Only she can't prove how that box got in Jamie Simmons's house. Everything you know about that comes from Hayden Simmons. Hayden Simmons. Ms. Brent wants to talk about obsession? Fine. Let's talk about it. Let's talk about the fact that it was Hayden Simmons who developed an unhealthy obsession with her aunt's disappearance. Hayden Simmons who spent up to ten hours a day doomscrolling an online forum filled with other people, strangers, who were equally obsessed with this tragedy.

"Hayden Simmons got popular online. She admitted she entered that forum under false pretenses. She didn't tell the other members who she was or how she was connected to Ellie Luke. She lured information out of them. She shaped a narrative based on it. She got attention. I submit to you that it's Hayden who is disturbed. Hayden who is obsessed. Hayden who has worked to destroy her family and poison them against her father.

"And yes. The box. What's in it? An earring? Underwear? Photographs. Photographs that show a very much alive Ellie Luke. Photographs that Ms. Brent never proved who took. We don't know. And it's not Jamie Simmons's job to prove that to you. It's not his job to prove anything. That's not how our system of justice works.

"George Luke, Ms. Brent's supposed star witness. A distraught, grieving father who has been put through hell for twenty-two years. George Luke admitted that his daughter's personal items were accessible to anyone and everyone for two years after she died. Her room was kept as Ellie left it. Her clothes. Her jewelry. Her earrings. Her undergarments. Even her hair brushes. All of it in that room. In a house where her friends gathered after her death. A house where contractors came in to complete a kitchen renovation. Where other family members stayed. Where Hayden Simmons herself stayed. In that very room. Ms. Brent has provided zero proof that any of the items in that box were actually taken from Ellie's dead body. Even if Jamie Simmons is the one who collected them, and that has by no means been proven, that's not a crime.

"And Holly Logue? I'm sorry. She has no credibility. This woman claimed to love Dane Fischer. Was willing to jeopardize her marriage for him. And she can't be bothered to give the man an alibi? I don't buy it. You shouldn't either. Holly Logue is the third lie Dane Fischer gave about his alibi. Don't be fooled. How convenient she just happens to show up here after twenty-two years. She's a liar. A prop."

Cutler walked back to the lectern.

"It's not a crime," he repeated, pounding his fist on the wood. "It's not a crime, ladies and gentlemen. Ms. Brent has done nothing more than peddle this family's grief to her own end. There's an election coming up. What a feather in her cap this would be. In Sheriff Cruz's cap too. The two people who got a hold of Hayden Simmons before anyone else did."

I vaulted to my feet. Judge Saul saw me and put a hand up. "Mr. Cutler," she said. "Please stick to the evidence. The jury should disregard Mr. Cutler's unsubstantiated conclusions about Ms. Brent's motivation."

Cutler laughed. "Sure. Of course. My mistake."

"Reasonable doubt," he went on. "There's no proof a murder was committed. No proof that the items in Hayden Simmons's infamous box were taken directly from Ellie's gravesite. No proof that Jamie Simmons was ever at that gravesite or abducted Ellie Luke from the side of the road. I, too, appreciate your time and attention. I don't envy your job. But I honor it. It would be a travesty of justice if you bought into the story Mara Brent is trying to sell. It isn't supported by the facts. The provable facts. I ask that you render a verdict of not guilty and allow this poor family to heal. Thank you."

I was still on my feet. Erin and Claudia Luke were in near hysterics. Jamie Simmons sat rigid, a stoic expression on his face. I turned to Hayden. Hojo had moved down one seat. George had his arms wrapped around his granddaughter, hugging her. And she had finally let him.

34

Gus and Sam waited for me after I gathered my things and walked out into the hallway. George Luke and Hayden left during jury instructions. As I closed the courtroom door behind me, Erin Simmons and Claudia Luke emerged from a side hallway. It was unexpected. No one was with them. They had turned away any help from the victim advocacy groups.

I practically ran straight into Erin. She took a step back. She'd been crying. Her eyes were puffy, the left one almost swollen shut.

"Excuse me," I said. I took a step back, wanting to give her room to pass me.

"Mom?"

Hayden Simmons came out of the bathroom. Time seemed to freeze. Claudia put her hands on her daughter's shoulders and tried to pull her back.

George Luke emerged from the men's room. His face dropped

when he saw his wife and daughter in range of his granddaughter.

"How could you do this?" Erin shouted to Hayden. "How could you do this?"

Erin broke free of Claudia's grasp and lunged at Hayden. I reacted. Dropping the files, I clutched to my chest. I stepped in between Erin and Hayden.

"Stop," I said. "Just stop. Just turn around and take the stairs."

Gus and Sam were there.

"She's a liar!" Erin screamed. "She has no idea what she's done!"

"Mom," Hayden calmly said. "I'm not a liar. Dad's the liar. He's made you believe things about me that aren't true. He killed Aunt Ellie. Someday you're going to have to accept that."

"Claudia," George said, his tone sharp and loud. "This needs to end. The two of you need to wake up. We've caused enough damage. What we've done ... what we've put Hayden through ..."

Erin let out a guttural scream. She drew her arm back and tried to claw at Hayden through me.

Sam moved with the speed of a freight train. He grabbed Erin's wrist and pulled her out of range. Two deputies stepped forward to help disperse the melee. Gus had his hand on my shoulder. He pulled me away from Hayden.

"She's ruined our lives!" Claudia yelled. "And you're all part of this. Every one of you. You should be ashamed of yourself!" She pointed at Gus.

From the corner of my eye, I saw two local news reporters. They'd pulled out their phones and were recording everything.

"I'm going to let you go," Sam said to Erin through gritted teeth. "But I need you to go down those stairs and get yourself home. My deputies will escort you."

"Mrs. Luke," one of the reporters said. "Do you still believe your son-in-law is innocent? How can you explain the box of things he collected from your daughter's gravesite?"

"No," Claudia shouted. "No. To hell with all you!"

My heart shredded. The hurt look on Hayden's face cut through me. This was her mother. Her grandmother. Jamie still had them believing she was responsible for all of this.

"Come on," George said, putting his arm around his granddaughter. "Let's get you out of here."

"No," Hayden said, shrugging him off. "No. Answer her question, Grandma? I want to hear you say it. Tell them what you think happened. Say it!"

Tears rolled down Claudia's face. She shook her head. Sam let go of Erin. She ran to her mother.

"Go home," Sam told them. He nodded to his two deputies. One of them quietly directed Claudia Luke toward the stairs. Mercifully, she didn't put up a fight. Erin followed her and the two of them disappeared through the stairwell door. Sam blocked one of the reporter's way when she tried to follow.

Four more courthouse deputies appeared.

"Listen up!" Sam said to the reporters. "You're going to let this family go home. I can't stop you from doing your jobs, but I can stop you from harassing these people in this building. Show some common decency, please."

"This is news!" I recognized the young reporter as Chanelle West. She was new to the northwest Ohio area. God, she barely looked older than Will.

"Maybe it is," Sam said. "But I meant what I said."

"Come on," I said to Hayden. "You can come with me. Both of you."

Reluctantly, Hayden followed me to the elevator. George came with her. The three of us were able to ride downstairs alone. Gus kept anyone else from jumping on after us.

When we got to the first floor, I took Hayden and George out through an employee exit. We got lucky. No other reporters were lying in wait.

"This is going to get worse," George said.

"Maybe," I said. "We can go back to my office if you'd like. If you have questions …"

"No," Hayden said. "I just want to get out of here. I don't want to see this building any longer than I have to."

"How long do you think it will take?" George asked. "Before they decide."

"I don't know," I answered. "I won't even guess. But are you going to be all right? Are you still in the house with Mrs. Luke?"

"No," he said. "She wanted me to leave. I'm staying with an old friend until we can all figure out what to do."

"What about you?" I asked Hayden.

"I've still got the apartment the Silver Angels helped me find," she said. "But when this is over, I'm not staying in Waynetown. A friend of mine from high school moved to Pasadena a year ago. She's offered to let me come stay with her for a while."

"Oh honey," George said. "That's so far away."

"That's the point," Hayden said, her tone flat.

"Is there anything I can do for either one of you?" I asked.

Hayden shook her head. "No. You've done enough. Will you let me know the minute you hear anything from the judge?"

"Of course. That goes for you too, Mr. Luke. All of it."

He nodded. But he looked so broken. It had to feel to him like he'd lost everything. Both of his daughters. His wife. Now Hayden's news that might have seemed like abandonment to him. But they were right. There was really nothing else I could do for this family. As long as Jamie Simmons still had a hold on them, things would never be all right for them.

I went to my car and watched the two of them go their separate ways. I couldn't stop myself from wondering how many more victims Jamie Simmons would claim. No matter what the jury decided.

35

After four hours of deliberation, the jury hadn't reached a verdict by the end of business that Friday. They asked the judge for permission to deliberate over the weekend. By Saturday dinner, I'd still heard nothing.

Will stood at the kitchen counter stirring a pot of chili he'd made. It was a recipe he'd learned in a life skills class he was taking. It smelled delicious. Every time Sam or I tried to see if he needed help, Will kicked us out. We'd been relegated to the living room.

"He smacked your hand away too?" I asked Sam, smiling.

"More of a body block," Sam answered. "In six more months, that boy's going to be taller than me."

No small feat. Sam stood just over six feet. I resisted the urge to say Will got his height from his father. Sam harbored no jealousy, but it had taken me a long time to reclaim my life after Jason tried to destroy it. I would not give him purchase in it again.

"Mara," he said. "You're gonna have to stop looking at your phone."

I hadn't even realized I'd been holding it. I kept checking for texts from Judge Saul's clerk.

"They said they wanted to go until noon today," I said. "It's almost five. They've been at it for ten hours. How could it take ten hours?"

He sat down beside me. "And you're the last person I have to tell how juries work."

"It means they weren't unanimous when they took their initial vote. It means some of them think he's innocent."

"Or it means only one person thinks he's innocent and the other eleven have common sense. Or something else."

"Ugh. You're right. I don't know why I'm torturing myself with this one. I've never done this before during deliberations. I always think my job is over after the panel is sequestered."

"It is." Sam leaned over to kiss me. It felt good to have him here. He'd been spending most weekends at my place lately. We'd gone slow, letting Will adjust to having him as a permanent fixture in his life. Now, my son was out there making dinner for all of us.

But there was something bothering Sam. Over the last months, I'd gotten used to his noises, his facial expressions. Right now, he had a crease between his eyes. I knew it meant he had something else on his mind.

"What is it?" I asked. He was getting used to my noises, tones, and facial expressions, too. He knew I wouldn't be brushed off.

"I've been meaning to ask you," he said. "Something Cutler said in his closing. That bit about you using this case as leverage to run for prosecutor."

I looked over Sam's shoulder. Will opened the oven. He'd asked me to pick up some garlic bread. He busied himself basting butter over the top of it as it baked.

"What do you want to ask me?"

Sam shifted so he was facing me. "When were you going to tell me you decided to run?"

"I haven't. That's the thing. That's what's been bothering me about it. I had one conversation with Kenya. The crux of that was me trying to bully her into coming back. I probably shouldn't tell you this. But she's going to. She just wanted to be sure I didn't want it."

"Wow," he said. "That's ... wow. She's coming back?"

"I'm pretty sure. She admitted her lost weekend needs to be over. We need her back in the game."

"Hmm. Well, that's interesting. And encouraging. But you didn't really answer me. And so I'm clear. It's not that you need my permission to make a choice like that."

"Don't I?" I said, quicker than I meant. A stab of fear went through me.

Sam took my hands in his and brought them to his lips. "That came out wrong. What I meant to say ... you know you would have had my support. Whatever you decided to do."

"Sam ... we've talked about this plenty. Me as prosecutor and you as sheriff. It could cause issues for you. That was absolutely part of my thought process."

The crease between his eyes softened. "I'm glad. Because ..." He looked over his shoulder. Will had a pair of earbuds in as he stirred his chili. My stomach growled.

"Sam, there's another issue with what Cutler said. I told you. I've discussed running for prosecutor with very few people. You. Kenya. Caro and Hojo. And those last two really briefly. Mostly trying to gauge if Hojo really didn't want it. Cutler got his information from somewhere."

"Or he didn't," Sam said. "He just took a wild guess and said it to rattle you. And it did. Here we are talking about it."

"And I *have* made a decision," I said. "I mean it. I want to stay where I am."

"You're sure?"

"I'm sure."

"Mara, I just don't like the idea that it was because of me."

I took a breath. Sam met my eyes. I thought of everything we'd been through in the last few months. He'd been a solid source of support. Never putting more pressure on me even though part of my job had added more stress to Gus. And there was Will. Somehow, Sam had found a balance with him. Not a replacement father. But a mentor. Someone Will knew he could trust.

"Yes," I said. "Part of my decision was because of you. I've been honest about that."

"Mara ..."

"Let me finish. It's important what we do. The county needs you. You're my sheriff too. I've seen good ones. I've seen lousy ones. I know how bad lousy ones can be. I think you're heading toward being a great one. That matters to me. You matter to me."

"You matter to me, too."

"And I liked what you said. As much as the county needs a good sheriff, they need someone good at that prosecutor's table, too. I think that's me. I think I can do more good where I am than dealing with union contracts and the county commissioners and all the administrative stuff that comes with Kenya's job. And it's not like it pays all that much more than what I'm doing now. So, Kenya's going to run. She'll win. And we'll get the band back together the way it was."

He smiled. "As long as it's really what you want."

"It is."

"Sam, will you just do it already?" Will shouted. He was way too loud on account of his earbuds. I gestured toward my own ears. Will pulled one out.

"Did you do it?" he asked Sam.

Sam's face lost a little color. "Uh ... we were kind of talking about something else."

"You want me to go back to the kitchen until you're done?" Will asked. "It'll be okay. She's gonna say yes."

I felt a jolt of adrenaline. What had the two of them been plotting?

I looked back at Sam. He'd subtly shifted his posture. He had one leg on the couch and the other slid down so he rested on his knee.

His knee. He was positioning himself down on one knee.

"Sam ..." I said.

Will's face dropped. "Oh. Sorry. My bad." He quickly turned and went back to the kitchen.

"Well," he said. "You can see I've got a bit of a co-conspirator. Maybe that's okay. Maybe that's perfect, actually."

"Just ... say it," I said, my heart thudding. I hadn't anticipated it. Hadn't really let the idea of it truly enter my mind.

"Mara," Sam started. "I love you. We were friends for a long time before this. I've known you for what, ten years?"

"Something like that."

"I'm not good at grand gestures. But if you ..."

Sam's phone rang. A second later, mine started to ring. Both of them sat on the coffee table next to us. We froze. I could see the caller ID on Sam's. It was Gus. The caller ID on mine was Hojo.

"The jury?" Sam said.

I shook my head. "It wouldn't be Hojo."

We both reached for our phones, fueled by the same concern. We answered in unison.

"Hello?" I said. I kept my gaze locked with Sam's as Gus told him the same news I was getting from Hojo.

"Mara," he said. "I've just gotten a call from Deputy Jaffee. He's over at County Hospital. Claudia Luke called 9-1-1. She found Erin Simmons unresponsive on her living room floor. It looks like she tried to take her own life. They're treating her now. But it doesn't look good."

"Dammit," Sam said as he nodded then hung up his call with Gus.

"We're on our way," I said. "Has anyone gotten a hold of Hayden or George Luke?"

"Working on it now," Hojo answered. I thanked him and clicked off the call.

"Come on," Sam said. "I'll drive. Will? Just keep the chili warm."

36

"He can't make decisions for her."

When Sam and I walked up to bed 8 in the ICU, George Luke was standing outside talking to a hospital employee.

"George?" I said. He turned to me, eyes red.

"Mara," he said, relief flooding through him. "Maybe you can explain."

"Anything I can do to help," I said. I read the employee's name badge. Emily Lansing. She was a social worker.

"I'm just trying to clear up who Ms. Luke's patient advocate is," she says. "Her husband is listed as next of kin."

"Her husband is in prison for killing my other daughter," George said, exasperated. "There's me. I'm her father. Anything you need me to sign, I'll sign."

"I'm Mara Brent," I said. "I'm an assistant prosecutor."

"Sheriff Cruz," Sam said.

"Oh dear," poor Emily Lansing said. "You didn't happen to bring the probate judge with you, did you?"

"No," I said. "But if you need some sort of court order, I can help Mr. Luke get that going."

"No," Emily said. "Of course not. We'll go with what we have. I'm sorry. Please let me know if you need anything."

Emily left to deal with another patient. George looked ready to fall over. I grabbed his elbow and led him to a row of chairs further down the hallway. Sam and I flanked him in the adjoining chairs.

"What happened?" I asked. "How is she?"

George shook his head. "She swallowed pills. Antidepressants, we think. A whole mess of them. She won't wake up. My God. I'm going to lose her. I'm going to lose my other baby."

"What are the doctors saying?" Sam asked.

"They don't know. They pumped her stomach. She was unresponsive when Claudia found her. Erin's next-door neighbor's an EMT. Thank God he'd just got home from work. Claudia got him in there right away. He started CPR. But they don't know anything. Something about lack of oxygen to the brain. They don't know how long she was deprived of it yet."

"Where's Claudia now?" I asked.

"They had to sedate her. She was out of her mind. Took a swing at one of the deputies when they showed up. Hayden's here with her. On another floor. She's coming back up here as soon as she gets Claudia sorted out. One of Claudia's cousins is on the way."

"Is there anything we can do?" Sam asked. "I'll talk to the deputies. Don't worry about Claudia as long as nobody was hurt. Let me go see what I can find out."

I clutched Sam's hand for a second as he got up. He gave an unspoken reassurance with his eyes as he headed back down the hall.

"He did this," George said. "Jamie's responsible for this, too. I tried to reason with them. Erin and Claudia have shut me out. That monster has jammed himself too far into her head. Erin lost her mind. I don't know how we get past all of this. Maybe we never can. And if they let him out? God. I don't know what to do."

"You're doing it," I said. "You're here for Erin. For your wife. And Hayden."

As soon as I said it, the elevator doors opened. Hayden walked through. Her face fell when she saw her grandfather slumped forward as he was in his chair.

"Is she dead?" Hayden asked.

"No," George reassured her. "She's still alive, honey. We just don't know how much damage she did to her brain yet."

"How's your grandmother?" I asked.

"They're not admitting her. They calmed her down."

"Did her cousin Carol get here?" George asked.

"She's with her now," Hayden said. "Let me text her. Let her know Mom's stable for the time being."

Hayden pulled out her phone and shot off her text. Then she sat in the chair Sam vacated and put her arms around her grandfather.

"You can't leave me now, baby," George said. "Promise me you'll stay for a while."

"I'm here now," Hayden said. "We're just gonna do this one minute at a time, okay? Grandma's better. She actually let me hug her. She thinks this is all her fault."

"Why?" I asked.

"She said she told my mom she was going to cook her dinner. She was running late. She thinks if she'd gotten there a half an hour earlier like she was planning, this wouldn't have happened."

Lord, I thought, trying to wrap my head around it all. Erin took a bottle of pills, knowing her mother would be the one to find her. The wounds of this family grew ever deeper.

"It's not her fault," George said. "It's Jamie's fault. Don't you ever forget that."

"I never will," Hayden said, with an edge to her voice. Of all of them, Hayden had been the only one who'd seen her father with clear eyes the moment she understood what he'd done. George Luke had been right next to Claudia and Erin against Hayden until only recently. But to her credit, Hayden seemed to have forgiven all of them. She was here today. She was holding them all together. I hoped she made good on her plans to leave. Get a fresh start. Her best hope at surviving any of this with her mental health intact would be to set hard boundaries with each one of them.

"Mara," she said. "There were a couple of deputies down there with my grandma. She assaulted one of them when they tried to ask her questions. I mean, she didn't hurt him. But ..."

"It's going to be okay," I said. "Sheriff Cruz is already taking care of it."

"Thank you. I don't condone what she did. It's just ... it's all just a mess."

"Mr. Luke?" A young doctor appeared. He held a tablet. "You're George Luke?"

George shot to his feet. Hayden rose with him and they linked hands.

"Is she okay? Is Erin going to be okay?" George asked.

"I'm her daughter," Hayden said. "Please. Whatever you can tell us."

"Erin's starting to come around. She's still got a tube down her throat so she isn't going to be able to talk yet. But she's starting to respond to simple commands. That's good. That's very encouraging. It'll be a little while before we know exactly how much ... or if any ... damage was done. We just don't know how long her brain was deprived of oxygen. But I'm optimistic. She's going to need time."

"Can we see her?" Hayden asked.

"One at a time," the doctor said. "And just for a few minutes. If she seems upset, I'm going to ask you to leave."

"Of course," Hayden said.

"You go," George said to Hayden. "Then if you think she'd be okay with seeing me, I'll go."

"I'll take you in," the doctor said.

Hayden kissed her grandfather on the cheek and followed the doctor back down the hall.

"Thank you for coming so quickly," George said to me. "I didn't know you would."

"I had to make sure you were okay," I said. "That you had someone with you."

"I'm okay." He smiled. "I'll be even more okay if you can tell me I don't have to worry about Jamie ever getting near us again."

"As soon as I know something about that, I'll tell you. I promise."

My phone buzzed with a text. I checked the screen. It was Sam.

"Can you meet me on the first floor? Claudia's heading back up. She wants to see Erin."

I showed the text to George. "I think maybe I shouldn't be here when she gets here," I said. "I don't want to further upset her. I know I'm not Claudia's favorite person."

George nodded. "I'm sorry. Maybe that would be best. I'm not her favorite person right now either, but she's not going to keep me from seeing Erin."

"Okay," I said. "You have my number. You let me know if there's anything else I can do."

"That goes both ways," he said.

I leaned in and hugged George Luke. He felt so fragile. Like if I'd squeezed too hard, he would shatter. He would need to be stronger than ever now.

"We'll be in touch," I said.

I left him and took the stairs, hoping to avoid running into Claudia. Sam waited for me in the first-floor lobby. He was talking to one of his deputies. As I approached, he left Sam's side so we could talk in private.

"How is she?" Sam asked. I explained what the doctor said.

"That sounds good," he said. "Let's hope this is the tail end of the drama. Claudia really walloped Deputy Jaffee. I hope I won't regret it, but we're not going to press charges."

"I don't even know what to think," I said. "Hayden says Erin knew Claudia was on her way over. She knew her mother would be the one to find her. I can't even fathom it."

"Something happened," Sam said. "Jaffee told me Erin's house was torn up. Like at first, they thought there'd been a burglary. All the dishes in the kitchen were thrown on the floor and smashed. The couch cushions in the living room were slashed and the stuffing covered the ground like snow."

Sam took his phone and opened a picture text he'd received. Three images popped up. Two of a kitchen like he'd described. Plates, glassware, and a coffee pot were shattered all over the place. The living room had been ransacked.

"What in God's name?" I asked.

"She had some kind of psychotic break, maybe," Sam said. "The whole thing just finally got to her. I don't know. But you said the doc thinks she'll pull through?"

"Probably. But it's going to be a long road to recovery. And if Jamie gets acquitted ... Sam ... I just don't even know what to think."

"Is there anything else you need to do here?" he asked.

"I don't think so. George has my number. So does Hayden. They know to reach out if I can help."

"Yeah. Same here. Come on. Let's head back. Will's got to be wondering what's taking us so long."

My stomach answered for me. I hadn't eaten since breakfast. "I'm looking forward to that chili," I said.

"Me too," Sam agreed. "The kid might have a knack in the kitchen. I was watching him. I mean, until he kicked me out."

I laughed. Sam looped his arm around me and we headed out to the parking lot.

I got as far as the ambulance bay before my phone went off again. I pulled it out, then froze mid step.

"Mara?"

"We have to call Will," I said. "The chili will have to wait."

"What?"

I turned my phone screen so Sam could see it. It was from Judge Saul's clerk. The jury was in. She wanted us assembled within the hour.

37

"Has he been told?" Hojo whispered to me. He raced into the courtroom on my heels. He was still tying his tie. A group of reporters set up along the back wall.

A moment later, the deputies led Jamie Simmons in. He wore a suit, but his hair was wet as if he'd just been pulled out of the shower before transport. Bennett Cutler was already at the defense table. Simmons leaned over and whispered something to Cutler. Then Simmons scanned the back of the courtroom.

Claudia Luke and Erin Simmons were obviously not present.

"I don't know," I said. Cutler straightened, then turned toward me, scowling. He whispered something back to Simmons then walked over to me.

"My client wants to know what you know about his wife's condition," he said. "What happened? The sheriff has been less than forthcoming."

"I don't have all the answers," I said. "But Erin made a suicide attempt. She swallowed a lot of pills. She's improving, but when

I left the hospital, she was starting to give limited responses to stimuli. That's a good sign."

"You were with her? Who else was there?"

"Her daughter, her father. There was ..."

Cutler's attention went to the courtroom doors. George and Hayden walked in together. Cutler frowned at me and charged over to them.

"On it," Hojo said. He got to George and Hayden before Cutler did.

There were harsh whispers. "Unauthorized!" I heard Cutler say.

"All rise!"

Judge Saul took the bench. Cutler was still trying to harass George and Hayden. Hojo physically pushed him back. Every reporter in the room took note of it.

"Mr. Cutler?" Judge Saul said. "Is there some sort of problem?"

Cutler shook his head and he stormed back to the table. "Your Honor, it's come to my attention that my client's wife is being harassed by members of her family against her wishes. Against Mr. Simmons's wishes. She is incapacitated in the hospital. But Mr. Simmons still holds her medical power of attorney. He's still her next of kin. While I know this is unusual, I'd like to move for a restraining order against them."

Judge Saul barely looked up from her notes. "And I know you're aware those aren't issues I have jurisdiction over. I'm sorry to hear about Mr. Simmons's wife. I wish her nothing but a full recovery. But those are matters you'll have to take up with the probate court. Are we ready to proceed with the matter at hand?"

"We are, Your Honor," I said.

George and Hayden moved into the row behind me. George had his arm tightly around his granddaughter.

"I demand to know what these people have been telling my wife!" Simmons shouted. Judge Saul looked up, startled. It shocked me too. Simmons was about to hear whether he'd been convicted of aggravated murder. He was worried about what George and Hayden were telling Erin? He didn't ask about her condition.

"Enough, Mr. Simmons. Mr. Cutler. Can you control your client? The verdict can be read in his absence, if not."

Cutler gripped Jamie Simmons's arm. Simmons gritted his teeth, but kept quiet.

"We're ready, Your Honor," Cutler said.

"All right. Bailiff, can you please bring in the jury?"

The side door next to the jury box opened. Each member of the panel filed in. Most of them looked at Simmons as they made their way to their seats.

I felt a tap on my arm. Sam was there. "She's awake," he whispered. "I've got a deputy with her now. She asked for it."

"What's going on?" I mouthed.

"Mr. Foreman," Judge Saul called out. "Have you reached a verdict in this matter?"

"We have, Your Honor," the foreman said. It was juror number seven. The retired plumber Hojo thought hated Dane Fischer.

Judge Saul's clerk walked over to the foreman and took the verdict form from him. She brought it up to the judge. Vivian Saul slid her readers up her nose and read the form. She folded the paper and handed it back to the clerk.

I'd known the clerk for a long time. Janine Bosko was famous for her stoicism. You simply could not read the woman's face as she held countless defendants' lives in her hands before she read out their verdicts.

"Is your verdict unanimous?" Judge Saul asked the foreman.

"It is," he answered.

"Read it into the record, please," Judge Saul instructed Janine.

Janine brought a fist to her mouth and coughed into it. Then she unfolded the paper and lowered the microphone to her level.

"We, the jury in the state of Ohio versus James Baldwin Simmons, Case No. G-83010-CR-23109, on Count One of the complaint find the defendant not guilty of aggravated murder."

I didn't dare breathe as Janine read the verdict on the second charge.

"On Count Two of the complaint, we, the jury find the defendant James Baldwin Simmons guilty of murder."

A rush of heat went through me, settling in my feet. For a moment, it felt like my legs didn't work. I gripped the table. Hojo grabbed my arm and shook it. Behind me, Sam put a hand on my back.

"Oh God," Hayden whispered. From my peripheral vision, I saw George Luke sink to the bench. Sam leaned over and whispered in George's ear. They didn't understand what they heard.

Murder. I hadn't proved premeditation. But he was guilty of murder. It meant he would still be in prison for the rest of his life. I would see to it.

"What did she say?!" Simmons shouted. "You tell me. Right now. What did Erin say?!"

"Mr. Simmons, I'm warning you," Judge Saul said. "You will be silent or you will be removed. Ms. Bosko, please continue."

There were other counts. Kidnapping. Abuse of a corpse. Obstruction of justice. One by one, Janine read the jury's decision.

Guilty. Guilty. Guilty.

"Mr. Foreman," Saul said. "Is this verdict unanimous?"

"It is, Your Honor," Juror number seven answered.

I couldn't take my eyes off Simmons. He glared at George Luke and his own daughter. Cold hatred in his eyes. Only it didn't seem to be about the verdict itself. Instead, he was more concerned about whatever he thought his wife might have said to them, or vice versa.

"All right," Judge Saul said. "The jury is discharged for now with this court's gratitude. Deputy Stryker, can I trust that you'll ensure the members will be escorted safely to their cars?"

"Yes, Your Honor," Stryker answered.

"This case has garnered significant media attention," Judge Saul continued. "You may be asked for interviews when you leave this building. Whether you choose to grant them is entirely up to you. Counsel, we will reconvene for sentencing in one week. Mr. Simmons is remanded back into the custody of the Maumee County Sheriff. We stand adjourned."

She banged her gavel. Two deputies stepped forward.

"You stay away from her," Simmons shouted. "You hear me? She doesn't need you. She knows who you are."

Hayden was closest to the aisle. George hadn't picked himself up off the bench yet. But as Jamie Simmons passed by his daughter, he spit at her. In full view of the retreating jury.

Sam sprang into action. He got between Hayden and her father. The deputies jerked him forward away from her. Hayden didn't move. She kept her back straight as they led her father out. When the door closed behind him, she finally sank next to her grandfather and wept.

38

Two hours later, I sat in Sam's office. Numb. Spent. But Jamie Simmons was probably going to prison for the rest of his life. The not guilty verdict on aggravated murder only meant that he would not face the death penalty. He would technically be eligible for parole depending on how Judge Saul sentenced him. But he would likely never get past a parole board.

"Are you okay?" Sam asked. "You haven't said much."

"I don't know how to feel. Happy? That doesn't seem right."

Sam came around his desk. He perched himself on the edge of it so he was right in front of me, our knees touching.

"Nobody else could have done what you did," he said. "Not even Kenya in her prime as a litigator. This case was tough. It could have gone the other way."

"Now you tell me that?" I said.

"Yep." Sam leaned forward and kissed me. "I'm proud of you. I hope it's okay for me to say that."

"Of course. And I get it. You saw me at my worst during this thing."

Sam smiled. "You think that was your worst? Woman, you're nuts. Come here."

He pulled me forward, so I stood between his knees. He was warm and strong, his arms completely enveloping me.

"It's been a long few months," I said. "I'm looking forward to things getting back to normal."

My phone buzzed. I'd set it on Sam's desk. I caught it before the thing vibrated itself off the edge.

"It's Kenya," I said, smiling. I showed Sam the screen.

"Great job," she texted. "Remind me to take credit for your success when I get my old office back in January."

"She's really running!" Sam said. "Thank God!" Then he grew quiet.

"Mara," he said. "You're absolutely sure you don't want the job?"

"Yes," I said. There was something else between us. A question he'd almost asked me before everything blew up. I could see it in his eyes now.

"Not here," he whispered.

I was about to tell him I wouldn't mind. But Sam looked up. Gus stood in the doorway, looking even more grave than usual.

"Gus!" I gushed. This case had driven a wedge between us. Taken us both to the edge. I didn't care about any of that now. I walked out of Sam's embrace and threw my arms around Gus.

He went rigid, but didn't pull away. "We did it," I whispered, then kissed him on the cheek.

"Have a seat," Sam said. "Close the door."

Gus was like a zombie. He took a seat on the couch along the wall. Sam reached into his desk and pulled out a bottle of bourbon he secretly kept there. He was off duty now. So was Gus. So were we all.

He poured three glasses and handed one to Gus. Gus took it, but didn't meet his eyes.

"Come on," Sam said. "You can be satisfied now. It's over, Gus."

"Yeah," Gus said, taking a slow sip of bourbon. I joined him, but truly hated the stuff. Gus finished his, then put his glass on the table beside him. He reached into his jacket pocket and pulled out an envelope.

"It's good that you're here too," Gus said. "It'll save me the trip over to your office."

Sam frowned as he took the envelope. He tore it open and read the piece of paper inside of it. It only deepened his frown. Sam handed it to me.

I read quickly, not really believing what I was seeing. It was a resignation letter.

"Gus," I started.

"Nice try," Sam said. I handed him back the letter. "But I don't accept this. You're not leaving me, buddy. Not like this."

"I've been eligible to retire for two years," Gus said. "It's time."

"Nope," Sam said. "I'll tell you when it's time. For months now, I've watched you carry the weight of this thing. Blaming yourself. And I've given you space to do it. Enough. The bad guy's going to jail. Ellie Luke can rest in peace."

"Peace?" Gus said. "I've ruined that family."

"Jamie Simmons ruined that family," I said. "You keep wanting to forget that. He killed Ellie. He wormed his way into the Luke family. Brainwashed them. And don't you dare start talking about Dane Fischer. He was innocent of this. But he wasn't innocent *in* this. He gave you every reason to think he was guilty. If I had been around twenty-two years ago, I would have thought he did this too. As for the Lukes, God ... you know ... I should take my own advice. I've been sitting here feeling so guilty about what they've gone through. But it's Jamie. Let's not forget who the villain is. It isn't you, Gus. So forget it. I don't accept your resignation either. And Kenya's coming back. She told me. She'll kill you before she lets you bail on her."

Gus buried his face in his hands. Sam and I went to him, each of us putting our arms around our dear friend. He let us.

"Sheriff?" Deputy Jaffee stood in the doorway, unsure of whether he should come in. Gus immediately straightened.

"What's the word, Nick?" Sam asked.

Deputy Jaffee had been the one to interview Erin Simmons at her request. I'd almost forgotten about it.

"I've got Erin Simmons's statement," he said. "I wanted to come straight here. Detective Ritter, I was actually looking for you."

Gus's face changed. Whatever emotions he'd been having melted away. He was all business.

"Mrs. Simmons's house was torn up," Jaffee said.

"We heard that," I said. "That it looked ransacked."

"It was," he said. "By Mrs. Simmons. She kinda lost her mind. But she said she found something taped under one of the register grates on the floor."

"The house was searched," Sam said. "After Jamie was arrested."

"It was hidden pretty good," Jaffee said. "Wasn't something you could have seen if you didn't know it was there."

"How did *she*?" Gus asked.

Jaffee pulled his phone out of his pocket. "She said she saw her husband messing around with this particular grate a few times. She didn't think much of it. I don't know what made her look there yesterday. I suppose that part doesn't matter. But she found something. She took pictures of it on her phone. The paramedics brought her purse when they loaded her into the ambulance. She had some pill bottles in it. They always think that might help the doctors ..."

"Jaffee, what is it?" Gus said, impatient.

"Right," Jaffee said. "I took some pictures of what she showed me with my own phone. You're gonna want to send a crew out to collect it. She said she put it back under the grate. As you can imagine, it shook her up pretty good. I think this is why she tried to take her own life."

Gus took Jaffee's phone. Sam and I crowded over his shoulder to see. They were pictures of pictures of pictures. Erin Simmons had carefully documented seven Polaroid pictures on her phone.

"My God," Sam whispered. Gus's hand shook. I grabbed Jaffee's phone from him before he dropped it. I scrolled each image.

It was Ellie Luke. She lay in a pile of leaves, her head at an unnatural angle, eyes open, staring vacantly at the spring sky. She was dead. Blood poured down one side of her face. Her hair was caked with it. I knew she would have had a massive head wound on the back of her skull.

The next image had been taken further away, so you could see the full length of her body. She was partially clothed, her pants off.

In the next image, she'd been moved and leaned against the base of the tree where I knew she was later found. She was wearing both earrings in this one, blood caking the one in her right ear. Another image showed her driver's license. It had been in her purse that the police had never found.

"The rest of his souvenirs," Sam whispered. "Christ, what a monster."

"It broke her," I said. "When Erin Luke finally saw these, it broke her. She knows what Jamie is. She knows what he really did. That poor, poor woman."

"Thank you, Jaffee," Gus said. "I'll get over to Simmons's house right away. Make sure the scene is secured. There could be more. We're going to have to go over it again. It's going to be a long night."

For now, though, Gus rose. Squared his shoulders. His expression hardened. His duty to Ellie Luke was not yet done. But I, for one, felt grateful that Detective Ritter was going back to work.

39

One week later, I stood in a courtroom with Jamie Simmons one last time. But for the first time, Ellie Luke's family spoke for her. And they were united.

"I know what he wants me to be," Hayden said. "He wanted me to be like one of those awful things he collected in that box. A souvenir. Something to own. Possess. I cannot begin to describe how that feels. How evil and manipulative Jamie Simmons is. He turned my family against me when I spoke the truth. They understand what he is now, but I can't say things could ever be the same.

"I know it may not mean anything. Not legally. But we're in a courtroom. And people are watching. Those reporters are going to write about what happened here today. So I want to make this as plain as I can. Jamie Simmons, you are not my father. You are nothing to me. And you will never see me again.

"It's a strange thing. You took away my chance to ever know my Aunt Ellie. But I know at the same time, if those terrible events hadn't taken place, I wouldn't be here. For a long time, that has haunted me. Made me feel like an abomination. Lately, I've started to feel differently about it. Therapy has helped. I still have a long way to go. But now, I think I'm not what you thought I was. Instead, I think I was put on this earth to do exactly what I did. Expose who you really are. A monster. A killer. An abuser and manipulator. Worthless. I think Aunt Ellie moved through me. And that makes me proud. Makes me feel close to her. I am not your twisted souvenir. I am the instrument of justice for Ellie. And I hope you rot in hell where you belong."

She didn't cry. Hayden held her head up and looked straight at Jamie the whole time. It was subtle. Had I not been looking at him at that exact moment, I would have missed it. But as his daughter condemned him to hell, Jamie Simmons flinched.

Claudia couldn't bring herself to take the stand. But George did. He spoke again about the person Ellie was. Her hopes and dreams. His pride for her. It was twenty-two years of suppressed grief. Of things Jamie had conditioned the family not to speak of. It all came flooding out that day. And I knew that the Luke family at least had a chance to heal now.

Finally, Erin took the stand. It was an eerie thing. She had Ellie's face. It almost seemed like Ellie herself had risen up to speak against Jamie. But Erin told her story plainly.

"You made me believe you loved me," she said. "Maybe you did in your sick way. But I know now what you are. What you did. You thought you owned Ellie. Made her yours by taking her from us. Hiding her away. Hurting me. Turning me against my daughter. But you didn't win. Ellie did. Do you hear me? Ellie won."

She showed the photographs she found hidden in the home. The ones that provided incontrovertible proof of what Jamie had done to Ellie. Each photograph was another hammer blow. Even Cutler knew they would make any meaningful chance at overturning the verdict on appeal impossible.

For once, Jamie Simmons's smug expression vanished. In its place, I saw true fear.

Judge Saul handed down his sentence. He would serve his prison terms for each charge consecutively. In a move that clearly shocked Cutler, she removed the possibility of parole. For murder and kidnapping, Jamie Simmons would spend the rest of his life behind bars.

When it was over, I turned my back on Simmons and Cutler. I wrapped an arm around Hayden and walked out.

"You were amazing," I told Hayden. I'd taken her to the side a bit, away from the rest of her family.

"I meant what I said. And he's not my father anymore. I filed a petition to change my last name to Luke."

"Good for you."

"I want to finish what Ellie started. I've applied to nursing school. I want to help people heal."

"Oh Hayden." I hugged her. She let me.

"But I'm going to do it in Pasadena starting next summer. I have to start over. They've got each other now," she said, gesturing to her huddled family. "They'll try to guilt trip me. But my mind's made up."

"If there's anything you need. A letter of reference?"

"I may take you up on that," she said.

"Count me in on that too," Sam said. He'd just joined us. "You're something special, kiddo. I hope I'm not overstepping by saying this. But I think you're right. I think your Aunt Ellie did move through you. And I think she'd be damn proud of you today."

Smiling, Hayden opened her arms and hugged Sam. It caught him a little off guard. His eyes glistened a bit. I felt a lump in my throat.

Hayden went back to her family. They had a long road of recovery ahead of them, but they would all commit to taking it together.

Later, Sam, Will, and I sat at my dining room table and ate the most delicious chili in the world. When we were through, Sam and I cleared the dishes. He washed. I dried.

Snow began to fall. Big puffy flakes, the kind that sparkle after they hit the ground. They'd already closed school for the next day. We'd be under a level one snow emergency by morning. The weather report said we'd get up to eight inches. Christmas was just three weeks away.

"Looks like we might be snowbound," I said. "The plow trucks aren't gonna make it out here until the afternoon."

Sam smiled. He came behind me as I stared out the bay window. Pulling me against his chest with his strong, solid arms, I felt safe. Warm. Home.

"Lucky for you," he said, "I happen to have some pull with the road commission."

I reached up and touched his cheek. "Do you have to use it? Maybe it wouldn't be the worst thing if all three of us took a snow day."

Sam kissed me. "I like the way you think, Mara. Come on. I've got another idea I've been meaning to run by the both of you."

He walked me into the living room. Will was scrolling through the channels, looking for a documentary he'd been waiting to see about the K-Pg boundary. Lately, he'd expanded his obsession out from the Titanic or the JFK assassination to the dinosaur extinction.

"Can you turn that off for a second?" Sam asked. Will hit the power button.

I sat next to my son, my heart fluttering. Will took my hand. Sam stood in front of us, then sank down so he was at eye level.

"You know I love you both," he said. "And I want to do this right. It's not just about your mom and me, Will."

Sam reached into his pocket and pulled out a small red box. He opened it, revealing a glittering, two-carat emerald-cut diamond ring with a white-gold band.

"Mara, will you marry me?"

Will squeezed my hand. Then he let go and threw his arms around Sam, nearly knocking him off his feet. Tears spilled down my cheeks as Sam hugged my son back.

"Yes," I said. Then Sam reached for me, and clasping my hand, we formed a circle.

This was the partner I wanted. I knew it. And I didn't want to wait.

So three weeks later, on Christmas Eve, my son put on a suit that Sam helped him pick out. He patiently taught him how to tie a Windsor knot. Then my son walked me down the aisle in Judge Donald Ivey's courtroom.

My mother sat in the front row, dabbing her eyes. Caro and Hojo sat beside her. Caro handed my mother a tissue, then took one for herself. Kat reached over to touch my mother's arm. Bree beamed as she saw Will and me walk in.

Gus stood beside Sam, serving as his best man. Kenya stood up with me. I wore a simple, light-blue dress. Sam looked so handsome in his gray suit. He smiled down at me as Judge Ivey had us recite our vows.

It was simple. It was perfect. It was my family.

WHEN A DEPUTY IS ACCUSED IN A heinous murder, it's up to Mara to bring equal justice to the courtroom. But when the case pits Mara against the entire Sheriff's Department, she'll have to take on the county's top cop himself, the man she just married. Don't miss Edge of Justice, the next page-turning book in the Mara Brent Legal Thriller Series.

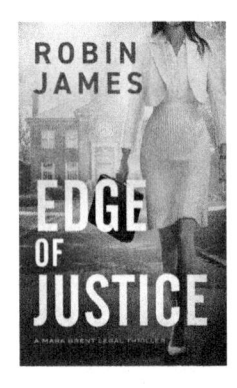

NEWSLETTER SIGN UP

Sign up to get notified about Robin James's latest book releases, discounts, and author news. You'll also get *Crown of Thorne* an exclusive FREE bonus prologue to the Cass Leary Legal Thriller Series just for joining.

Click to Sign Up

http://www.robinjamesbooks.com/newsletter/

ABOUT THE AUTHOR

Robin James is an attorney and former law professor. She's worked on a wide range of civil, criminal and family law cases in her twenty-five year legal career. She also spent over a decade as supervising attorney for a Michigan legal clinic assisting thousands of people who could not otherwise afford access to justice.

Robin now lives on a lake in southern Michigan with her husband, two children, and one lazy dog. Her favorite, pure Michigan writing spot is stretched out on the back of a pontoon watching the faster boats go by.

Sign up for Robin James's Legal Thriller Newsletter to get all the latest updates on her new releases and get a free bonus scene from Burden of Truth featuring Cass Leary's last day in Chicago. http://www.robinjamesbooks.com/newsletter/

ALSO BY ROBIN JAMES

Mara Brent Legal Thriller Series

Time of Justice

Price of Justice

Hand of Justice

Mark of Justice

Path of Justice

Vow of Justice

Web of Justice

Shadow of Justice

Edge of Justice

With more to come...

Cass Leary Legal Thriller Series

Burden of Truth

Silent Witness

Devil's Bargain

Stolen Justice

Blood Evidence

Imminent Harm

First Degree

Mercy Kill

Guilty Acts

Cold Evidence

Dead Law

The Client List

Deadly Defense

Code of Secrets

With more to come...

AUDIOBOOKS BY ROBIN JAMES

CASS LEARY SERIES

Burden of Truth

Silent Witness

Devil's Bargain

Stolen Justice

Blood Evidence

Imminent Harm

First Degree

Mercy Kill

Guilty Acts

Cold Evidence

Dead Law

The Client List

MARA BRENT SERIES

Time of Justice

Price of Justice

Hand of Justice

Mark of Justice

Path of Justice

Vow of Justice

Web of Justice

Printed in Great Britain
by Amazon